Archangel Revenge

Laura Prior

Laura Prior

The Falling series

Laura Prior

ISBN-13: 978-1502552143

ISBN-10: 1502552140

Dedication

As always, dedicated to my whole family for their support on this adventure. Special thanks to Simon for encouraging me to reach for the stars—*Falling for an Angel The Movie*, anyone? To Max, for forcing me to leave the computer and enter the outside world—where I often come up with some of my best ideas/murder plots. To Ian and my dad, who pimp out my books to colleagues, customers and strangers; and to my mam, who proofreads and complains there's too much 'naughtiness' but secretly likes it.

To Sheree and Tanya who scheme and plot alongside me and to Lauren McKellar—editor extraordinaire—who picks holes in my plots and deletes all my exclamation points. Special thanks to Paul for designing my website.

Thanks for supporting me . . . and if there's a movie—premier tickets all round!

Laura Prior

1

'There are devilish thoughts even in the most angelic minds.'

Rachel Wolchin

Pain roared to life through my nerve endings. It had started as a niggle in my mind; the beginnings of a headache that grew steadily worse, pulling me from my dreams where I was dark and warm and safe. It blossomed into shards of pain that ran down my neck, greedy grasping talons reaching for my soul. With each contraction of my barely beating heart, glass spun through me, shredding and tearing until I woke, screaming.

I knew the high-pitched shriek was coming from me; I could feel my mouth stretched wide, my lungs burning for air. The fear and agony built further, fueling hatred, rage and desperation until the pain consumed me.

My stomach lurched as gravity tilted, bright hues flashing at me like fireworks, portals starting to open, while a thousand voices laughed and shouted in my head. Flashes of white, electricity crackling along my skin, gave way to fire sparking from my flesh, hissing at me with anger. How could I let it happen? It was all my fault.

Pressure on my arms; a voice in my ears echoing in my mind. I took a breath, sucking in the thick air and screamed, throwing my arms outward, trying to surface from where I was trapped. I was lost, and so scared.

I gasped as my eyes locked onto Sam's. He looked as though he were in pain; his eyes were straining, his mouth in a grim line beneath which his teeth were clearly gritted, the tick of a muscle clenching along his jawline.

Well, he could join the club. Pain, terror and fire burned through me like dragons.

"Jasmine, stop. Come back to me."

I heard his voice, and while part of me wanted to reject his order, I softened. I felt my body still. My power began to recede back under my skin, absorbed into my flesh and bones.

Sam knelt in front of me on the bed, his clothes torn. I turned my face away slightly, taking in the wider picture. His makeshift bed on the floor beside mine was singed, smoke trailing up from it in wisps.

Trev stepped into view, dust and flakes of paint covering his clothes, a line of blood running freely from his forehead. I frowned at the fire extinguisher he held in his hands, only now noticing the white flakes covering all of us.

"What happened to you?" I tried to ask. My voice came out hoarsely, as though I had been screaming.

I had been.

Trev's smile was slow in coming. He was annoyed at me, but in his usual way, his stern expression soon melted and he sighed. "You threw me through a wall . . . *again*."

I hissed in my breath, not knowing the full story but aware it was true. "I'm sorry."

He shrugged, and dropped the fire extinguisher on the end of the bed. He patted me on the shoulder before throwing himself down onto the pillows and sheets in his own makeshift bed, parallel to Sam's. He lay down, keeping his eyes on me; keeping watch in case I flipped out again. Yes, this had happened before, many times. Now I could remember.

"Next time it's definitely Sam's turn to wake you up from your nightmares," he said softly, half-joking.

Sam smiled, squeezing my hand, trying to ease the situation as he always did. "You heal quicker than me, dude."

I turned away from their camaraderie and stared at the bedside table, which held a number of objects now covered in a light dusting of the contents of the fire extinguisher, including the clock. It was one-forty, and only nine days since . . .

I shut that thought down immediately.

"It's not been long enough," I whispered, hoping I didn't need to say anything else. Sam could read my mind for all I cared—then he'd know I spoke the truth. I needed more time.

I pulled away from him, feeling cold the instant his hands left mine. I turned on my side, lying in a ball on the charred sheets. With the smell of smoke in my nose, I pulled my knees up to my chest and closed my eyes, blocking everything out. I wasn't here, I was somewhere else. Anywhere or nowhere, I didn't care, as long as it wasn't here in reality. It wasn't time.

Sam's fingers touched my face and sunk into my hair, trailing down the dirty tangle of strands to my neck.

“There’s things to do, things that we started but haven’t finished. Everyone’s asking for you,” he whispered.

I closed my eyes tightly and counted to ten. He would go away when I didn’t answer; he always did. He’d get back into his own bed and leave me to the emptiness.

“Jasmine, this can’t go on.” He persisted.

I frowned; annoyed that he wasn’t following the standard pattern. Couldn’t he see it wasn’t time? It was too soon, too early, too everything.

“There’s nothing to do, nothing that has to be done ever again. It’s all finished; it’s all gone,” I replied in a shaky voice. I hated the fact that I could hear every note tremble.

“There are people counting on you. People who need you,” Sam said, continuing with his calm, soothing tone.

I shrugged. “I don’t care. I don’t want anyone to count on me, and I’m not planning on helping anyone do anything ever again, so they’re wasting their time. I’m finished.”

I felt the presence of another person, an angel, powerful and mysterious. I could feel my power reach out, assessing and judging. No threat; not at the moment, not this angel. I held myself tightly inside, frightened I might shatter into a thousand pieces. An angel, here. It wasn’t him; it would never be him again, so what use did I have for whoever it was? What did any of this matter? Nothing that they said meant anything to me. There was only one thing they could say that would breathe life back into me and it was impossible, it would never happen. Why did they keep asking for more of me when I had nothing left to give? Hadn’t I given up enough?

I felt Machidiel's mind with mine. I knew when he sat down on the bed beside me. I almost wanted to tell him to leave, but that would be acknowledging his presence, and that seemed like giving in. He would leave soon when I continued to ignore him.

I heard his breath blow out lightly. His body moved on the bed as he looked down at me for a moment. I knew when he looked away. I expected him to move, to leave me, like everyone else did. Except Sam. Sam continued to sit on the other side of me. I could feel his thoughts, though I tried to block them.

Machidiel moved slightly. "If you refuse to come back to this world, then what would you have us do about James?"

2

'I've been called rebellious, wrong, a black sheep, different . . . because I refuse to be what everyone else is. I stand by my beliefs.'

Egypt.

I clenched my teeth; hatred and denial washing through me. Why, when I wanted to wallow in misery and self-pity, did my selfish, pathetic half-brother insist on dragging me into his trouble? When someone you loved died, wasn't there a rule that gave you a free pass to remain in bed alone with your memories and dreams for at least a month or two? I didn't want to be busy or distracted. I didn't want a new crisis or dilemma to keep me occupied, or to focus my mind on something other than the fact that everything had been perfect for a while, and now I had lost the only thing that made life worthwhile, the only thing that made me want to be alive.

I swallowed deeply. Oh, if only I could have just one more moment with him; the things that I would say to him, the promises I would make if I could keep him.

My eyes flew open. What about the promises I would or should make myself? This was Asmodeus's fault. If he hadn't caused this mess and dragged me kicking and screaming into the middle of it, Zach would have never been there.

I sat up, feeling the bed bounce slightly under my weight. Sam and Machidiel were right; I *did* have things to do. I had demons to kill, Asmodeus to torture and rip apart in the most painful way possible, and the Horsemen to dispose of in what I was sure would be a difficult and bloody fight. I would enjoy gouging out Mnemosyne's eyes, and when I found the Goblin King and Lucifer, I would have my revenge and it would be bloody and glorious . . . *I promise.*

My promise may have seemed far-fetched and extreme, but I wasn't alone in this; I had allies, and I had Gabriel. I hadn't forgotten that she was the one who had sent me, the *old* me, here in the first place. If blame was being handed out, she would be next in line to get hers. She would help me; she didn't have an option.

I would start by asking the witches to make some kind of talisman to protect me against Mnemosyne's powers. The valkyrie were already down with destroying demons and the human rebellion, so I could ride on their tail and take as many out as I could along the way. I'm sure they would be on board with an attack on the Horsemen of the apocalypse.

I pursed my lips and pondered harder. Taking on the Goblin King and Lucifer would be much trickier. For them, I would need an army. Which army was expendable? Thinking like this, I knew I was expecting death but who would go up against Lucifer and not expect it?

I bit my lip as a grim smile pulled at the corners of my mouth. *Werewolves*. The werewolves were expendable, and they would do exactly as I told them; they owed me.

I guess that was the advantage of finding out you used to be and technically still were, an archangel and that everyone around had either fucked you over or had been keeping secrets from you; leverage.

Not everyone, Sam said, telepathically.

Then you know? I asked, meeting his eyes.

He bit his lip. *That you're a reincarnated version of the archangel Jophiel? With an army of angels, lycan, werewolves, valkyrie, witches, harpies, have I missed anyone, at your disposal? Yeah, Machidiel and Drew filled us in.*

Hearing him list my allies like that had the same effect as handing me a sword. I slid off the bed and stood, not looking at anyone in particular.

"I want to know what James knows about the apocalypse. He knows something. Where is he?" I demanded, fisting my hands on my hips.

"He's in a safe house for now." Machidiel stood, towering over me, too close. "But Jophiel, you need to have a plan before you see him."

"Don't call me that!" I shouted. I closed my eyes and took in a lungful of air, blowing it past my lips slowly. "Don't call me that; my name's Jasmine, and I *do* have a plan. He'll tell me what he knows willingly or I'll make him."

Are you? Sam whispered in my mind. *Are you Jophiel or are you Jasmine?*

I lifted my chin and stared at him. *Jophiel and Jasmine are one and the same. One doesn't exist without the other. I used to be Jophiel, and I have those memories—when I can access them—but I'm still Jasmine. I was a complete fuck-up in both lives, so it shouldn't make any difference which name I'm called but it does; I'm still me. I'm still Jasmine,* I added.

Was it true? Did either of them exist anymore? Had I discovered who I was only to become someone else entirely? Should I care if they called me Jophiel or Jasmine?

Then I realized; it was because Jophiel was pre-Zach. If I was called Jophiel, if I accepted that I was *she*, then it was as if I had never had Zach at all. I couldn't do anything about losing Zach in the flesh, but I would never give him up in my dreams. No, that wasn't something I was prepared to do at all. Revenge, was my new game plan.

3

'You're all geniuses and you're all beautiful. You don't need anyone to tell you who you are. You are what you are.'

John Lennon.

I looked up at Machidiel, meeting his eyes, daring him to say something.

He gave me a lopsided grin. "Threatening torture is definitely something Jophiel would say, rather than Jasmine."

"Trust me, when I say it comes from both of us," I replied.

I pushed past him and purposefully strode to the door. Drew stepped out of the way, perhaps sensing the mood I was in. I walked out into the hallway, jogging down the stairs.

I was in the valkyrie house, where my father had taken me after I had exploded in grief post the loss of Zach. The battle against the Horsemen had been epic. When Haamiah had been kidnapped, we had traced him to where he had been held. We hadn't expected to be betrayed by Elijah, another angel who had discovered that Sam was the nephew of hell's gatekeeper and his alter-ego was the Dagger of Lex. Elijah had handed him over to the Horsemen in exchange for his nephilim son.

Despite that betrayal, we had been winning; the lycan and valkyrie had stormed in at the last minute, adding their weight to the battle and flipping us to the strongest side. When I had killed Lilith, the demon armies had fled into the forest, the horsemen deciding to abandon the fight soon after.

That's when I had discovered that Zach had been killed. We had tried everything human and mystical we could think of. When trying to turn him into a vampire had failed, Caleb, my father, had brought me here. Catatonic, I had remained in this room for nine days, unable to summon the energy or reason to get up . . . until now.

I turned the corner, running my hand down the bannister with me as I descended another flight of stairs. The valkyrie house was large at three stories, and it needed to be; dozens of valkyrie lived here together, laughing, drinking and fighting. They were warriors—shield maidens of Norse Gods, whose duty it was to harvest the souls of fellow warriors and somehow send them off into storage to be used when the apocalypse took place. Which conveniently, seemed to be happening now.

Somehow, the house was clean and orderly. Each valkyrie took their turn doing chores, guarding the house, and killing off their neighbors when necessary. As the daughter of their sort-of leader, I had been welcomed with open arms. My semi-psychotic nature and death-wielding abilities had helped, and ensured I fitted in well with the extensively tattooed and pierced multi-colored brawlers.

Three floors down and into the kitchen I found my father and another valkyrie sitting on the table, swigging from a bottle of tequila. Bright lights reflected upon the white bench tops of the expansive room, creating a spacious yet homely feel. Shmaz, a pink-haired valkyrie was laughing at something Caleb had said.

Caleb smiled at me and extended the bottle in my direction. I took it without a moment's hesitation and downed a good amount, wincing at the burn even as I relished it, licking my lips.

"So, you finally found out who you are," he said with a knowing grin.

I considered that for a second, mocking my younger self. I had thought that knowing where I came from, who my parents were, what my abilities were, where I fitted in and belonged was all that mattered. Actually, it meant nothing. I had belonged to Zach and he had belonged to me so now, when I thought back to my frantic efforts to discover who I was, the whole situation was laughable.

After all of these trials; betrayed by werewolves, the Tournament of Ascension, being abused by Asmodeus, imprisoned by angels and the countless battles and bloodshed, I was the same person I had always been. Only now, considering the plan I had decided upon, I could safely consider myself as a borderline sociopath.

"I've always been who I was; I just never believed it," I said to Caleb.

He frowned, unsure what to make of that glib comment.

"You mean . . .?"

I laughed coldly. "I mean that parentage, money, accolades, all mean nothing. They have no influence or meaning to who a person is. You are who you are, and you shouldn't expect to be anything else."

I knew what I had said was mean, rude, even, but I meant it. It was true what they said—whoever *they* were—that friends are the family you make for yourself. Sam, Gwen and Trev were my siblings,

Haamiah was my leader, and Zach had been my home. I just hadn't seen what I had until it was too late.

Caleb rolled his eyes and snatched the glass bottle back from me. "Is this archangel Jophiel we're hearing from? Have we been accompanied by royalty? Or are you Jasmine? Because you sound way too depressed for this time of the morning . . . or night." He leaned back and looked over Shmaz's shoulder at the kitchen clock. "Morning," he confirmed with an easy grin.

"Maybe they don't exist anymore," I answered, swiping the tequila from him. I paced further into the kitchen, glancing absently at the worried looks Trev and Sam gave each other as they loitered in the doorway in front of Machidiel. "I'm clearly not a high-up, all-mighty, peaceful angel, am I? Not with what I have planned." I waved the bottle at them before swallowing some. "Neither am I goody-goody Jasmine, desperate for love and a place to belong."

Caleb quirked his eyebrow. "Are you sure?"

Black mirth bubbled up through me, escaping as a chuckle. "Well, I had both, and I lost them. So yes, to answer your question, I am sure I'm no longer looking for love or somewhere to belong."

"Then what are you looking for?" He folded his arms across his chest and regarded me seriously.

I smiled. "Revenge."

The swift intake of breath from the group at the door ensured I was aware my friends weren't on board with that. It didn't matter to me.

"Revenge," Caleb repeated, narrowing his eyes. "Who are your targets?"

"Everyone who has wronged me," I answered simply. In truth, the answer was a lot more convoluted. Anyone who had said or done something that had resulted in Zach lying lifeless in front of me, would be paid back in full. No matter how long it took, they would get what they were owed.

"Jasmine, think about this," Sam pleaded.

"I have thought about it," I snapped. "I understand you might not agree, and you don't even have to help, but know this; everyone who has hurt me or someone I loved is going to pay, and no one will get in my way."

"The way you're acting, I'd imagine you have a pretty long list," Caleb said.

"The valkyrie owe me allegiance; you already swore to be my allies. I will be cashing in on that promise," I said firmly.

Caleb grinned. "I have a feeling this is a fight we won't want to miss out on. We already have armies in strategic places, as I told you before. Our people are moving to intercept targets of our own as we speak. Possibly a few of our targets overlap; who are you going af-"

"Asmodeus," My eyes flashed with fire. Lightning flashed outside, adding eerie punctuation to my voice. "The four Horsemen, the Goblin King and Lucifer, to start with."

"I'm sure your adoptive parents will feature somewhere along the way," Caleb added.

I smirked. He was on the same page as me now. The valkyrie wouldn't stand in my way; they *lived* for battle. "I'm sure they will."

Caleb and Shmaz grinned at each other.

“Now you’re acting like one of us. I thought you must have been mostly angel with only a drop of valkyrie, with the way you’ve moped, crying and hiding this past week,” Shmaz said sarcastically.

“She’s been grieving!” Sam snapped.

I shrugged off her comment. It was true; I had wallowed for long enough.

“How do you plan on killing the most evil of creatures in existence?” Machidiel asked.

I scowled at him, curling my lip up in anger.

He held his hands up in surrender. “I’m asking seriously. What’s your plan?”

I smiled. “I killed Lilith; I can do it again. I have allies across the universe; no one can stand in my way.”

“I won’t,” he assured me. “But you will need to find them.”

“That’s why we’re going to find James, and learn what he knows. You said he’s in a nephilim safe house.”

Machidiel nodded. “On the other side of Melbourne, hidden in Toorak.”

I caught Caleb’s eye. “I need a car.”

He grinned and stood up. “I’ve got a few.”

He led us into the garage through a door at the back of the kitchen. The others trailed in behind us.

I had thought the valkyrie house had a double garage, not thinking that of course they would need many more cars to suit the number of people that lived here, but the garage was more like a car show room. Numerous vehicles were parked up inside, from the Saleen I had seen previously, to a Mercedes, to a basic Ford Focus.

"I want this one." I patted the bonnet of a seven-seater SUV. It would fit everyone in, and certainly looked like it could withstand a battering if necessary—not that I was anticipating James to put up a fight. When I had last seen him, he'd looked as pathetic as any young schoolboy.

Caleb selected the keys off a hook and threw them to me. I tossed them to Sam, who sighed with indecision.

"I take it I'm driving?" he asked.

I nodded. Driving lessons hadn't featured in my teenage years of alcohol and drug abuse, nor had I managed to fit it in between being captured by my enemies and learning how to control portal travel.

Sam pressed the button, unlocking the doors electronically. As Caleb and Shmaz stepped back into the kitchen, Drew, Machidiel and Trev piled into the back of the car.

Sam turned to me hesitantly. "Jas, are you sure you want to do this? This revenge . . . I'm scared for you."

"I'm strong enough to take them," I said calmly.

He shook his head. He looked sad, his eyes filled with sorrow. "I'm scared you will, and I'll lose you. You're wrong when you say you're not still Jasmine. I never knew you as Jophiel, but I know Jasmine is still here. I can hear your thoughts; I'm inside your mind, and as much as you're trying to convince yourself that you can never be yourself again, I *know* you're still in there. I don't want to lose you."

I bit my lip, his words tearing through me like ice. "This is something I have to do. When it's over, we'll see if there's anything left of me to lose."

4

'The price of being a sheep is boredom. The price of being a wolf is loneliness. Choose one or the other with great care.'

Hugh Macleod.

I pulled the car door open and jumped into the passenger seat. I reached back for my seatbelt, taking hold of it when Machidiel pushed it forward into my hand. I plugged it in and stared expectantly at Sam. He started the engine and gave a long, drawn-out sigh. When the garage door slid open seamlessly, Sam maneuvered the car out of the garage and rolled down the driveway.

Though Sam was driving, Machidiel was the only one who knew the way to the safe house. He told Sam to head left, and a second later we pulled out onto the road and began to pick up speed.

The valkyrie house was located in a suburban area of Melbourne. The neighboring houses were large, expensive-looking, and well hidden behind long driveways, high walls and green, leafy trees. Lining the sidewalk, more trees were placed equal lengths from each other, providing additional coverage.

I peered at each house we passed. A secret well-guarded was that a supernatural being inhabited each house on this road. Besides the valkyrie, witches, gypsies, harpies, and even a phoenix – a crotchety old man who tended to set fire to his neighbors' gardens when they were too noisy—lived in this private and mystical area. I guess they thought they had more protection from an attack that way. It would be the perfect place to live and raise a family; somewhere safe, surrounded by friends.

Self-preservation kicked in, and I shut that train of thought down. That would never happen for me, so I shouldn't waste time thinking about it.

I stared straight ahead, and ignored the glimpses of the life I could have had as they flashed by.

Drew stared out of the window while Machidiel rattled off directions. Trev and Sam sat silently—at least, they thought they were being silent. I had lost the ring Zach had given me to mute my powers, in the fight that had cost him his life. Even as I fought to control the emotions that soared through me, my abilities wrestled with each other to be heard. I had managed to force the portals to one side but my telepathy had gotten free, making the thoughts of those in the car whisper in my mind freely.

That was one of the valkyrie traits. As well as harvesting souls, valkyrie harvested abilities from creatures around them. Due to my supped-up genetics, aided by the Star Mist that had been the prize in the Tournament of Ascension, I acquired abilities at an alarming rate, and they strengthened rapidly. The ring had been a way of dimming them, and without it I had found my fallen angel rage consuming me, and my powers spiraling out of control, endangering everyone.

I rubbed my forehead as the telepathy pulsed through me in waves. Despite his calm, outward appearance, Trev was playing scenarios over and over in his mind. He was anxious that James would say something that would push me over the edge. He thought I was losing it, that losing Zach had unhinged me. There was no condemnation though, no anger or disgust. He only hoped that he and Sam could pull me back from the same insanity that he had faced when he was turned into a vampire and he'd lost control.

I tuned into Sam, rolling my eyes as the same thread continued. He was wondering what happened to a soul when it was separated from its mate. Was the damage reparable or would I be like this—cold and vengeful—forever?

I didn't want to hear any more. I didn't bother listening to Drew or Machidiel; their thoughts were more difficult to understand, and they would undoubtedly be repeating what the boys had been thinking.

Unhinged. Damaged. Words used to describe me now were unnervingly similar to those that described the old Jasmine, the one pre-angel, in school, searching for someone and something to believe in. I wished I could go back and advise myself to stop looking. There was nothing out there that made this pain worthwhile. Maybe it would have been best to give in back then.

Sam soon pulled off the main road and into a side street, stopping the car outside a run-down house, overgrown with bushes and trees. The stone of the building was dark grey, with cracks running the length of the building, decorating the brickwork and the windows, everywhere.

"*This* is the safe house?" I asked, turning to scowl at Machidiel. Was he playing me? There was no way the angels would have holed up here.

He crooked his eyebrow and slid out of the car, letting Trev clamber out his side while Drew got out of the other. I stood on the sidewalk beside Sam, glaring up at the dark building.

Machidiel stared at me for a moment. "See what is beneath the illusion," he said quietly.

Drew, Sam, Trev and I focused on the house with renewed interest.

"An illusion?" Sam breathed, eagerly looking for the secrets it hid.

After a moment, I gave in. Like everything else, I would need to practice to control the illusion, and now wasn't the time. The house still looked like it was about to collapse, and I was beginning to get a headache.

"Can we go in already?" I asked irritably.

Machidiel shrugged, and approached the wooden gate along the sidewalk. He slid his hand through a broken slat and unhooked the latch on the inside. Swinging the gate open, he entered the garden first, striding confidently through the uncut grass to the house.

I followed closely behind Machidiel, distantly hearing the gate close behind us as the others pushed through the grass. We reached the doorway; despite the rest of the house seeming battered, it looked solid. Machidiel knocked in a pattern that made me roll my eyes. A code knock? How *spy movie* of him. Regardless, the door swung open immediately, an angel warrior beckoning us inside.

Crossing the threshold had an instant effect on lifting the illusion hiding the safe house. The hallway was spacious with modern black and white tiles on the floor, and whitewashed walls with mirrors amplifying the space it held.

The warrior remained by the door and Machidiel continued leading us through the house to the living room, which peeled off from the kitchen. Again, it was modern, clean, and presumably because of the time of morning, empty, apart from our leader.

“Haamiah, friend,” Machidiel greeted him with a grin, clapping him on the back.

I stepped forward, keeping my expression neutral. If I was planning on taking revenge on everyone who had caused Zach’s death, Haamiah wasn’t far along that line.

Now I had most of the memories from my life as Jophiel, I knew that Haamiah, along with Machidiel, Gabriel, Bëyander, the commander of the angelic army and a captured lycan leader among others, had banded together in a secret group, opposing Raphael’s threat to rid the human plane of nephilim and every other mystical creature, hoping to prevent the threat to humans and angels by uniting the warring factions there. They had plotted and planned and come up with a solution; Gabriel would be sent to the human plane as a hybrid, a creature able to make allies of the factions and create one super army to drive back the evil forces, providing a solution that kept everyone safe—not just humans and angels.

I, as Jophiel, had agreed to care for a nephilim baby—Sam. In a bizarre twist of events, Gabriel had been imprisoned and I had been sent to a seer in her place. After being shown a vision where my soul mate, Zach, had been killed, I had immediately offered to go to the human plane as the hybrid. I had been sent there without any of my angelic memories, and had been created in the form of Jasmine, half valkyrie and half fallen angel; a hybrid who could delve and would be able to be accepted by all factions, given the right circumstances.

Haamiah had sent Zach to me as my guardian angel, possibly not knowing that he was my soul mate, but even so, he had set in motion the events that would lead to his death, an event I had given up my angelic existence to try to prevent. If only he had sent someone else . . . Although as a result of his decision, I would be fulfilling my purpose in one aspect; I would unite the armies of the supernatural world, destroy the creatures that had killed Zach, and prevent the apocalypse by default.

Of course, the reasonable part of me knew that Haamiah wasn't really to blame, and perhaps that would save him from my anger. It wasn't his fault that he had trusted Mnemosyne, the Goddess of Memory, and fallen for her charms, or that he had been kidnapped and tortured to discover the Falchion of Tabbris and the Dagger of Lex—two objects that would open the gates of Hell and Heaven, and allow the demons of the underworld to rampage through the human and Heavenly planes.

The angels had healed him. Though Elijah had no doubt been imprisoned somewhere for treason, there were other angels gifted in healing available.

I let my eyes run over Haamiah. He looked the same, yet different; weary and sad. Physically he was unchanged He was tall, dark skinned with thick, black dreadlocks. I could almost smile that despite our home being burned down, he had still managed to find beige trousers and a loose, white shirt.

He nodded to me, pressing his lips together grimly. "Jasmine, I'd like to give you my condolences."

I held my hand up to stop him, or to ward off his words, I didn't know. "I don't want to hear it. Where's James?"

"Jas!" Sam gasped, aghast.

I bit my lip. I didn't care if I was being rude. I didn't care.

Haamiah shrugged it off anyway. "It's not even three in the morning. He's in bed."

I stepped closer, threateningly. "I want to speak to him."

"What you have to say can wait a couple more hours."

"No, it can't," I growled.

Sam grabbed hold of my arm and forced me back a couple of steps. "Enough," he hissed.

"We have something to discuss. Sit down," Haamiah said. His voice was stern enough to brook no rejection, but soft enough that I wavered in my resolve to grill him.

I sat up straight for a moment before relaxing into the cushions involuntarily. Sam and Trev breathed a sigh of relief and sat down. Drew sat on the chair arm, while Machidiel hovered in the background. Haamiah relaxed back onto the sofa he had been sitting on, wincing as he did so. So he wasn't fully healed, then.

He stared at me for a moment before speaking. "A number of spirits have escaped from the Pool of Kali. Somehow, they have been released into the human plane. They need to be found and returned."

I grimaced, my body tensing up. That was *my* fault. In order to rescue Aidan from Lilith, I'd had to bring Zanaria back from the dead—the only person who had known that Sam was actually the Dagger of Lex. I hadn't explicitly confessed to what I had done. Lilith and her henchmen had killed the guardians of the pool, giving us access to the souls. I hadn't told anyone the pool was now unguarded. I hadn't given it a second thought once I was out of there.

"What kind of spirits?" I asked hesitantly. "And how many?"

"Two. One is the spirit of a werewolf and the other a zombie."

I closed my eyes in defeat. A werewolf I could have left; I had no alliance to werewolves, except Valentina. Her people had betrayed the angels and me, and deserved no compassion or help. The zombie however . . . that would need to be taken care of.

"This doesn't fall in with my plans," I said angrily. Surely someone else could catch them and send them back. Why did I have to do this? Yes, it was my fault they had escaped, but there were thousands of warrior angels capable of completing this task.

Haamiah shrugged. "This is the mission I'm giving you."

Everyone in the room seemed to be holding their breath, waiting to see what I would say.

"You've given me many missions over the years, and they certainly haven't ended the way they should have. Why should I do this for you?" I scowled.

Haamiah sat up stiffly, fixing me with his black eyes. "Because if you do this for me, I'll help you break Gabriel out of her prison."

5

'Always do what you are afraid to do.'

Ralph Waldo Emerson.

He would help me break Gabriel out? She definitely figured into my plans, and I hadn't given much consideration as to her situation. She was still in prison? She'd been locked up before I had come to the human plane. Did that mean she had been locked up for more than twenty-five years? Surely the angels wouldn't do that to one of their own?

"Why would I want her to be free?" I baited.

He gave me a knowing smile. "You might not remember everything, but you know she's your sister. You wouldn't leave her there."

"*Jophiel* wouldn't leave her there . . . I'm not sure what I would do," I corrected.

"You'll free her. I know you will," he replied, unfazed by my devil-may-care attitude.

"Wouldn't that put you in trouble?" I asked.

He shrugged. "I'm always in trouble with someone. If you're questioning my reasons, then perhaps you need reminding that I am a principality."

I sneered. “Yes, always playing games with the puppets around you.”

He shook his head. “I’m one player; there are hundreds out there all pulling strings of their own. You need to decide which one you will back, which one you will support. Our team has let you down, and for that I am more sorry than you will ever know, but you need to remember your reasons for joining us in the first place.”

“The apocalypse? Joining the allies together to create one super army to defend the heavens?” I smirked. “That was never the reason I joined you. I joined because I saw a vision of Zach being killed. I thought if I came here I could prevent it. I failed, and now I have no reason to do anything for you.”

Haamiah’s face fell. He stared at me in a subdued horror, before glaring up at Machidiel. Drew shifted uneasily next to me.

“You were never with us?” Haamiah asked, hesitantly.

I swallowed deeply. “You all presumed Jophiel would just do as she was told. That because she always did what Michael told her to do she would jump through hoops for Gabriel. You thought I would be easily controlled when I was reborn here, that I would be your weapon. Perhaps you didn’t expect me to be reborn as I did. I have my own will, my own game plan, and you feature in it, but not the way you expect. You’re no longer my leader. I don’t need a leader.”

Jasmine, think about what you’re saying. You’re pulling away from the angels? We’re your family, Sam thought loudly.

His words battered at me from the inside and I paused, taking some deep breaths. I could feel my fallen-angel anger influencing my words, my attitude.

I took a deep breath and shocked them all by admitting it, forcing the words out. “I lost the ring Zach gave me in the fight, and I’m fighting my own battle to stay in control. Don’t push me to say something I’ll regret.”

Haamiah’s expression softened. “I would never presume to give you orders, and I would never want to diminish the horror of what you have gone through, nor tarnish Zach’s memory in any way, but these spirits need to be contained. If you took the time to track them down you might be able to gain some distance and time to think about your . . . *game plan*, further.”

This could be my bargaining chip. I nodded slowly. “Fine. I’ll track down the spirits, and make sure they’re no longer a threat. In return, you will help me find a way to get Gabriel released, but I will speak to James before I go.”

Haamiah consented, and the tension in the room immediately lifted.

“So we have time for breakfast, then?” Trev cut in.

I relaxed, grinning at him before anxiously wondering when he had last had blood. Since turning, he had only fed from a live source when in the midst of a fight. It was as if all of the sweat and adrenaline had triggered feeding instincts within him. He had mostly been living off blood bags kept in the fridge. He’d had his own stash kept in the safe house, but while I was recovering from this last battle, I had no idea how he had been getting any.

Trev caught my eyes and smiled, though hurt flashed in his eyes. “Cereal will be fine.”

“Coffee for me,” Sam added quickly. He had noted the sadness in our friend’s expression and as always, tried to steer the conversation away from any awkwardness.

“Me too,” I chimed in.

“Oh, so you’re actually going to eat and drink something now? Is my food not good enough for ye?” Drew joked, his Scottish lilt evident.

Flashes of Drew standing over me, coaxing me to eat a few bites of bread or take a few sips of water echoed through my mind. The past nine days had been rough, and not just for me.

I bit my lip and tried to block the wave of emotion that threatened to break free. It seemed to take forever, when actually only a few seconds later I managed to smile and say, “Diet’s over.”

He nodded with a returning smile and stood.

“It’s okay.” I quickly slid out of my seat and stepped around him towards the door. “I’ll get it. You having coffee or tea?”

“Tea,” he replied.

I could feel his eyes on me as I left the living room and stepped out into the hall. I edged around the warriors who suspiciously stared at me while I peered through into the kitchen.

The black and white tiled floor continued from the hallway through the kitchen to a door at the very back, guarded by two warriors. The kitchen was wide and airy, not even half the size of the kitchen in our old safe house. The counters had a dark granite top with some sort of sparkly sheen to it, and they were cluttered with dishes from the day before.

I was still unsure how they could fit so many nephilim in this one house—our last home had been a mansion and more like a boarding school than a home. I thought to the other nephilim I had lived with; Samantha, Abbey, Lisa, Will and Joe among others . . . what had happened to them all? What had happened to Valentina, who lived among the nephilim now, after being cast out by the werewolves? Had she been given a place here or at another safe house? What about Daton, our fighting teacher, or any of the other teachers who taught us angelic ways?

It was easy to be sucked down into how this affected me, about how I had lost my home and my peace was threatened, my family and my friends killed in battle, but what about everyone else? They had all lost people in the numerous fights that seemed to follow us.

I braced my arms against the kitchen bench and closed my eyes, taking a deep breath in. I let it out, blowing it past my lips slowly, seeing how long it could last. I opened my eyes again and reached forward to switch on the kettle, flinching when I realized someone was standing next to me.

"You're doing the right thing," Sam whispered.

"What am I doing?"

He smiled and opened a cupboard above us, pulling down an assortment of cups and mugs. "You're not giving in."

I grimaced. "It would be so easy to just let it all out." I met his eyes. "You have no idea the battle going on to keep the magic, everything inside of me."

Sam dropped his hand to mine and squeezed my fingers. "But you'll do it, because if you don't, you'll endanger everyone."

I snatched my hand away. “I *know* that.”

He sighed. “Maybe we can get another ring, something to keep the worst of it back.”

I shrugged. “It was old, *really* old. I don’t even know if that kind of magic exists anymore.”

“It doesn’t matter about the ring, as long as you can get by without it for a little while longer.” Trev’s smooth voice spoke behind me.

I spun round, catching up with his words. “Why?”

He smirked. “You brought Zanaria back from the Pool of Kali; can’t you do the same to Zach . . .?”

I froze. I couldn’t believe it. Caught up in all my plans of revenge, I hadn’t even considered it. I could bring Zach back. I could bring him back to life.

6

'Damaged people are dangerous. They know they can survive.'

Unknown.

"We have to go there. We're leaving now," I said immediately. I pushed past Trev roughly, knocking him aside as I ran out of the kitchen.

The boys caught up with me in the corridor. Trev dug his fingers into my upper arm and dragged me up against him.

"Wait!" he hissed.

"No." I shook my head. "He needs me. He's waiting for me; I'm not just going to leave him there." My voice trembled as my eyes flooded with tears. This wasn't the time to get emotional; I needed to remain cool and calm.

Trev glanced over his shoulder at the warriors hovering beside the door. He grimaced and turned back to me, lowering his voice. "We can't tell anyone."

"Haamiah can help us. We can get to New York with a portal, but the pool is guarded now; Haamiah can make them let us through."

Sam shook his head. "I don't know if he will."

I blinked, my mouth falling open as I stared in utter confusion. “Why wouldn’t Haamiah help bring his best friend back?”

Sam and Trev gave me worried looks before Trev finally took a breath. “They were furious that you brought Zanaria back. Angels don’t agree with bringing anyone back from the other side; you think they’re going to help you bring one of their own back?”

I frowned. “You think they’ll stop us.”

Sam shrugged. “I think they’ll put even more guards on the pool and warn you to stay away. Zach’s soul is in Heaven, they’re not going to want you to drag him out of there.”

“*Drag* him out?” I narrowed my eyes, feeling the familiar rage seethe through me, acid burning through my stomach as my magic began to twist and turn. “You think that’s what I’m going to do?”

Sam turned slightly to check the warriors were keeping their distance. “No, but it’s what *they’ll* think you’re going to do.”

“What’s going on?”

I flinched and pushed away from the wall I was backed up against. Machidiel rested his shoulder against the wall his ankles crossed, and his lips curving up.

“Nothing,” I said, daring him to question us further.

He didn’t; he sighed and shook his head. “When are you going to realize, whether you’re Jasmine or Jophiel, you can count on me?”

I bit my lip. “I’m Jasmine, and I don’t need your help.”

I glared at Trev and Sam and turned back into the kitchen, stomping over to the bench to make the world’s strongest cup of coffee.

I wasn't going to change my mind; I was actually devastated that I hadn't even considered bringing him back earlier than now. If our roles had been reversed, I had no doubt he would have brought me back already. I felt terrible . . . and I had so much adrenaline rushing through me I could almost feel my magic fighting to be released. I imagined a fire blanket smothering my powers, cooling and sedating. I took a deep breath and held out my hand, watching my fingers shake as I poured out the hot water.

The next two hours went by painfully slow. Every second seemed to last a minute, and every minute an hour. While the boys scoffed any food placed in their reach, I picked at some toast then left it to go cold on the side table, downing cup after cup of coffee. Haamiah sat with us for a while, conversing with Machidiel about people I had never heard of. Drew occasionally joined in with a sarcastic comment, but he seemed to sense the somber mood Sam, Trev and I were in, and remained quiet and observant.

We seemed to have a mutual agreement that we would hear James out first then agree on a plan of action, without telling any of the angels what we were planning. I racked my brain, trying to think of a way to ditch Machidiel when the time came, and came up with nothing. I couldn't just leave without him—it would be a little too obvious when we all disappeared, plus the giant portal that would appear to pull us all through. Neither could I disable him in some way, although if he kept giving me that perceptive look, as though he could read my mind and knew what I was planning, I might just be tempted.

When I didn't think I could stand waiting any more, the house started to waken. I breathed a sigh of relief when I heard footsteps above us, doors opening and closing, chattering, and finally the clatter of feet down the stairs.

I rolled my eyes when Will and Joe stomped into the room first. In unison they froze, their expressions darkening in disgust as they took us in. Known as heavyweights in our safe house, popular and opinionated, they were right up there with Gwen in their hatred of anything un-angelic. They ruled the safe house and had been active in turning everyone against Trev and I. I was used to the dislike—it wasn't exactly new for me, but for Trev, having the other nephilim back away from him when he entered a room was humiliating.

After glancing at Haamiah, they backed out of the room, I expected, to go and whinge to each other about us being back. Lucky for them, and us, we weren't staying long. Daton entered soon after, as expressionless as usual, a big hulk of man-flesh dressed in the warriors' usual black clothing, swords strapped across his back. Daton taught self-defense to the nephilim and having him here, just seeing him served as a reminder of everything we had lost; our home, friends, routine and safety.

He met my eyes and looked away. He jerked his head towards Haamiah, and the two of them left the room.

"Secret meetings all 'round, then," Machidiel grumbled.

Drew looked up in surprise. "Secret meetings?"

I bit my lip and remained silent.

"We'll fill you in later," Sam said.

I sensed Drew wanted to question us further, but a group of giggling girls entered.

"Jasmine?"

I looked up and smiled as one tall, blond girl skipped towards me with her arms outstretched. I pushed forward out of the chair and let her wrap her arms around me, squeezing me tightly. I didn't like the contact; until Zach, I had never been someone who liked to be touched by anyone. My friends I adored, and I had learned to allow them to comfort me, and to give comfort, and I was friends with Samantha—she was one of the few nephilim who actually accepted other creatures without judgment, and she had good reason for it.

Samantha was the girlfriend of Valentina; a werewolf and a close friend I had met in another realm while running from Zach and Aidan. She had been betrayed by her brother and her pack, and had been injured as we made our escape together. She had returned to the safe house with me to be healed, and had fallen for Samantha. I missed her terribly.

"Where's Val?" I asked as soon as Samantha let go.

Her face clouded with hurt. My heart skipped a beat and began to pound, hammering painfully inside my chest. When the safe house had been attacked, dozens of nephilim and angels had been killed, and even more had been hurt. Was Valentina one of them?

"Just tell me." I forced my words out stiffly. I needed to know.

"Oh my God, I'm sorry." Samantha gasped. "I didn't mean for you to think . . . I mean . . ."

"What's the problem? Where is she?" Sam asked, standing up beside me.

"Who's Val?" Drew asked.

"Her ex-lesbian lover," Trev whispered.

I shot him a scowl as Sam stifled a laugh.

"She's fine," Samantha finally said. "Honestly she's fine."

"She's not hurt?" I gasped.

"No, I . . . *we* broke up." She shrugged. "Maybe she was never really over you, maybe it was the fighting and the attack, the stress from running and hiding, and I don't know . . . it just didn't work. We've all been through such a lot."

"Oh." I wasn't sure what to say. Should I apologize? Should I say something else?

She let out an awkward laugh. "Don't worry about it. Just didn't work."

I pursed my lips. "So, umm, where is she?"

"Oh." She shook her head. "She didn't come here—she stayed in a safe house in the U.S."

Relief poured through me. "Why? Why didn't she come with everyone else?"

"Not everyone's here. The nephilim were split up and spread out, just in case . . ."

"In case you were attacked again," Sam finished.

Samantha nodded. As I watched I noticed her eyes redden. She was upset. She'd lost her home and people she loved too. Everyone had.

Here I was, wallowing in misery, completely self-obsessed, thinking that I was the only one affected when everyone had been affected to some degree. At the very least everyone in my safe house had lost their home, and a lot of their friends, teachers and guardians, while nephilim across the world were in fear of their lives, whether they'd been attacked yet or not.

I could do what Haamiah needed me to do, and still get Zach back. I would hunt zombies, track werewolves, return them to the Pool of Kali, or whatever it was I was supposed to do with them—I should really clarify the procedure for that—then I would pull Zach's gorgeous self right back out of the Pool of Souls and into real life. Then, we would tackle the Horsemen, Asmodeus and Lucifer together.

Yes, that was the new plan, and I would get right on that, just as soon as I'd interrogated my annoying, half-evil half-brother.

7

'Don't confuse a smile with someone baring teeth.'

Unknown.

Oblivious to my newfound self-awareness, Samantha hugged Sam and Trev and left us alone, going to the kitchen with her friends where I could hear more nephilim had gathered. The kitchen was the heart of the home, and all that.

I tilted my head towards my friends. "Judging by the noise, everyone seems to be down here."

Sam nodded and together, we headed back into the kitchen. James wasn't there. There were tons of kids, some I recognized and some I didn't, eating breakfast, talking, laughing, and joking around with each other, but not him.

I backed out of the room and slid through the corridor, ignoring the gaze of the warriors as they narrowed their eyes at me. One stood in front the stairs, frowning.

"I need the bathroom," I said, attempting to smile.

The angel stared at me for a second before stepping to the side, letting me past. I walked up the first few stairs calmly before running up the rest to the first floor. I grabbed the handle of the first door and pushed it open, scanning the interior. There was no one; the room was empty aside from furniture.

“Damn,” I muttered.

I pulled the door closed quietly and pushed open the next one. This irritating procedure was repeated over and over until the bedrooms and the bathroom on the first floor ended. I ran up the next flight of stairs and skidded to a stop. The whole floor was open plan—a dormitory. A variety of beds were crammed up here; bunk beds, single beds, even camp beds on the floor. There were piles of clothes, toiletries and books everywhere. To say it was messy was an understatement.

I huffed out my breath. Haamiah had said that James was here—I was going to kill him! We had wasted hours sitting downstairs, waiting for a reasonable time to question him. I could have tracked the spirits by now, and be on my way to Zach.

I was so angry. I was fuming. I was—

“Jasmine? Is that really you?”

I narrowed my eyes at the beds, moving slightly to try and see better. Who was there?

“James?” I called.

It was. James stood up at the far back of the room and stood, looking at me. Anger fueling me, I stormed towards him, pushing past blankets hanging over the edge of the bunk beds, kicking books aside until I stood in front of him.

He looked terrible, still. The last time I had seen him he had been pale and sweaty, his clothes ripped, and his skin blistered and dirty.

He had been so afraid. I remembered thinking he looked like he had narrowly escaped the jaws of hell.

Now, he looked different, and yet the same. He looked like the other nephilim with clean, non-descript clothes. He looked stronger and more in control, yet he still looked afraid. There were shadows in his eyes, lines around his mouth that couldn't be hidden. He was definitely scared.

I couldn't be weak; he was the only thing standing in my way. I raised my chin. "What do you know?"

"About?"

My eyes flashed. "I'm not playing games with you. Tell me what I want to know."

"There's so much you don't know, I don't know where to begin."

"Then tell me!" I shouted.

I took a few deep, calming breaths. "James, you said you knew something about the apocalypse. You said you knew what we're up against, something about a secret division. What the hell were you talking about?"

"I told you to get them to trust me. They don't. Haamiah and the others don't want to know what I have to say."

"You wanted to talk to an angel about what you know, so talk."

He snorted. "I wanted to talk to someone important and an angel. Someone high up. Sorry, sis, but that's not you."

I nodded, letting out a short laugh. “So you feel safe, hidden away here with warriors to protect you, and you don’t need to spill your little secrets any more.”

“No, I just want to speak to someone with authority.”

“Maybe you didn’t get the memo, but I’m the reincarnated version of archangel Jophiel. As myself, I also have an army of valkyrie and lycan behind me. In case you don’t get it, I’m kind of a big deal. Now spill.” I folded my arms across my chest and tried to look intimidating.

“*You’re* an archangel?” He sneered.

Yeah, there was the tosser I knew was lurking under that scared little boy act.

“I was,” I corrected him. Holding up my hand to wave at him, I continued, “I also lost the ring that keeps my powers under control. You remember what I did in the tournament? My powers are a thousand times stronger, so if you want to keep all of your body parts, tell me what I want to know.”

James glared at me, worrying at his lip. *Now* I had gotten through to him.

“Fine. I want your promise though.”

I groaned. “What promise?”

“That you’ll take me with you back to the Heavens when you go,” he said miserably.

I glared at him. Could I promise that? Did it even matter?

“Agreed.” A voice came from behind me.

I spun around. "What do you want?"

Machidiel shrugged, smirking at me. He tilted his head towards James, looking him up and down, sizing him up. "If I'm correct in my assumptions of your plans for the foreseeable future, I'm fairly certain you won't be in any kind of condition to fulfill your promise. I'm just here to assist in holding up your end of the bargain."

I shrugged. "So, you're just here to help me . . . at what cost?"

Machidiel grinned, his white teeth flashing at me with mirth. "So little trust. You *used* to trust me."

I stiffened. "When I was Jophiel? I'm not her anymore." I turned away from him to face James, noting the anger on his face. "I've trusted people before, and it's been proven how wrong I was about them. I can't—I *don't* trust anyone."

Machidiel frowned, the enthusiasm and mocking happiness fading out of his voice. I turned back sharply. "Okay, you want to know the cost of my help? You'll tell me exactly what you're doing and when you plan on doing it. I want to be involved in decision making, and I will be by your side when the fight goes down."

I shivered at his cold tone. "Why?"

If I hadn't been staring so intently at him I probably wouldn't have noticed, but I saw the very tip of his lip curl upwards just a millimeter.

"You're not the only one with a soul mate on the line."

I froze. My blood seemed to turn into ice in my veins. "You have a soul mate?"

He nodded. “That is something we can talk about another time. For now, let’s get the information we need to get out of here.”

I still felt stiff, cold. Had I misjudged him all of this time? Was he hurting like I was? Had he lost his soul mate? God, was he relying on *me* to bring her back? I guessed that was why he was helping me. It seemed a better reason than most. I had to decide—did I trust him? I almost laughed at my thoughts. I didn’t really have a choice, did I?

I bit my lip, tasting blood, and turned my back to Machidiel, firmly concentrating on James. “You have your promise, so tell us what you know.”

He sunk down onto the nearest bed and looked at his hands. They were shaking. “When I was with the fallen they spoke of things, of demons, wizards, vampires, ogres and the unspeakable evil they’re going to unleash. You’re so far behind in bringing your side together, in preparing for the fight, and they’re already ready. They’re just waiting for the right time. They have everything they need.”

“What—”

Machidiel silenced me. “Let him finish.”

“There’s a secret division, hidden deep inside the fallen. You’re all so self-righteous, you don’t even realize that most of the fallen aren’t even evil. They were just at the wrong place at the wrong time.”

I rolled my eyes.

“The ones that are evil,” he continued, “aren’t even the worst. Most are happy to kill, maim and torture, but a few want revenge.”

"Now there's a concept I'm familiar with," I said.

James looked at me warily. "They're opening the gates between hell, earth and heaven and letting the demons loose. It's a bad time to be an archangel; in particular they're going after *them*."

"Why?" I demanded, ignoring Machidiel's exasperated sigh.

"I already told you—revenge! He's going to make them pay."

"He?"

"Lucifer," Machidiel answered angrily. His eyes darkened and a scowl took over his face.

James nodded slowly. "He wants payback. The archangels were apparently pretty instrumental in having him cast out."

He paused, watching me, waiting for me to say something. I couldn't stop the suspicion crawling through me; he wasn't telling me everything. There was more.

"You were beyond terrified when you came to me. You saw something. What aren't you 'fessing up?"

James sucked on his bottom lip as his chin trembled. "I saw their army in a vision." He shook his head, wide eyed, horrified. "It's huge. There's no way to defeat them. I'm sorry if that's not what you want to hear, but it's not possible. They've got monsters like you've never seen before, the size of skyscrapers, with teeth as big as cars, waiting to be let out. You can't kill them, and that's why the fallen who aren't so evil are trying to find their own way into Heaven, for protection."

"Asmodeus," I whispered.

He nodded. "They know that Heaven is the target, but some figure defending the Heavens will gain them forgiveness, and some figure they'd just prefer to be on the other side of the gate."

"The gate?"

"The Heavenly gates." Machidiel narrowed his eyes at my brother. "They think they can close them once they're broken open?"

"There's a way." James ran his hands over his face. "A sacrifice."

I laughed. "Of course—a sacrifice!"

"Jasmine," Machidiel said harshly. "What sacrifice?"

"An archangel," he said. "I heard them say that the only way to close the gate completely is to kill an archangel with the same weapon that opens the gates. That's why . . ."

"That's why they're going to hunt us down?" I said, guessing the end of his sentence.

James shook his head. "No. That's why they've already started killing off the archangels."

I gasped, hearing Machidiel's shock echo my own.

"What do you mean? Who have they killed?" he demanded. He stepped forward, bringing clenched fists up, fury radiating off of him in waves.

James flinched away from his anger and shrugged. "I don't know. I swear, I don't, but I saw . . . it was a male."

"What did he look like?" Machidiel leaped forward and grabbed him by the throat, shaking him.

"I don't know; they'd almost finished with him when they showed me. He'd been tortured; there was almost nothing left of him." He began to cry, tears spilling down his cheeks.

I felt sick. Nausea rolled through me, churning and biting. My first thought wasn't for myself—I probably should have been concerned that the same fate awaited me—but despair poured through my body at the thought that one of my brothers had suffered so badly. I could have saved him; I *should* have saved him. Wasn't that why I was here, in the human plane?

Machidiel let go of James and took a step back, almost stepping into me. "Why did they let you see?"

"I don't know. Maybe they thought I would help them if I saw how invincible they were. Maybe they wanted me to tell you they were coming after them." He met my eyes. "I did everything I could to find you. I had to tell you what they're planning, try to help you in some way. They're going to keep killing them off until there's none left for the Heavens to use to close the gates with."

"The angels won't turn on their own people. There's no way they will sacrifice an archangel to close the gate," Machidiel spat. "You're an idiot to think that helps us."

As they began to argue, I churned things over in my mind. Which weapon opened the gates? The Dagger of Lex? Or the Falchion of Tabbris? We had both, so they couldn't be used against us, but wait . . .

"*Any* archangel?" I interrupted.

"No!" Machidiel shouted. "I'll not let you sacrifice yourself; not when I swore to protect you."

I held my hand up to silence him. "That's not what I was thinking, although if it comes to it . . ." I shrugged. "If killing *any* archangel will close the gates, then we all know one which is disposable . . . Lucifer. And as it's he who is opening the damn gates in the first place, the punishment kind of suits the crime."

Machidiel nodded. "It could work."

"It *will* work." I folded my arms and clenched my hands, digging my nails into my palms. "I was planning on hunting him down anyway, so that will just kill two birds with one stone. Speaking of birds . . . Asmodeus does not get to hide in the Heavenly realm. His ass is mine."

"I'm okay with that." Machidiel flashed a smile.

"If you think you can take them on, you're crazy," James spat.

"Are you done being helpful now?" I asked. I stepped closer, threateningly.

"No, he's not." Machidiel pushed past me and narrowed his eyes on James. "What else made you so scared when Jasmine spoke to you last?"

James paled. That's when I knew there was one final blow coming. After a long minute, he flicked his eyes up to mine. "They've already released the hell hounds. I saw them. Nothing can stop them. You're so excited about the idea of killing Lucifer, but you haven't even seen him. He's a hundred times bigger, ropes of muscle, and he can breathe fire. He's the King of Hell, and even the most evil of creatures are terrified of him." James stood up and clenched his fists. "You sound so brave that I almost want to have hope—I almost want to believe in you, but you don't know . . . you haven't seen what I've seen."

I began to reject his words, telling myself that he was still the scared, traitorous schoolboy I had first met until his words started making sense, and then something clicked.

"Wait," I growled, my voice coming out in an unearthly snarl.

Machidiel and James looked at me in surprise, flinching away as flames began to lick over my skin.

"Jasmine . . ." Machidiel warned, edging away from me.

"What do you mean; the hell hounds have already been released? How? How have they gotten out of Hell if the gates aren't yet open?"

If it was possible for him to pale further, he did. "The gates are already open."

"Then they have the Falchion." I gasped.

No, no, this wasn't possible. *We* had the falchion. I'd had it in my hands.

I backed away from them and jumped down the stairs, running down the next flight until I skidded past the warriors and into the living room where Haamiah stared at me in shock.

"Where's the Falchion?" I shouted. "Where is it? Tell me you have it."

Haamiah's eyes dropped to the floor as he shook his head. "It was lost. During the battle . . . it was lost." He looked up, catching my eyes with his. "*They* have it."

8

'Far too many people are looking for the right person, instead of trying to be the right person.'

Gloria Steinem

"What?" Sam and Trev exploded.

"We've been sitting here all of this time, doing nothing, while you knew about this? They could open the gates at any moment." Sam gasped.

I glared at Haamiah. "They already have. The hell hounds are out, the demons will be next."

"We need to make a plan," Trev said, urgency in his tone. "Where are the warriors? Where is the Heavenly army to defend us?"

Haamiah closed his eyes for a second. "We have a plan; we're going to evacuate."

"What?" Machidiel appeared next to me. "Why didn't you tell us?"

"You knew it was coming," Haamiah replied.

"You're just going to give up? You're not even going to try to fight?" My voice trembled.

Haamiah shook his head. "It's out of my hands. We've been ordered to evacuate the nephilim and the angels into the Heavenly realm. None of the angels will risk their lives and their souls for this.

There's little hope of anyone getting out of this alive. The angels have been ordered to fall back and defend their home and families."

"And leave the humans and the rest of us to burn," Trev added bitterly.

I frowned at him. "You'll go with them—" I broke off as I took in Haamiah's pained expression.

He swallowed. "*Only* nephilim and angels."

Trev sneered. "Vampires not allowed."

"And valkyrie?" I asked Haamiah, my voice laced with sugar.

"I'm sorry; I'm out of ideas," he hissed. "The only thing I could think of was to comply with the Heavens, evacuate everyone we can—"

"And send me on a wild goose chase?" I asked, tears filling my eyes. "This was your game plan? This is how you predicted we would go out? This is *not* the way I'm ending, abandoned by my own people. I kept telling myself not to trust anyone; I've known for years that trust gets you nowhere. I should never have put my trust in you."

"I'm not going," Haamiah whispered.

I paused, shocked. "What?"

He shook his head. "I swore to look out for you. You only remember flashes, parts of the past, but you, Machidiel, Gabriel, Bëyander and I swore to stick together, no matter what. We knew it could come to this. There's still a chance—we just need more time and a much bigger army."

Hope surged. “We have an army; the valkyrie, lycan, harpies and the human rebellion are our allies,” I said.

Haamiah shook his head. “You’ve done well, but we need more. Remember we’re facing vampires, fallen and demons in the human plane, as well as hell’s prisoners.”

“Who else is there to join us?” Trev asked.

“Witches,” Sam said.

“Werewolves.” Samantha’s voice came from behind us.

We spun around, shocked when we saw nephilim crowding into the room behind us, obviously listening to every word. Most of them looked terrified, and some were even crying.

“You shouldn’t be listening to this,” Haamiah chastised.

She shrugged. “It’s our fate too. It’s our lives or deaths you’re discussing. We should know what’s going on. But, for the record,” she looked at me, “Val could talk to her wolves and make them come around; they’re not all bad.”

“Isn’t there a way to persuade some of our enemies to be our allies?” Will asked.

I snorted. “Yeah, like who? Do *you* want to reason with a bunch of demons while they’re trying to kill you? Maybe list off your attributes?”

Joe glared at me, immediately in defense of his best friend. “Asmodeus seems to be controlling most of them—can’t *you* talk to him and make him join us?”

I blanched. “No. No way.”

Careful, Sam's voice flickered in my mind.

I glanced down as the floor tilted and rolled. I felt pressure on my arm and looked back up to see Sam and Trev clutching onto me from either side, not to control me, but to make sure I didn't go through any portals alone.

That revelation, that feeling of support—that's all it took to calm me down. I wasn't alone. I could breathe again. I could see.

I took a few calming breaths. "Asmodeus is our enemy," I finally replied to Joe. "He's not joining us."

"What about the vampires?" Someone called out.

I shrugged. "What about them?"

"I'm not evil. Maybe we can find some others willing to join forces," Trev suggested.

I looked at Haamiah hopefully. Finally he nodded.

"Okay, we have a plan. The nephilim still need to be evacuated though." Through a chorus of groans, he continued, "If we don't comply, they'll know something's going on. Jasmine, you still need to go after the zombies; meanwhile, find Valentina and send her through a portal to her people and see if she can persuade them to join us. Trev, use your contacts to find other vampires, see if any of them are willing to fight alongside us. Drew, get the lycan army on standby. I'll work through my contacts to see if any warriors will be willing to stay behind."

"What about the human rebellion?" Sam asked.

Haamiah groaned. "I don't see how they can help. They're so weak compared to the rest of us."

"They have equipment and weapons; they can help," I said. "They deserve to be given a chance to save their world."

He flashed a small smile at me. "Fine, contact them and tell them to get ready. Give them the heads up that this is going south quickly."

I nodded, and took a deep breath. "Looks like we have a plan."

"No, we don't." Sam grabbed my arm and swung me towards him. "This plan involves splitting up. We're not splitting up."

"I need to track the zombies, Trev needs to find vampires and you—"

"I need to what? Hide?" Sam glared at me.

"Daton!" Haamiah shouted. Immediately the warrior angel and two others pushed past the nephilim until they stood in front of us. "It's time. Send a message, we need to go."

The nephilim were gathered up and pushed out of the living room, and the door closed firmly, leaving Sam, Trev, Haamiah, Drew, Machidiel and me.

"We're not splitting up," Sam repeated.

Haamiah took a deep breath. "They're expecting you to go with the other nephilim. As the Dagger of Lex, we need you to be kept safe."

"What does it matter? The gates are already open," Sam argued.

"They're open a fraction, but not fully. The Falchion can open them, but the knowledge you have, or at least, *can get*, can get the gates wide open. At least only a trickle of evil is coming through, not a full-blown river." Haamiah grimaced. "You need to be far away from anyone who can use you."

I searched his face; he was telling us the truth. He was genuinely worried for Sam. I turned to look at my friend, who stared at me with horror.

“You agree with him, don’t you?”

My heart ached. “I don’t want to do this without you. I need you with me.”

His face softened and he pulled me into his arms, burying his face into my hair. I could feel his warm breath blow over my skin. “I’m with you. I’ll always be with you.”

“But Haamiah’s right.” I pulled back, dreading the look of betrayal I knew would be in his eyes.

I was right. He stepped away. “What?”

“If they get hold of you, it doesn’t matter what we’re doing, who we get to join our army, we’re screwed. *You’ll* be screwed.” I pleaded with him to understand. “I love you. I don’t want to be without you, but I also don’t want you to be hurt, and I don’t want you to be used against us, because I know how much that would hurt you too.”

He swung away, and stomped over to the chair, sitting down on the arm. “Fine.”

“Please don’t be like that,” I begged.

“It’s done,” Haamiah said firmly. “Sam goes with the rest of them. You focus on building our army and getting the escaped spirits back where they’re supposed to be.”

“You’ll make sure the guardians of the Pool are expecting us?” Trev quickly asked.

I sent him a silent thanks. I'd forgotten about that aspect.

"Why would they be expecting you?" Haamiah asked.

"So we can return the spirits," I said brightly, forcing a smile on my face.

Haamiah shook his head, his dreadlocks swinging over his shoulder. "No, there's no need. By now they'll have taken corporeal form, so the only way to return them is to kill them . . . again."

"I'm not going to the Pool?" I whispered.

The floor tilted, despair, agony and anger rippling through me. No, this couldn't be happening. I couldn't be given hope only to have it ripped away again. I couldn't live without him, I needed him. I couldn't be without Zach; he was mine! This was all my fault. If only I had done something different, any small action, he could still be with me.

God, I missed him so much; the way he touched my hair, the way he said my name, even the way he would snarl and growl at me when he was mad. I missed his smile, his humor, his anger, his frustration, his kindness, the way his soul shone through his eyes, the way he didn't care how strong or powerful I was, he was determined to keep me safe and carry me through the storms. Through his actions more than his words he showed me he loved me, and hell, I knew I wasn't easy to love. I had many flaw, many weaknesses, yet he was my guardian angel, my lover, and my soul mate. He promised he would never leave me, but because of me he was dead . . . and I couldn't bring him back. There was no way to bring him back.

It's amazing how quickly your mood can change, how deep your heart can sink and how much one person can affect you. How extinguishing hope can literally seem like ending the world, the end of you and your heart. I could see him; I could feel him. His face was right here, burned into my mind, his body a memory I would never forget. God, what if I forgot him? I closed my eyes tightly, my head throbbing as tears burned behind my eyelids. *Oh my God! Please, baby, I'm sorry, please come back. I'm so sorry. Don't leave me!*

"It will be easier to return them to the Pool of Souls," Machidiel said, his voice cutting through my mind like a knife.

My head whipped around and my eyes automatically found him, an anchor in the storm. Did I hear him correctly? Was he helping me? Was he helping us?

Jasmine, hold on. Sam's arms found me again. I hadn't even heard him move but he was here, holding onto me as the floor continued to slope downwards.

"Why?" Haamiah questioned him.

"It just will be. Trust me." Machidiel's soft voice brushed over me. "Just make sure they know we're coming."

"Fine. I'll call them now." Haamiah moved on. "I take it that means you're staying behind. Make sure you get up there before the gates close. I'll speak with Bëyander, see if she can buy us a little more time, or think of a way out of this."

"Good. We're heading out now." Machidiel tugged me out of Sam's arms, and I let him lead me blindly out of the room, down the corridor, and out the front door into the garden. Drew and Trev followed quickly and bundled me into the car we had parked outside the gate.

As we pulled off from the curb, I curled up on the back seat and buried my head in my hands, feeling waves of emotion poured over me. Loss, so much loss. I was drowning. It really sucked when the only person who could make you feel better was also the reason why you cried.

9

'Souls recognize each other by the way they feel, not by the way they look.'

Unknown.

I sighed, rubbing my face along the light dusting of hair on his chest. Soft, yet raspy on my cheeks, I rubbed lower, feeling the ropes of muscle beneath my skin. He was so silky and smooth, yet hard, the most powerful of all men. A warrior; my warrior. Oh, I felt so safe with him. So loved.

His lips gently touched my forehead, softly pressing a kiss to my skin. I surged up, turning my face upwards, shivering as he trailed kisses down the side of my face to my cheek. No more teasing.

His lips found mine and I opened, letting his mouth sweep into mine, dueling with me. His warm tongue stroked mine, soothing yet scintillating at the same time. Butterflies swept up through my abdomen, flying through my chest as he rolled me under him, sweeping the sheets out of the way. He caged me in with his arms on either side of my body, leaning down on his forearms to stay connected to my mouth.

I reached up, trailing my hands over his shoulders and up the back of his head. I loved the feeling of his shaved head beneath my palms. The strength of him as he rolled against me, his weight pushing me into the bed as his thigh slipped between mine, pressing between my legs.

I gasped. "Zach."

"Did you say something?"

I sat up straight, panting for breath. Trev was sitting beside me in the back of the car, frowning.

"What?" I whispered.

"I thought you said something." He yawned and rested his head back against the headrest.

I pressed my hand to my chest, feeling the pounding of my heart as the pain pulsed through me.

"You okay back there?" Drew turned around to face me, slowing the car.

God, I wanted to cry. I bit my lip, digging my teeth in to try to force out the pain of my heart. I scrunched my eyes closed, and turned to face the window. I would never be okay again, not until I had Zach back. I shivered at that thought. I needed to focus on that. Machidiel had made it so we had a way to get to the Pool. I would pull him out and bring him back. That's all there was to it. That's all that mattered.

I just needed to get a hold of these zombies first . . .

"Where are we going?" I asked.

I felt the weight of Machidiel's eyes on me. "The airport."

"Why? I hate airports. Can't we just use a portal?"

Machidiel snorted. "Not when you're as unstable as you are now. Who knows where we'd end up?"

I scowled. "Again, *where* are we going?"

He sighed, irritated with my questions. "Unless you have another idea, we're heading to meet a coven of witches who may or may not be able to point us in the direction of the zombies," he said.

I nodded to myself. *Oh yeah, zombies. Right.* "I don't see why it even matters if we find them. In the grand scheme of things. What difference will returning a zombie and a werewolf make, when demons the size of skyscrapers are about to be unleashed on us?"

"The size of skyscrapers?" Trev echoed.

"Haamiah may be irritating at times, but he knows what he's doing," Machidiel answered, very blasé. "If he says it's still important we hunt them down, then that's what we're doing. He's a principality; this will all figure into his game plan somehow."

I scowled. "I don't like where his game plan has gotten us so far." I sat up straight and looked around the car. "Where's Sam?"

Trev grimaced. "He's going with the other nephilim, remember? You kind of spaced back there, we needed to get you out."

I slouched back into my seat. "I didn't say goodbye."

Trev reached over and linked his fingers with mine. "You don't need to say goodbye. You'll see him again. *We'll* see him again."

I shook my head. "You don't know that. You know what we're up against. Demons and vampires are the easiest of what we'll face. We're up against the four Horsemen, Asmodeus and Lucifer, among the rest of Hell's vomit." Trev tightened his fingers around mine. "I'm sorry, I know you all want to think we're getting out of this, but

I just don't see it happening. Best outcome, we take them down with us."

"That's a really great motivational speech," Drew drawled.

I stayed quiet, staring out the window at the passing houses. Where were we? Did it even matter any more?

"It's going to be okay," Trev whispered.

I squeezed his fingers between mine. He was my anchor now, the only thing keeping me sane.

"So, who are these witches?" I heard my voice shake.

"Friends, allies, really," Machidiel corrected himself. "They're the good sort."

"As in, less evil than the rest," Drew added, sarcastically.

"It's all relative." I could hear the smile in Machidiel's voice. "We're going to see one particular witch; Marjorie. She's going to help us."

"By doing what?"

He turned around to smile gleefully at me. "She's going to do us a little conjuring spell. She's going to tell us exactly where they are, and then we're going to go hunting."

"Then what?"

Machidiel pinned me with a frown.

"I just need to know. I need to have it clear in my mind what we're doing," I said.

“If you need to know exactly what we’re doing, then I want to know exactly what you have planned...no secrets,” Machidiel said.

Drew lifted his hand off the steering wheel. “I second that.”

I exchanged a look with Trev and sighed. I didn’t really have the option to keep our plans secret. When Machidiel had seen how shocked I was that Haamiah wasn’t going to get us access to the Pool of Kali, he had spontaneously backed me up without question. I needed to be straight with him.

“We’ll track and kill the zombie that got out, then we’re headed for the Pool of Kali and we’re going to bring Zach back,” I said quickly, clarifying my goals so there was no misunderstanding about what I was in this for. I grimaced, waiting for Machidiel’s reply.

There was a heavy silence for a moment.

“Is that even possible?” Drew asked in a shocked voice.

I shrugged. “Of course. I brought Zanaria back.”

“What if he isn’t there?” Machidiel said.

I scowled. I didn’t even know that was a possibility. “Why wouldn’t he be there? It’s the Pool of Souls.”

He laughed without humor. “Didn’t you learn anything in your lessons?”

I gulped. “Why wouldn’t he be there?”

I saw his shoulders shrug in front of me.

“Souls don’t all go to the same place. Zach’s a warrior in the Heavenly army, and he died doing his duty; it’s unlikely his soul went anywhere besides Heaven,” he explained.

I bit my lip. “Then why was Zanaria there?”

“It was unprecedented. Her death came as a shock, completely unexpected. Sometimes when that happens, souls get sucked in the wrong direction, flowing into other areas, and sometimes they’re purposely placed somewhere, such as in the Never Ending Forest.”

That was another name for the Throne’s waiting room; a place where souls were sent to be judged. “You think he’s in the Never Ending Forest?”

“No, I don’t. I was just using it as an example. Zach’s soul could be anywhere.”

Blinding pain crushed through my chest, peeling, bleeding, agony. No, it wasn’t true, it couldn’t be. Zach needed me to find him, to bring him back, but if he wasn’t in the Pool I might never find him. He’d be lost forever. He couldn’t be gone. I pressed my hand to my throat, gasping for breath, needing air. I like I was drowning, my soul being ripped into shreds again. *Zach could be anywhere.* He could be in Hell. He could be facing an eternity of torture, and I wouldn’t be able to rescue him. God, I would do anything, I would pray every day, I would give up everything I had, devote my life to the sick and the poor. I would do anything to have him back.

Please come back!

“Machidiel, shut up!” I heard Trev shout through my hazy mind.

“He *might* be in the Pool of Kali.”

I heard the words, I let them sink in. I needed them, believed them. I would bring Zach back. This would work; I just needed to concentrate on all of the little steps I needed to take before I could get there.

Looking up, I frowned as my eyes remained fuzzy. I could hear the guys coughing, spluttering. My door was pulled open, and someone reached over me. As astounded as I was, I didn't put up a fight as I was pulled from the car onto the road.

Smoke billowed from our vehicle, streaming up into the sky. Cars and lorries beeped their horns as they sped past, giving us a wide berth. Any moment now, there would definitely be a fire truck heading our way; there was no way this hadn't been reported.

I sheepishly glanced at Drew. "Sorry. That was my fault."

"Don't worry about it; we're close. We're in walking distance." Drew grinned.

Trev grabbed my hand and pulled me away from the car onto the grass beside the road. Together, we started walking, Drew and Machidiel trailing behind.

"Guys." I took a deep breath, concentrating on marching onward. "I have to believe it's possible, okay? I need this to work."

Trev squeezed my hand. "It will work."

I gave him a grateful smile, the tension in my body relaxing a notch.

"Zach knew you'd come for him, just as you know Zach would always come for you if anything had happened. He would go somewhere he knew you'd be able to find him," Machidiel added, relaxing me further.

"You're right," I agreed. "He would know I'd come for him. He *knows* I'll come for him. And we have more of a chance of defeating the evil coming at us if we have him by our side. He won't want to miss this fight."

“You’re right. He was always vicious,” Machidiel agreed.

My mind pulled me back to the thousand times I had seen Zach in action. He was more than vicious, he was majestic, powerful, and magnificent. He would take on this serious, deadly expression and you knew he would win whatever fight he was in. He’d have dozens of weapons strapped across his body, swords across his back, knives attached to his ankles—I even once saw him with a mace, though that was more Maion’s weapon of choice. Oh, and his wings; beautiful, white, billowing wings, with feathers as soft as cloud. They were stronger than they looked, and made for an excellent pillow, though he normally tucked them away when he slept, which wasn’t often. He usually only came to bed to be with me; angels only slept if they were injured or exhausted. It didn’t happen often, but waking up curled under his arm, with his sleepy kisses on my lips, were the most peaceful, idyllic moments of my life. I’d trade away the rest of my existence to experience just one more moment like that.

Zach *would* be in the Pool of Kali and I *would* bring his soul out. The only thing I needed to worry about was where he would be made corporeal. Zanaria’s soul had flown out of my hand seconds after I had pulled her out of the vortex of nothing, and vanished. The angels had located her, thankfully, and brought her to safety, and I’m sure they would do the same for Zach. I just hoped he would be safe until they found him and brought him home to me.

We left the roadside and weaved our way through a large industrial estate at the edge of the airport compound. It took a good half an hour to work out how to reach the airport by foot, but after a few dead ends, we trudged onto the path leading up to the multistory car park.

“We’re here.” Trev tugged me out of my musings.

I looked up from the pavement I had been staring at, and followed Trev as he pulled me along beside him into the airport terminal. We dodged the families with mountains of suitcases piled up on top of metal trolleys, and walked around rude businessmen who almost ran us over as they practically sprinted out of the terminal with their small black cases. Screaming children ran amok with shouting parents rushing after them, and the noise was almost deafening.

I looked back down at my feet, remembering the way Zach would touch my cheek, pushing strands of hair behind my ear before he kissed me. I missed him.

Machidiel had apparently already bought tickets and checked us in online, and he pulled us towards security. We passed through the scanner without hindrance and headed straight for the gate. I kept my head down the entire time, letting Trev push and pull me in the right direction until I found myself being led onto the airplane and pushed into my seat.

I pulled the seatbelt across my lap and buckled it, sliding the material to make it fit snugly. I glanced around, noting the flight was only half full, empty seats surrounding us.

“Where are we going?” I asked Trev, who buckled his seatbelt next to me.

“Back to the United States.”

I settled in, leaning my cushion against the window to sleep, blanking out the bright lights, the noises and the annoyingly loud rumble of the engine. I just wanted to sleep . . . because then I would see Zach again.

10

'The animal in you is no match for the demon in me.'

Unknown.

After too many, and yet not enough, hauntingly realistic dreams I woke up to find a steaming hot cup of coffee and a breakfast muffin on the small pullout table in front of me. I squinted at Trev, smiling slightly at the sight of him sleeping with his mouth open, snoring softly; it had been a hell of a long day/week/month for all of us.

I looked past him to see a little old lady bent over in her seat, sitting on the very edge of it, across the aisle, her mouth gaping wide open as she stared at us.

I shot up in my seat and nudged Trev awake, knowing exactly what that nosey old bitch was looking at. He jerked awake and scowled at me.

"So you're the only one who's allowed to sleep?" he grumbled, shuffling around in his seat.

"Your fangs!" I hissed.

He paled and surreptitiously glanced around, shooting a glare at the woman and sending her scuttling further back into her seat.

"Way to stay undercover," I joked.

He rolled his eyes and swiped my coffee from my fingers, gulping some down. “Not exactly loving the plane ride, just weeks after almost being murdered on one.”

I shrugged and began to pick at the muffin, pulling off a piece of bread to chew on. “We could have tried a portal—”

“But you’re not exactly Miss Stable.” He grinned. “I’d prefer to take my chances on the airplane.”

I laughed. “You can talk.”

“Not planning on a repeat of the problem in the car, are you?” Drew drawled.

I turned around to catch him grinning down at me from the chair behind. He reached over to touch me and seemed to think a little better of it, pulling back.

“No, I’m okay,” I said, not exactly sure if it were true. I just needed to concentrate, focus on the end game—bringing Zach back. “How much longer?”

“We should be there soon,” Drew said. “Better finish your coffee before it’s time to land.”

I turned back around, and with a guilty expression Trev handed my coffee cup back. I shook it slightly, feeing the significantly lighter fluid slosh around inside. I quickly finished my snack and sat back, waiting for an announcement that we were going to land.

A full hour later, we had dropped into L.A. airport and were being steered through the terminal towards security. Machidiel led the way, seeming to know where he was going. He avoided the travel escalators, preferring to weave through the other passengers. Trev and I bumped into each other when a group of men stopped suddenly. Quickly apologizing, we ducked past them, jogging to catch up with Machidiel and Drew.

I turned to glance back, dread running through me as I caught the eyes of one of the men. He lifted his chin, a hint of a smile on his lips, before his friend nudged him. I didn't recognize him from the plane, but the instinctive shiver that ran up my spine told me he certainly knew who I was.

"That guy . . ." I whispered to Trev. I dug my fingers in his forearm to get his attention.

He shot a look behind us, disregarding them soon after, and pulled me along to keep up with Machidiel. I looked back again, biting my lip with uncertainty. The men had disappeared behind obvious tourists in loud T-shirts, laughing and joking, silently dragging luggage behind them as they kept up with the fast moving crowd.

Spotting the security sign ahead, I took a deep breath and pushed forward to join the queue that snaked around rope and metal barriers designed to keep us orderly. I gripped the passport Drew threw to me, flicking to the picture page.

"Huh."

"What?" Trev asked, looking at his own.

I rolled my eyes and turned the book toward him, flashing him a picture of me that somehow looked as though it had been taken recently, though I didn't recollect anyone asking permission to take my photo. I wouldn't have complained—after all, to randomly produce a current and legal passport was a pretty cool feat—however, the angels had clearly decided that anonymity was the way to go, and had given me a name that wouldn't look out of place in an Amish town; Martha Miller.

As Trev stifled a laugh, I hissed at Machidiel, "Really? Was that your idea?"

He flashed a grin. "You've had more than enough excitement for both of your lifetimes."

Trev choked. "Seriously, dude?"

"What did you get?"

"Keep your voices down, people!" Machidiel hushed us.

I squeezed closer to Trev, pulling down the book he held tightly to his chest.

I gasped, my eyes flying to Machidiel who was trying not to laugh. "Lucian Blood? Seriously?"

I turned to Trev, my mouth gaping wide. "He's obviously crazy, right?"

He shook his head in amazement and pushed me forward, shuffling down the line into the gap that had widened while we had been busy learning our new names.

Within a few minutes we walked towards the immigration officer who was impatiently gesturing us to come closer. We went up as a group, holding our passports out to be viewed. The young yet balding officer took Drew's first, flicking through the pages. He ran it under a small scanner at his booth desk and looked up, glaring at the lycan.

"Boris Wolfgang?" He quirked his eyebrow sarcastically.

My mouth dropped open. What was Machidiel thinking? This was no time to be playing pranks on us. I wanted to cringe at the embarrassment, maybe angrily hissed at Machidiel for being an idiot and drawing attention to us when we needed to be flying under the radar. Tired and emotionally drained as I was, I would have probably been unable to hold that anger in, and then we would have had a problem. Having a shotgun pointed at my face made my blood run cold so anger was the last thing on my mind.

Time slowed, froze, actually, as I stared down the barrel of the gun into the eyes of evil. Where the eyes of this immigration officer had appeared normal just seconds ago, the black of his pupils now seemed to flood past his irises into the whites of his eyes. As his finger tightened on the trigger, I was knocked to the floor. An explosive boom silenced all noise after, my ears ringing sharply.

Feeling the weight of Trev pushing me into the floor had oddly made me feel safe—until I realized despite the screaming and further gunshots, he wasn't moving.

I slid out from under him, crouching near his head as he coughed and spluttered. Seeing the blood seep from under him, pooling around his torso, I shrieked.

No, not again.

My eyes clouded, mist pouring from my body, from every orifice, rising up from my skin as though I were sweating a glittery shadow. All noise still muted, I faced a group of men rushing towards us with vengeance in my blood. As I narrowed my eyes at them, the ground tilted and leveled.

I opened my lips slightly, just enough to blow out a sliver of air. In response, flames licked up the clothes of the men facing me. I smiled coldly, distantly, as I saw their mouths open in expressions of terror and excruciating pain as they swung around, slapping at each other, dropping to the ground to try to put out my angelic fire.

Drew jostled me back to attention, dragging me by my arms. I dropped my gaze to Trev, lying face down on the cool, white tiled floor, blood continuing to leak out of his body. Machidiel picked him up, the bulk of muscle on his arms very much evident as he threw my friend, my brother over his shoulder and roared at us to go while other travelers screamed in terror.

“Let’s go!” Drew shouted. At least, I presumed he did; his mouth opened and I read the words as clearly in his mind as if he had had subtitles.

We sprinted towards the turnstiles, the metal designed to keep us here so we could be murdered. I kept checking to see that Machidiel still had Trev, only truly concentrating when Drew took on his lycan form, his body elongating, bulking up, his eyes changing color as adrenaline turned him. I stared at the gate before us and bent my knees, throwing my body high up into the air to leap over it, landing in a run, and heading for the next blockade—the declarations queue.

The ringing in my ears began to subside, and was replaced by a shrieking alarm through the airport sound system. The screaming and wailing of terrified passengers didn’t faze me; I pushed on, gearing up to jump again. Drew snarled, tackling an officer, punching out at another. While he was on the offensive, I maintained defense—ducking, diving, and sprinting as fast as my legs would carry me, keeping Machidiel and Trev in my sights up ahead.

Passengers fled from us, giving us a clear path. I turned back to check on Trev, and was punched in my jaw. My head snapped around to the left and I stood, stunned out of my senses for a slow second. Another punch was aimed at my stomach and I fell forward, held up by my attacker. I lifted my head, horror flooding me as I took in the black, soulless eyes that seemed to swallow my oxygen. For a moment I paused . . . Would it really be so bad to give in? It would all end; it would all stop.

I lifted my arm to block the next punch and slid to the side, turning to kick him in the back, knocking him off his feet. I wouldn't give in, not while there was still a chance to get Zach back. I pressed my right foot to the floor and pushed off. I grabbed hold of the metal barricade and twisted my body, flying over the top. The others were still ahead of me, Machidiel and Trev running through the airport, almost outside. Drew was fighting off a group of men, thankfully hand to hand combat was his specialty, and because their own men were too close to get a clear shot of the lycan, the armed officers held their guns back, holding their fire.

Drew is my friend. Drew is my ally. He needs me. Trev needs me, I spoke to myself sternly, forcing my mind to act, pushing aside the rage coursing through me. I needed to stay calm.

I ran and slid across the floor, taking down one of the men. While on the floor I kicked my heel out, cracking him in the face. I knelt up and rolled, flipping up to my feet in front of Drew. In the heat of battle he was still able to grin, a feeling of comradeship making me grin back. Backs to each other, we lashed out, knocking our assailants out one by one.

When the last one dropped to the floor with a thud, blood spurting out from a head wound, Drew and I ran for the exit and out into the daylight. We saw Machidiel up ahead, pushing past disgruntled pedestrians on the sidewalk. We crossed the road, dodging oncoming taxis, and continued on.

Keeping the angel in our sights, Drew and I ducked and weaved, trying not to follow the exact same steps, making a fresh trail.

When Machidiel disappeared from view, I panicked, screaming, “We’re losing them!”

Drew took my hand and led me on, shoving people out of the way. We ran through an arcade, customers in the small boutique stores and coffee shops gasping in shock as we passed by. Back out on the street, with the tall buildings surrounding us blocking the sun, we joined up with Machidiel and Trev.

Machidiel abruptly turned down a narrow alleyway and stopped beside a red car; a sedan with rust splatters on the doors and a taped up, broken rear window. Drew threw his elbow through the glass, smashing it in one go, and punched his hand through to reach for the handle. He pulled the door wide and quickly released the lock on the front door. Machidiel almost threw Trev onto the back seat and I leaped in with him, clambering over his prone body while Machidiel and Drew jumped into the front.

Drew reached down, breaking apart the hard material hiding the electronics, and hotwired the car with an ease I would have thought suited a hardened criminal.

Not bothering with a seatbelt, I crouched over Trev, pulling his T-shirt up over his chest to see where he was injured. As blood bubbled up out of the hole in the center of his chest, I pressed my shaking hands to his skin, covering the wound. I closed my eyes, gritting my teeth as Machidiel swerved the car around a corner, throwing me back against the door.

Power surged to life, magic churning through my stomach and up through my chest. Reaching my heart, it gushed through my hands, seeping into Trev.

I couldn't fail now, not again. I couldn't lose Trev, not when he'd thrown his body over mine to shield me from the gunman. He was so good, so selfless. He didn't deserve what life had given him, but I *would* heal him and bring him back.

I felt platelets joining together to clot, blood able to channel through his body correctly. The tissue reconnected, healing, forming a barrier and ever so slowly, I became aware of his eyes staring up at me.

"Be careful back there," Drew shouted. "Remember he's a vampire and he's lost a lot of blood."

I didn't need any warning. I could tell how hungry he was just by looking into his eyes, feeling the rigidity of his body as he held himself still while staring at me. He was ravenous—his jaw ticked as he locked his muscles so he wouldn't move. His breath hissed in and out and he groaned.

No, I didn't need to be told to be careful; I was leaning over a ravenous, injured vampire and I was well aware of it.

11

'Your intuition is a muscle. To develop it, you must listen.'

Phil Good.

"Is he okay?" Machidiel aggressively turned the wheel and slid around another corner, horns beeping at us in outrage as we narrowly missed crashing.

I was flung against the backseat and slid off down the well in the center of the car. I grimaced as I pushed aside cigarette cartons and empty drink bottles and scrambled up again, straddling Trev with a knee on either side of his body.

I bit my lip, keeping my eyes on him. "Like Drew said, he's lost a lot of blood," I answered slowly, appraising his blood soaked T-shirt. Even with the wound now closed, he had lost so much. The seat beneath us was saturated. Where my knee pressed into the material, a shiny pool of liquid seemed to be squeezed out on top.

What was I going to do? What would Zach do? What would Sam do? I wasn't as good as they were; I could kid myself and pretend to be heroic and knowledgeable, I could pretend to be an archangel or a valkyrie warrior or whatever else but right now I was just a scared little girl with a thousand mental and physical problems.

My problems at the moment centered on the starving and injured vampire who was also one of my best friends. He needed blood, and I needed to get out of here alive. Or did I? Out of the two of us, despite the fact that I was an archangel and Trev was a vampire, he was a thousand times better than I was. He was honest, kind, loving, brave, and deserved a hell of a lot more than what he had been given. Out of the Ten Commandments, I had broken most of them; as a valkyrie I was supposed to believe in a completely different set of Gods, I coveted other people's lives all of the time, I stole, I lied, I kind of cheated in the whole Aidan versus Zach problem a couple of years ago, I planned to kill my adoptive parents as soon as I got my hands on them, and said "Oh, God" in almost every sentence. No, if anyone got given a second chance, it should be Trev.

His eyes were emotional as he stared up at me. He was struggling, and he was losing the battle against his nature. I could hear his thoughts, and though they were jumbled and confused, in this moment he hated himself. He hated what he had become, what he knew he was going to do. He was devastated because he knew he couldn't hold on much longer.

I took a deep breath and pulled at the neck of my T-shirt, dragging it down my shoulder.

"Shit, are you really going to do this?" Drew growled.

I turned my head to see Drew had turned fully in his seat and was anxiously looking from me to Trev, guessing the situation correctly.

"I would do anything for my friends," I replied honestly.

He narrowed his eyebrows, scowling at me. "Anything?"

"*Anything*," I repeated. "My friends are everything to me. They're my family; they're who I am."

"Good to know." Drew ran his hand through his shoulder-length, dark hair. Blood had matted through the ends, and it fell back in his eyes again. "I'm asking you a favor, then."

I groaned, exasperated. "Don't ask me not to do this. He's in control at the moment, but the hunger will get too much and you know it. I couldn't live with myself if he did something that I could prevent. He would hate himself if he hurt someone, Drew. He's not a bad person. He doesn't deserve this."

"Just make sure he doesn't take too much," Drew said, his eyes flashing.

"I might have to rely on you for help with that," I muttered, eying Trev as his body began to shake.

I pulled my T-shirt further so it remained in place, stretched over my shoulder. I took a deep breath and slid my hand around Trev's neck.

"Do it."

Trev shook his head, squirming away from me . . . for a second. Maybe it was the smell of my blood, or the sound of my heartbeat, but his arms pulled me down, almost suffocating me and he turned his head into my neck, his teeth sinking deep.

I gasped, trying not to scream as pain spread through my neck, up my jaw and down into my shoulder. My fingers grew numb, searing heat scorching the rest of my body. I screeched when Trev rolled, pulling me underneath him, one hand gripping my throat and the other holding my shoulder still. His lean, yet heavy body held me captive beneath him, one of his legs between mine, anchoring him.

The stories I had read about a vampire bite feeling amazing, about the sensation of teeth sinking into your body being erotic had it completely wrong. The pain roaring through my veins was hideous. I was sweating with the effort to pump whatever blood remained to my limbs and organs, fighting to stay conscious, though my mind screamed at me to let go, to avoid the throbbing agony I had inflicted on myself.

"Enough," I hissed, a grey haze not of my own making alerting me I was fading out.

Trev groaned and kept drinking, and the suction on my neck became unbearable. I heard a yell, shouting, arguing, and a moment later Trev's fangs were ripped out of my throat and he was shoved away. Drew dragged me up against him, stroking my neck, feeling for my pulse.

"I'm fine," I moaned.

"You don't look fine," he snarled. "You nearly killed her!"

"No, he didn't mean to." I gasped, trying to defend him, even as I slumped against the lycan behind me.

"I'm so sorry. I took too much." I vaguely heard Trev say.

I felt bodies shift on the backseat. Trev's hands were on my hips as he moved me inwards, away from the ledge. I smiled to convey my thanks, even as a twinge of pain pulled at my neck when he and Drew moved me into a safer position. Trev pulled my legs out over his lap and reached forward. His fingers never touched me though, as Drew knocked his hand out of the way.

"Don't touch her," he snarled.

I knew his lycan had risen with his need to protect me and I just couldn't understand it. I began to roll my eyes at their ridiculous male protective instincts when I realized I had done the exact same thing. It felt a little odd in my mind that I had just risked my life to save Trev's, but I let it pass, not wanting to waste my energy thinking about anything so confusing. Trev was alive and no longer psycho with hunger; I was a little drained, literally, but again, alive, so Drew should just relax and wait for Machidiel to get us out of this mess. Which reminded me . . .

"Did we get away?" My voice was hoarse, raspy.

Drew stroked his fingers down my face. "We're almost out of the city; they're not tailing us anymore, which is something to be pleased about."

I smiled, resting my eyes. "Good."

Their voices faded in and out for a moment before I opened my eyes again as something tugged on my hand.

"You still with us?" Machidiel's clearly worried voice reached me.

"Yep. I'm still here, in the car, fleeing from whoever those guys were. Any ideas?"

Drew tilted my head to look down at my neck again. "We have a long list of enemies so it could have been any of them. Initially I thought human rebellion, but their eyes were clearly demonic."

"They were trying to kill her, so that rules out Asmodeus; he wants her alive," Trev added, running his hands down my legs, squeezing my calf occasionally as if to remind himself I was still there. Normally I didn't like people touching me but I could shake this one off, or at least, I couldn't somehow find the energy to actually care. A grey haze took over and I only came out when I felt eyes on me.

I had zoned out again and missed something.

"What?" I asked.

Machidiel turned his head to look at me, worry creasing his forehead. "I said it was probably Mnemosyne. The Horsemen seemed to enjoy the fight too much; they wouldn't want anyone else to take away their fun. Mnemosyne seems more the type to get others to do her dirty work." There was a slight pause. "We're going to have to pull over, I need to heal her."

"Me? No, keep going," I insisted.

Machidiel growled low in his throat. "Have you seen your neck? You're still . . . *leaking*!"

I lifted my hand to my neck, touching the sore area delicately. I brought my hand in front of my face, moving it until it came into focus. "Ew." I wrinkled my nose at my bloody fingertips.

"Exactly," Drew grumbled.

"I can just heal myself." I lifted my hand again, though it felt heavier by the second.

"You will not!" Machidiel ordered.

I flinched and dropped my arm suddenly.

He turned to glare at me and I hunched back into Drew. "You'll drain the last drop of energy out of yourself if you do that. Concentrate on breathing."

I rolled my eyes and huffed out my breath. "You can't tell me what to do; I'm in charge here."

Laughter met my ears. "Yeah, how's that working out for you? You able to even sit up on your own?" Drew sniggered.

"Jas, you did an amazing thing. Giving me your blood was selfless and so brave. I could have killed you—I don't know if I would have stopped if Drew hadn't pulled me off you," Trev said, his fingers circling my ankle. "You were exhausted before we even set out on this mission. Now, I've drained most of your blood. I know you're used to being the one in charge and doing your own thing, but now you need to let us help. Let us take care of you just for a little while."

"I'm fine." I sighed. I took a deep breath and let it out in a whoosh, sinking deeper into Drew's arms. *That felt better*. "Okay, you can look after me, but don't tell anyone."

My body felt so heavy, so tired. My eyes wouldn't stay open so I tilted my head against Drew's neck, breathing his scent in deeply. I heard him shouting at me to stay awake, but I just couldn't summon the energy to reply. I didn't know why he was so worried; I was fine and so was Trev. We would get out of this okay; I just needed to have a little sleep. Okay, a *lot* of sleep. I felt a smile pull at my lips and I sighed into Drew's warmth, letting my eyes shut and my breathing slow.

12

'How can a person give you so much strength, yet still be your only weakness?'

Unknown.

I knew I was under, I knew I was dreaming; shadows swept across my eyelids, dark, grey and sometimes black. Images swirled about my mind; horrific dreams about Zach and Trev, demons and fallen angels. In one dream I imagined that Lilith had been turned in to a vampire and was murdering my friends. When I wasn't dreaming vivid massacres, I felt as though I were drowning in a sea of grey. My body was heavy, my mind floated. I could hear voices, people talking to me, saying things I couldn't understand. The voices were low, muffled and disjointed.

I tried to surface, I knew there was something I was supposed to be doing but I was dragged down, chains holding me at the bottom of the sea, drowning me, filling my body with weights despite the voices calling to me. I heard my name many times but couldn't respond. There was no energy.

Black eyes flashed in my mind, startling me out of my reverie. Like an anchor they held me still, forcing me to stare into them. Unblinking, they drifted back, zooming out so that I could see a nose and lips. Soft lips moved, shaping words I couldn't hear. They were demanding something from me, barking orders.

I surfaced, swimming up out of the darkness, letting the beautiful, black eyes pull me awake.

"She's come around!" A voice yelled in my ear.

I groaned, lifting a hand to my face. I felt stiff and sore all over. I shifted trying to roll onto my side, but was pulled into a sitting position, a hard body cushioning me from behind.

A cool cloth was pressed to my face, jolting me awake. I pushed it off, squinting at the face directly in front of my own.

"What?" I whispered.

Machidiel broke into a relieved grin. "Thank God."

"That was the longest few hours of my life. Don't do that again!" Drew chastised me, scowling, more than a little irritated.

I smiled. Yep, as much as he tried to play the cool guy, Drew hated not being in control.

"What happened?"

"You were unconscious. Do you remember anything?" Machidiel asked.

I stiffened, sitting up on my own, and looked at our surroundings. We were sitting on a bed in a very nondescript room, probably a motel. There was a plain wooden desk, complete with telephone, a small television in the corner of the room, two double beds, and the heaviest black drapes ever dragged haphazardly across the windows.

"How did we get here?" I mused, still feeling faint.

"Drink this." Trev pushed off the wall he was leaning against and handed me a carton of orange juice.

I downed it in three huge gulps, panting for breath after. "I'm so thirsty."

"I nearly killed you," Trev whispered.

I looked up, crunching the carton in my palm. "What?"

He shrugged forlornly. "I took too much blood. You've been unconscious for hours. I thought I'd killed you."

I tilted my head, frowning at him. He looked gutted. I slid to the end of the bed and stood, ignoring the wave of dizziness that threatened to send me falling to the floor. I quickly stepped closer and grasped him by the hands, staring up at him.

"I made the decision to give you my blood. I gave it to you freely. You didn't *take* it; I gave it, and I would do it again."

He shook his head. "You shouldn't. I couldn't stop and in the car you . . . you looked . . ."

I waved his words away. "I'm sure I looked pretty bad, but I'm fine now. I take care of you, you take care of me. That's how this thing works."

He dropped his gaze, staring at the floor. "Maybe I should go. I need to find vampires willing to fight with us anyway."

"No," I barked. He flinched. "No, you're not going anywhere. The only reason you think you want to leave us is because you feel guilty and sorry for yourself. Well, stop it. I need you in this fight. I need you to stand with me. Running off and getting yourself killed isn't going to help anyone. We'll find the zombies, kill them, bring

Zach back, and together we'll find some vamps who don't want to slit our throats." I shrugged. "Can't be that hard . . ."

A ghost of a smile appeared on his face.

"Where are we, anyway?" I turned to Machidiel.

He puffed up his chest, looking suspiciously proud of me, as he sat on the bed beside Drew. In fact, both of them had an odd, disconcerting look about them.

"Four hours drive north of L.A. We had to stop for petrol and a couple of healing sessions on you which hindered us, but we made a good dent in our journey," he said.

I narrowed my eyes. "A *dent*?"

He shrugged. "We're near Sacramento."

"And we're going where?"

"The coven's in Portland."

I gasped. "We couldn't just fly directly there? We could have avoided the whole L.A.-airport-massacre thing!"

"You're being a little dramatic don't you think?" He sighed. "There were no direct flights out from Melbourne, hence our arrival at L.A."

"Yeah, it's no big deal . . . in a stolen car!" I scowled, tossing my hair over my shoulder.

Drew laughed. "Jesus, didn't figure you for a prude. You know, you say you're a bad ass, but really . . ."

I stuck up my middle finger and tilted my head. "No one else have a problem driving halfway up the country in a stolen car?" The boys continued to grin at me, albeit Trev's a little forced. "Then neither do I. Though, if we get pulled over by demonic police officers—I told you so."

I flounced into the bathroom and turned on the sink tap. I grimaced at myself in the mirror. I was beyond pale, probably more grey than white. Black bags circled my eyes as I stared at myself. I checked out my bruises, wincing as I found a hundred of them in all sorts of weird places.

I tested out my muscles, stretching and flinching as they protested. Turning my neck, I could see two red wounds in my neck. Though healing wasn't Machidiel's natural talent he had done a good job healing them. Though healing wasn't his natural ability, he'd done his best and gotten some result; at least Trev's fang marks had stopped bleeding and had begun to scab over.

After splashing my face a few times, I decided I'd just go ahead and have a shower. The bathroom looked pretty clean and had a pile of free soaps and shower gels begging to be used, plus a rack of plush looking white towels. Locking the door, shedding my clothes and stepping into the shower gingerly was all worth the effort as the hot water began to pound on my skin. I dropped my head back, letting the water splash on my face, soothing and massaging.

The weary effect seemed to be washed away with the bloody water, pooling around my feet and sinking down the drain. I shuddered as I rubbed at the blood that had dried on my skin, picking at flakes and scrubbing them off. I picked up the complimentary shampoo and lathered my hair up, scrunching my face at the very male scent I now reeked of. Still, it was better than smelling of old blood.

I picked up a small tub of shower gel and rubbed it across my shoulders and down my chest, lathering the liquid over my skin. I leaned my head against the cold, white tiles and closed my eyes, letting my shoulders drop, and the muscles in my torso relax with the rhythmic beating of the water. I moaned with pleasure, completely uncaring if the hot water ran out for the boys.

Black eyes flashed at me, taking over my entire vision and I screeched, jerking my head up away from the wall. I dropped the shower gel to the bottom of the shower, tensing as it clattered loudly on the tiles.

Immediately the boys began to bang on the bathroom door, shouting, while the handle squeaked loudly as it was turned and jerked forcefully.

"Don't come in!" I squealed, angling my body away from the door and covering myself with my hands.

"Are you okay? What happened?" Drew yelled.

"I'm fine! I just dropped the shower gel," I shouted back.

"We heard you scream!"

"I dropped it on my foot, that's all. Don't come in!" I pleaded.

There was a silence, and while I was still uncertain if they were going to barge into the bathroom, my heart continued to race painfully, beating against the inside of my chest as though it wanted to break free. After a moment, when it was clear they weren't coming in, I lowered my hands and bent to pick up the tube. I straightened again, shooting a nervous glance at the door. I let out a breath I didn't know I had been holding and tried to loosen my tense muscles.

Of course, my heart didn't settle. I wasn't dreaming, I wasn't imagining it. I saw eyes.

I saw *his* eyes.

13

'If you're still looking for that one person who will change your life, take a look in the mirror.'

Roman Price.

I hurried the rest of my shower; rubbing conditioner into the ends of my hair and running my fingers through the strands to get the tangles out as well as any leftover blood. I tentatively rubbed at my neck where the worst of the blood had stained my skin.

Was it really Zach? Was he reaching out to me somehow? Did he need my help? Machidiel had said that we didn't truly know where he was; what if he was trapped in a Hell dimension, enduring an eternity of torture?

"Breathe," I whispered to myself. I needed to calm down, to focus. It didn't matter that I saw him—well, it did, but it didn't change the plan. *Zombies, Pool of Kali, Zach. Zombies, Pool of Kali, Zach,* I chanted in my head.

I stepped out onto the cool floor and pulled down a towel from the rack, ignoring the others that fell to the floor in a pile. I roughly dried my skin, trying not to wince like a girl when I rubbed too vigorously over the bruising. I picked up my black trousers and T-shirt off the floor and scowled at the state of them. They were disgusting; torn, the horrible red-brown color of dried blood and a little singed from where I had played with fire in the airport.

I clutched the towel to me when someone banged on the door again. “Who is it?”

“Machidiel went shopping.” Drew laughed.

Hope flared to life. Surely he couldn’t mean what I thought he meant? I shook my head. There’s no way the thought to buy me clothes would have even entered Machidiel’s mind. I was obviously still delirious.

I wrapped the towel around my body, tightly tucking the corner under my arm. I unlocked the door and pushed it open a fraction, peering around the edge expectantly.

Drew held a white carrier bag towards me. I snatched it and pulled it back inside gleefully, closing and locking the door behind me. I pulled out faded blue jeans and a black T-shirt. A dark blue hoodie fell out onto the floor. I grinned, stunned by how thoughtful Machidiel had been. I felt a little guilty at how surprised I was that he had done this; I guess I wasn’t such a good friend after all.

“Ew.” I grimaced when I realized I would have to wash my underwear in the sink and pray the blood came out, due to the lack of clean underwear in the bag. I actually wasn’t that upset that Machidiel hadn’t had to guess my bra and panty size, it would probably have ended up being embarrassing or insulting anyway.

I scrubbed and dried them with the tiny, automatic hair dryer in the bathroom, and dressed quickly, scraping my almost dry hair up into a top knot. I shoved my gross, bloody clothes into the carrier bag and threw them in the bin and sauntered out into the bedroom, feeling a thousand times better.

I felt a million times better just an instant later when I saw the McDonald’s paper bag on the desk waiting for me.

Drew chuckled as I ripped the paper in my desperation to get to the contents.

"I didn't know what you wanted, so . . . I got a mixture," Machidiel finished lamely, staring at me in mock horror as I shoved a burger in my mouth.

"I don't care. You're amazing!" I said around a mouthful of bread and meat. "Thank you."

The boys were equally enthusiastic about their own burgers and fries, and we had collectively finished eating within minutes of starting. One by one, they took showers and changed into fresh clothing until finally we were clean, clothed and fed, and no longer looking like we were involved in some kind of murder cover-up.

By the time we gathered together again around the beds, it was dark outside. With the time difference between Australia and America, the flight, the fight in the airport, our manic drive up the country and my unconsciousness, the whole day had gone by in a flash. I almost couldn't believe it, and I dreaded getting back into the bloody car, which I presumed was sitting outside the motel in the car park. How had they concealed the blood across the backseat? Anyone looking in the window would know something awful had happened. I was surprised the police weren't knocking the door down right now.

"Stop worrying," Machidiel said.

I looked up at him, catching a half-smile on his face before he turned away to look out of the window. "Huh?"

"Your facial expressions give you away. You were moments from panicking about something."

I frowned. "I wouldn't exactly say 'moments away'." I lay back on the bed, stretching my arms up above my head. "Do we have a plan?"

Drew and Trev expectantly looked at Machidiel. I rolled my eyes; somehow Machidiel had jumped into *my* mission and taken over.

The angel turned away and faced me, crossing his arms across his chest. He hadn't bothered to put on his own non-descript T-shirt, instead standing bare chested, his tattoos thick and dark, standing out against his brown, smooth skin.

"Do you have a plan?" he asked me.

I bit the inside of my cheek, thinking. Planning had never really been my strong point. Fighting, or jumping straight into trouble was more my thing. I sat up straight. "Zombies, Pool of Kali, Zach."

Machidiel nodded thoughtfully. "That's more of a goal than a plan."

I shrugged. "It's what I've got. What've you got?"

He pursed his lips. "We stay here tonight, at dawn we head up to Portland. We've got another nine or so hours drive. We find my contact who will lead us to the coven and persuade them to assist us in finding the zombies; a tracking spell should suffice," he added, in response to my silent question. "We can also see if they would be happy to join forces and if they know of a vampire colony less evil than most that we can approach."

"Then what?" Trev asked.

He shrugged and turned away to look out the window. "Let's start there, shall we? The rest really depends on how quickly we find the escapee zombies and if there are any vampires worth contacting."

I felt antsy with anticipation. That was certainly a more detailed plan than the one I had, but why wait? The longer we sat around, the longer Zach had to wait for me.

"Why wait? We can take turns driving. Surely if we've still got another nine hours drive ahead of us, we should set off sooner rather than later," I suggested, pacing the carpet beside the bed.

Drew shook his head. "It's better to stay indoors overnight."

"Afraid of the dark?" I asked sarcastically.

He smiled. "No, but there aren't many cars on the road overnight, so if we're out there and get pulled over by the cops . . ."

I shrugged. "So what if we don't get pulled over? The chances of that are pretty slim."

Trev stirred. "I don't know. Surely our pictures are all over the news? There's got to be people out there looking for us."

"All the more reason to head off now, under the cover of darkness," I insisted.

"We need sleep. We need to rest, recuperate and gather our strength. We wait until morning," Machidiel decreed.

I stomped my foot angrily. "You're here because of me. This is my mission."

"And without me, you wouldn't have even made this far," he said calmly, with a smirk.

"Chill out, guys." Trev stood up and placed his hand on my shoulder. "I drank a lot of your blood, Jas. I know you heal quickly but you need some time to recover properly. If we go off this fast and get into another fight . . . well, you won't have the blood I need, will you?"

I knew he was saying it to calm me down, but it worked. Picking the one thing he knew I would agree with—my friends' safety—was sly, but he got his way and I backed off. I doubted he would ever willingly drink from me again after taking so much, but I knew I would make him. That's what friends did; you had something someone needed, you gave it, they had something you needed, you took it. That's how families worked.

I felt my anger dissipate, though anxiety remained ripe. "Okay, fine. But we set off *first thing*, right?"

Machidiel's face softened and he nodded. "I promise."

14

'Sometimes what you want isn't always what you get, but in the end what you get is so much better than what you wanted.'

Unknown.

Trev flicked the television on and we took the bed closest to the bathroom, sitting up against the headboard. Drew lay on the second bed, raising his eyebrows in a, 'don't even think about it' kind of way, at Machidiel.

Machidiel rolled his eyes and pulled out the desk chair, lifting his feet up to rest them on the desk. We watched re-runs of *Friends* for an hour, then channel hopped between a documentary about volcanoes, a history channel, and a black and white movie. One more channel flick and the news came on with a young male reporter informing viewers about a train that had derailed near Chicago.

I closed my eyes and rested my head against the material headboard, sure it would be another pointless, filler news story.

While the passengers saw nothing amiss, the train driver insists a creature, around four meters in length with wings spanning one meter each, ran across the tracks causing the deadly accident. The driver has since been taken into police custody and tested for drugs and alcohol. Lawyer Brant Johnson is already involved, and as we have seen many times over in cases of this nature, the train driver will most likely be acquitted of any wrong doing.

All four of us stared at the television in unison, shocked.

“Who’s that lawyer guy?” Trev asked grimly.

When Drew and I shrugged, Machidiel sighed. “He’s working with the human rebellion, getting them out of all sorts of trouble.”

I flinched. “By trouble you mean . . .”

“He’s had people cleared of the most solid cases; murders, witch hunts, stakings and drownings—some were humans mistaken for demons, and some were innocent creatures targeted by human fanatics.”

“How can he do that?”

“He’s good, and he knows people high up in the judicial system.”

“So he’s a bad guy?” Trev asked, meeting my gaze. *Do we seriously have another enemy to add to the list?*

Machidiel stood up and stepped up to the television, blocking our view. He switched it off and stalked back to the window, looking out between the blinds.

“It depends on how you look at it,” he replied absently.

“How’s that? If he’s getting murderers out of prison then surely he counts as a bad guy?” Trev asked, amazed.

“He’s only a ‘bad guy’ if the human rebellion are also bad. Aren’t they now our allies?” Machidiel said.

I bit my lip. He was right. The human rebellion was only trying to defend their world from the creatures of their nightmares; the creatures which had destroyed the White House, among other landmarks. Though the government maintained an official story of a terrorist attack, those of us in the supernatural world and humans witnessing the attacks knew the real story. The events hadn't been random; they had been directed at carefully guarded, maximum-security facilities in an attempt to find the Dagger of Lex and the Falchion of Tabbris, one of which they now had.

With part of Hell's gates now open, more and more creatures would be emerging into the human world, resulting in more incidents like this. Was this Brant Johnson really a bad guy, if he was helping the humans to defend their lives? If he was on the side of the humans, then surely he was also on the side of the angels.

"What about the creature? The four-meter long, winged thing?" I asked.

"Could be a Kregl⍰r Demon," Drew suggested.

Machidiel nodded. "Or a dragon—a small one."

I pulled up my knees and dropped my head onto them. "God, this is insane. Sometimes I can't even believe this is happening."

"We've been waiting for this for a long time. Now it's finally here we can only do what we can," Machidiel murmured. He turned around to face us. "There's no point stressing over what we can't change. Focus on your goals, make your plan and execute it."

Trev and I exchanged a humor-filled look. It was all well and good saying that, but to actually do it, as if either one of us was capable of not stressing over something out of our control? Maybe that kind of restraint came with age. How old was Machidiel? Like, a thousand years old?

“We should rest,” Machidiel decided.

As much as I didn’t like being told what to do, I was exhausted and sore, and couldn’t think of anything better to do right now.

Trev and I jumped off the bed and got back in together, pulling the sheets up high. I sneakily watched as Drew and Machidiel grumbled before each lying on top of the sheets on the other bed.

“Don’t even think of snuggling; I’m not that kind of guy,” Drew commented, making Trev and I laugh.

Machidiel snorted. “Just don’t hump my leg and we’ll survive this.”

I smiled into my pillow, linking hands with Trev under the cover, thankful that no matter what lay ahead, I was going into it with three wonderful, strong, courageous men by my side.

***

After an hour of unsuccessfully attempting to get to sleep, tossing and turning, partly due to the loud, incessant snoring, and partly due to the fact that every time I closed my eyes I saw Zach’s eyes flashing at me. I crept out of the room, pulling the door closed quietly behind me.

The air was much cooler in the corridor, the lighting dim, and no one else in sight. I took a deep breath and exhaled, leaning against the wall outside our room.

The door clicked closed next to me and I jumped out of my reverie, spinning around with my fists held up, ready.

Trev raised his eyebrows, lifting his hands up in mock surrender. "Just me."

I sighed, dropping my hands to my sides. "Couldn't sleep either?"

He grinned sheepishly. "Not with *that* noise." He turned and leaned back against the wall exactly where I had been moments ago. "And not after what happened earlier today."

I nodded in agreement and copied his stance, dropping my head back lightly against the wall.

"Jasmine."

I turned my head to look at him. "Trev."

"If that happens again . . ." He shook his head. "Please don't . . . just don't."

I rolled my eyes. "Oh, okay, I'll leave you starving and happily watch you turn into your psycho vampire alter-ego in your desperate need for blood, running off to murder everyone in sight. Is that what you want?"

He dropped his head into his hands. "God, I hate myself. I'm so selfish. I just couldn't bear it if you looked at me the way . . ." He trailed off miserably.

"The way Gwen did?" I guessed. I reached over and took his hand, ignoring the way he flinched. "You never have to worry that I'll turn away from you. You could do just about anything and I would never abandon you. You and I are on the same side. We both walk this uncomfortable line between sanity and our murderous impulses. Don't think that I don't know what you feel because really, I'm probably the only one who actually knows *exactly* how you feel.

And if anyone's selfish here, it's me, not you." I hushed him as he tried to deny it. "I couldn't bear to lose you. If I didn't have you and Sam as my anchors, I don't know where or who I'd be right now. I couldn't let you fly off the handle back there because I *need* you. I love both of you so much; I couldn't bear for anything to happen to either of you. I gave you my blood because I was being selfish." I shrugged, my eyes filling with tears. "Just like usual."

"What happened wasn't your fault."

I didn't need him to clarify; I knew what he was talking about. I was furious that I'd managed to turn the conversation into my own pity party instead of trying to comfort and reassure Trev. I bit my lip and turned my face away, trying to steady my emotions. "I'm not saying this because I want your pity or because I want comfort, but I could have done something differently. I could have done *anything* differently and it might have changed what happened."

"*Might have* being of importance here," Trev said. "You can't think like that. I've been there—hell, I'm *still* there. It doesn't help; blaming yourself—nothing changes."

"Oh God, I'm so scared," I whispered. I clapped my hand to my mouth and took a shaky breath.

Trev stood straight and linked his fingers with mine. "We're going to win, I promise. We'll get through this."

I left out a short, maniacal laugh and pulled away. "I wasn't even thinking of the battle. What I'm so selfishly terrified of . . . Trev, what if Machidiel's right, and Zach isn't there? What if I can't bring him back?"

Trev tensed. "He didn't say he wouldn't be there."

I bit my lip and glared. “I’m not stupid.”

He pushed his dreadlocks back over his shoulders and rubbed his face with his hands. “Okay, he might not be there, but it doesn’t mean he’s not somewhere else.” He stepped closer and took hold of my shoulders. “We’ll get him back.”

I nodded and pulled away, swinging my arms around me. I needed to pull myself together; this wasn’t going to get us anywhere. I closed my eyes. *Focus on the plan; Zombies, Pool of Kali, Zach.*

Black eyes flashed and I flinched, gasping. I opened my eyes wide, trying to dispel the image.

Trev was there instantly, grabbing my shoulders. “What is it? What’s wrong?”

I shook my head. “Nothing, just a headache.” I stepped back and looked up, pursing my lips together. “We should get to bed. We’re setting off in a few hours.”

I turned away from him and twisted the door handle, pushing the door open to slip inside. I looked back to see if Trev was following then headed into the motel room, pretending I didn’t see his perturbed expression. He was worried for me. Maybe he thought I was losing it.

Maybe I was.

15

'I love you with all the madness in my soul.'

Unknown.

I moaned, tilting my face up. Soft, warm kisses were pressed to my throat, teeth nibbling down my neck to my shoulder. Arms circled me and pulled me so that I was on top, straddling him, my legs splayed wide across his thick body, his body hair tickling my thighs. I leaned forward, pressing kisses of my own to his chest before surging forward to meet his lips, pillowing cushions mashing with my bottom lip, opening just enough for me to sweep my tongue inside, sparring with his.

He clenched his arms around my buttocks and dragged me down his body, filling, stretching. We rolled over . . .

"Jasmine, it's time to leave."

I sat up, the sheets restricting my movement. Twisting and turning in bed, I'd managed to wrap the cover around my body so tightly I could barely breathe. My body was tense and tingling all over. I had been on the verge.

Mortification rushed through me like a fireball as I peered around the room. Machidiel was staring out of the window again while Drew channel hopped.

Trev raised his eyebrows at me from where he stood at the bathroom door. He held out a toothbrush.

“Complementary brush; comes with the smallest amount of toothpaste *ever*.”

I closed my eyes for a second, praying I hadn’t made any noises in my sleep, then grimaced and pulled the sheets off me, wrinkling my nose at the sweat that shone on my skin. I slipped to the edge of the bed and stood. Looking down at my wrinkled and sweaty clothes, I felt the urge to moan at my current state; I stopped myself after seeing the grin on Trev’s face . . . that would have been a little too girly for a hybrid like me.

As the boys had washed up while I was being lavished in passion in my dreams, they were ready to go, and were just waiting on me. I quickly stepped into the bathroom, competing for space with Trev to brush my teeth. As soon as he had finished, I pushed him out of the small en suite, stripped down to wash, and within fifteen minutes I joined them, ready to go.

Drew pulled the door behind us and we began to quietly walk down the corridor towards the stairwell. The cheap motel was the same as any other; neutral colors, plain, threadbare carpet, and small lights outside each identical door. At this time of the morning there was no one else up, no one else making a sound, so we tried to be as quiet as possible. Perhaps it was the silence that made it so eerie, but when the light at the end of the corridor nearest the stairwell began to flicker, I jumped, slivers of fear rushing up my spine.

I didn’t want to be the first to say anything, to show that I was frightened over a faulty wire, if anything. So I bit the inside of my cheek hard, lifting my chin.

Machidiel nudged me sharply. I cranked my neck up to look at him. I didn't like what I saw.

His normal smirking, mocking expression was gone. His eyes had narrowed and he seemed to glide in a predatory way down the corridor, slinking in front of me. He handed me a knife—God knows where he had gotten it. I clenched it in my palm, wrapping my fingers around the thin handle and followed the angel, absently noting that by this point Drew and Trev had realized something was wrong and had fallen in line behind us.

We slinked up the corridor, keeping to the walls, glancing behind us to check for anyone who might be sneaking up. We reached the door; room number two. The light continued to flicker, a low hum of electricity filling my ears. I listened with my other sense, hoping to hear thoughts, but there was nothing, not a single sound to be heard once I'd blocked out Drew's snarl and Trev's chant which mostly consisted of the word *fuck*.

I looked up at Machidiel as he stiffened, passing the door painfully slowly.

Move to the side of the door to the stairwell, but don't go through until I give the word, Machidiel's voice came at me.

I scowled. What I wouldn't give to have Sam here so I could converse freely. I had a million questions running through my mind. What was Machidiel expecting to be inside the stairwell? Wasn't there another way out? If he was right, and there was something or someone there, how did he expect us to get out of here? Did he want us to fight our way out?

A sliver of doubt entered my mind. What had Machidiel been looking at through the window just now and last night? Had he known something was coming? Was he leading us into a trap?

Fuck, fuck, fuck. I entered Trev mode. There was nothing I could do except follow Machidiel's orders and hope for the best.

I crouched at the side of the stairwell, turning so I could see right up the length of corridor, the flickering light just beside me. Trev and Drew stood to my left, watching Machidiel with confused expressions.

I'll go first, check it out. Don't come unless I tell you, he cautioned me again.

He reached his hand to the metal patch on the door and began to push forward slowly. I held my hand up to stop Drew when he went to follow. He frowned at me, but remained still.

Machidiel entered the stairwell, disappearing out of sight, the door falling closed with the smallest yet loudest squeak of the hinge. I cringed at the noise and looked up the corridor. I waited for a noise, anything to tell me we could continue, while staring up at that corridor. After a moment, my face fell, my body locking into position.

One by one, the small lights outside each room switched off, slowly creeping closer towards us.

"Oh my God," I hissed, my eyes widening painfully.

Drew and Trev turned their heads to look, cursing when they realized that whatever was coming for us wasn't in the stairwell with Machidiel—it was here with us.

16

'You don't have a soul; you are a soul. You have a body.'

C.S. Lewis.

Throwing Machidiel's instructions out of the window, we belted through the door, slamming it against the wall with a bang. We turned to the left and ran down the stairs as fast as our legs would carry us, almost falling. We crashed into each other halfway down and turned back, seeing the door crash open again. We thundered down the steps, our feet slapping loudly.

"What the hell are you doing?" Machidiel hissed from the bottom of the stairs. He stared up at us aghast.

"There's something up there!" Drew hollered.

Machidiel glared up the stairs, at the darkness that spread through the door. He screamed as he was thrown against the wall. I should have guessed that the threat would be coming at us from all sides, but in our attempt to flee, we had jumped right into the fire.

I was thrown from where I stood halfway down the steps to against the far wall, smashing the bricks as I landed against them. I dropped to the floor in a heap, gasping for breath while I took stock of my injuries. My head throbbed, blood running into my eyes, and my left shoulder was shot with pain. Something grabbed my arms and pulled me up, throwing me down the remaining stairs. Trev caught me and pushed me behind him, preparing to take on our attacker.

Black mist circled us, obstructing our view. I gasped as Trev was kicked, knocking him on top of me. I hissed in a breath and pushed him off, jumping to my feet. A fist connected with my face and I flew to the side, spitting blood out of my mouth. I ducked and swung the blade upward, catching something with the edge. The black mist receded and I released what I was up against.

A Horseman stood before me, an axe in his hand. I sucked in my breath, stiffening. I ducked, rolling to the side as he attacked again. I punched out, hitting him in the face, and then once again in the stomach. He hit me and I fell to my knees. Drew jumped over the top of me and kicked him, sending him crashing into the stairs. Powdered brick fell down on top of us.

A scream had me on my feet and running to Trev. He bent over, clutching at his shoulder, his face twisted in agony. I took hold of him, reaching for his shoulder.

“Don’t!” he groaned.

An arrow protruded through his shoulder and out through the back. I glanced around, seeing Machidiel and Drew fighting with one of the Horsemen—the one who had pounded on me just a minute ago. I felt a whisper of movement, and as I knocked Trev to the ground an arrow shot past my face, burying into the wall behind us.

I looked up, seeing a second Horseman at the top of the staircase. A bow and arrow was his weapon of choice; I presumed he was Conquest. I wasn’t sure which one the other demon was, and really, what did it matter? I did want to know, however, where the last two were.

Drew snarled as he landed on the floor next to me. I gasped, watching in horror as Machidiel received punch after punch, and was pummeled onto the ground. He curled up, covering his head, trying to deflect the kicks coming at him.

I shrieked and lit myself up, fire rushing through my limbs as smoke filled the stairwell. I ran towards the wall and used it to run up, pushing off to flip over the top of the Horseman. I landed side on, and kicked high, catching him in the chest, just before his axe was thrown into the angel at my feet. As my foot connected with him, sparks caught on his black clothing, and he hit the wall heavily, landing on his knees.

Arrows began to rain down all around us, skimming our bodies. I was able to incinerate some before they hit us, but Conquest scored one savage hit on my thigh, scratching off a layer of skin, blood soaking immediately through my new, now torn, jeans.

Machidiel and Drew launched themselves at Conquest and began to hit and stab at any part of him they could. I pulled Trev to his feet and dragged him towards the door. I was torn between joining the fight with Machidiel and Drew, and getting Trev to safety. With both Trev and I injured, we'd be better getting a head start; at least Machidiel and Drew could take care of themselves.

Another arrow narrowly missed us as we pushed the door open and fell through onto the floor. I crawled forward, looking up as something grabbed my head, launching me across the reception area, smashing through the glass window that would house the receptionist later during the day.

I hit the far wall and fell through a desk to the floor, broken glass and wood underneath me. The Horseman was on me again, attacking viciously. I let my rage take over, my body on fire again, and shrieked as loud as I could. Any remaining glass—the computer screens, the shards still attached to the reception window, even trinkets on the shelves—shattered into pieces as lightning struck, echoing my valkyrie war cry. With the Horseman momentarily distracted, I closed in, shoving the blade I miraculously still held into his gut. I sliced up and stabbed again in his face, sinking to the hilt.

With the most horrific cry the demon fell to his knees in front of me, his arms up in denial. He opened his mouth and to my terror, his mouth expanded, growing wider and wider. I jumped up onto the desk, screaming as hands reached me from behind, dragging me over the counter. I fought them off, shrieking with relief when I realized it was Drew, and turned back to face the Horseman.

The black mouth grew grotesquely huge and folded outwards, devouring the demon, leaving nothing behind.

"Go!" Machidiel roared.

We turned, spotting him running from the stairwell, two Horsemen chasing after him. I swiveled in place, and sprinted for the motel doors. They automatically opened and we ran into the car park, heading for the rusty red car we had parked in the shadows. Drew got there first and unlocked the door, slamming it shut behind him when he jumped in, immediately starting the engine. I threw Trev into the backseat and got in beside him, locking the back doors. It's not as if it would make any difference, seeing as the Horsemen could probably just rip the car in half if they were of a mind to, but it made me feel just a fraction safer.

Drew reversed the car and we watched Machidiel as he sprinted out of the motel, throwing himself through the door Drew had pushed open.

Revving, we skidded out of the car park and sped down the road away from the motel. Trev and I turned in our seats, staring out the back window in horror as two of the Horsemen appeared at the bottom of the car park, staring to run after our car.

"Faster!" I screamed at Drew.

He put his foot down and we ran straight through the next set of lights, and down the dark road. I heard a bell ringing in the distance and turned, leaning forward between the front seats to see what was going on.

"What's that noise?" I asked.

"Train," Drew replied grimly.

"No," I said, in shock. "If we stop, they'll catch up with us!"

The lycan didn't reply. Instead, he put his foot to the floor and we zoomed down the road towards the train crossing, seeing the lights of the oncoming train as it approached. I sat back in the seat, staring, my mouth open in fear as we raced the train for the intersection where it crossed the road.

I reached over and took Trev's hand, needing someone.

"Oh my God," Trev muttered. "Oh my God!" He squeezed my hand so hard, I was sure he would break something as the train horn blasted us.

With only centimeters to spare we flew across the metal tracks and landed on the other side, skidding across the road as the train roared behind us.

I burst into tears as Drew righted the car, flooring it away from Sacramento and onto the highway. We were thrown back in our seats, the road bumpy and uneven. It soon flattened out and we left the town behind. I sat facing backwards, sure that at any moment the Horsemen would follow, that I would see them flying towards us.

“You alright?” Drew shouted back to me over the noise of the over-exerted engine.

“I have no idea.” I gasped. “How did we even survive that?”

I looked down at my hands; they were coated in blood, *my* blood, and they shook.

“How did they find us?” Trev growled.

I faced him, knowing it was a valid question, but equally concerned by the angry look he was directing at Machidiel. I reached for the arrow.

“Don’t.” He pulled away.

“If I don’t get it out and heal you, you’re going to bleed out. We don’t want to deal with that situation again, do we?” I said, pointedly.

My face wet with tears, I leaned over him and glared at the point that came out the back of his T-shirt. I snapped the pointed end off of the arrow, then pulled the wooden stick back through.

“Do you think it’s poisoned?” I asked, thinking back to lessons we’d learnt in the safe house.

He shook his head. “I’d be able to smell it, if it were.”

I nodded, not questioning him, and placed my hand over the wound on his shoulder, blood coating my palm. I pulled my magic through my pores and let it seep into him, knitting his flesh together from the inside. He flinched as muscle reattached and bone re-grew.

I sat back against my seat, letting my hand drop to my side.

“Are you okay?” he asked, staring at me with concern etched onto his face.

I shrugged, and shook my head. “I don’t think any of us will ever be okay again.”

“I meant are you hurt?”

I shrugged again. “I don’t think so. I’m a little sore, and Conquest got a good shot at my thigh but it’s healing.”

He sighed. “How did they find us, Machidiel? You knew they were coming for us.”

“I could sense them following us,” he replied.

“And you didn’t think to tell us?” Trev asked angrily.

“It wouldn’t have made any difference. At some point we would have needed to stop, and they would have caught up with us then.”

I clenched my fists. “You could have given us a heads up. We could have left earlier.”

He turned around with a slight smile. “I think things went as well as we could have hoped.”

I rolled my eyes. “You hoped I’d get thrown through a glass window?”

“And have an arrow shot through my chest?” Trev asked dryly.

He chuckled. "One down, three to go."

"One down . . . *one down*?" Drew cried, turning to look at us.

"Eyes on the road, lycan!" Trev shouted, as we veered across the lane.

He turned back with a grunt before repeating his question. "One of you took out a Horseman?"

Machidiel turned to grin at me. "Jasmine did."

I blushed, hiding my smile before biting on my bottom lip. I *was* proud, but I was also terrified. Meeting them in battle with an army raging all around me had been different. Fighting them with Zach at my side made it different. I'd had Trev, Machidiel and Drew with me this time, but it wasn't the same. It wasn't that I didn't think they would defend me, or even that I thought they *should* defend me; it was different because if I died in battle in the arms of my soul mate, I wouldn't care. I'd be in the one place in the whole world where I felt safe, even if I was dying.

At that thought, momentary indecision rocked me. Zach had died like that. He had died in battle, and been held in my arms with my love reaching for him, trying to hold him. Would I really try to erase that and bring him back? I had just told myself that that would be the way to die; defending the ones I loved, and being held safely by my soul mate. Would I take it back? Did it make me a hypocrite?

"No way," Drew cried, oblivious to my inner turmoil. "You killed a Horseman?"

I nodded absently. That Horseman had nearly killed me, and the way that it had died, seeming to devour itself . . . I was petrified of seeing one of them again, and there were three more. Three more of those demons searching for us.

"Which one did you kill?" He asked gleefully.

"I don't know," I replied. "Machidiel?"

He shrugged. "Conquest was back on the stairs with the bow, and Death wasn't there, so it had to have been either War or Famine."

"Why wasn't Death there?" Trev asked.

Machidiel looked out of the window. "Death is the most difficult of the Horsemen to track down. He's very similar to a Principality; he plots and schemes, and is very much the game master. He won't show himself until the end."

I gulped. "So we should be expecting Conquest and one other to show up at our next stop while Death waits until we've got our backs against the wall?"

The car fell silent as we considered that. Though I couldn't wait for the journey to be over, I dreaded getting out of this car again, because the things that would be waiting for us at the next stop would get their next try.

17

'Sometimes the hardest thing and the right thing are the same.'

Unknown.

It wasn't for another twenty minutes that I realized or at least, *remembered*, the state of the backseat. To say that the seat squelched was an understatement. I kind of presumed the blood would have dried overnight while we were in the motel, but no, it was as sopping wet, as it had been yesterday. Between Trev and I, we must have lost a bucketful of blood.

With most of the blood saturating the middle of the seat, I kept myself firmly squashed against the door, not wanting to wreck my new clothes any more than they already were. As much as I prided myself on being totally un-squeamish and far from girly, I'd had these clothes less than six hours and they were already singed, bloodied and ripped. *FML*.

We passed through a number of smaller towns which all seemed to look the same; small timber and brick houses with messy, fenced gardens, small motels with neon signs flashing *Vacancies*, closed pharmacies, and the ever popular Walmart. Each one we drove through, we sped through to the other side and disappeared into the early morning darkness of the motorway again, passing the occasional truck and campervan, each time tensing in case we were rammed or driven off the road.

I saw a sign stating we were now in Redding, and rested my head against the window, hoping for another unexciting drive through. It took a few moments before I realized we were slowing. I frowned at Trev, and moved slightly so I could see through the front windscreen.

“You do realize we’re slowing down, right?” Trev voiced the question running through my mind.

Drew snorted. “We need to ditch the car, mate.”

“Why?” I exclaimed.

He turned to raise an eyebrow at me. “You want to drive in a stolen car all the way to Portland?”

I shot him a glare. “Oh, I’m sorry, are you planning on buying a car at five a.m.?”

He chuckled. “You want to continue sitting on that seat for the next six hours?”

“Fine.” I smiled. “But if we pull over and get jumped, I’m telling.”

Redding seemed a little bigger than the other town; maybe it was, or maybe it was just that we were heading into a more suburban area; you know, looking for a car to steal.

We pulled up at the curb outside a house surrounded by tall and thick bushes. Machidiel opened the door and jumped out, poking his head back through.

“Trev, you’re with me,” he said with a grin.

"What?" I shrieked. At the wounded looks, I lowered my voice and whispered, "We're splitting up? You seriously think that's a good idea? Are you insane?"

Trev squeezed my hand. "It's okay, I'll go with him."

"That's not the point; a few hours ago we were nearly killed. There are three more of them out there somewhere, hunting us down!"

Machidiel laughed. "Trev and I are going to scout around for a car while you and Drew dump this one somewhere. We'll meet up again in less than fifteen minutes."

I dropped my head into my hands. "Anything could happen in fifteen minutes. Why can't we just leave the car here and all go together?"

I looked up at Machidiel miserably, seeing a glint in his eye.

"Scared?" he teased.

I immediately stiffened. I had been through too much to be patronized by this arrogant know-it-all.

"No," I denied. "It just seems pointless."

"If we leave this car in the same place we pick up the next, the police will link the two stolen cars and we'll be back in the same position of being hunted down by demons *and* the police," Machidiel said.

It did make sense, but I still didn't like it.

"Where are we meeting up?"

Drew ran his hand down the stubble on his face. “It would be better to ditch the car at the very edge of the town. We’ll meet up on the motorway there.”

I rolled my eyes. “Could you vague that up for me?”

“They’ll find us.” Drew turned to Machidiel. “See you soon.”

Trev flashed me a smile, and slid out of the car. I climbed through the middle of the car and jumped into the passenger seat beside Drew, looking back at Machidiel and Trev as we pulled away. I ran my hands through my hair and lifted my feet up to put them on my seat. At Drew’s insistence, I plugged in my seatbelt and peered up at him.

“So, I hope you remember the way out of this town.”

He smiled. “Lycan senses, Jas.”

I rolled my eyes and rested my forehead on my knees, praying there was no one lying in wait for us.

Drew drove swiftly through the streets and we ended up back on the main street, heading north. Despite it being a larger town than the others we had driven through, there wasn’t a single car on the road, the shops were all closed, with not one light to pierce the darkness.

We headed through the town, coming to a stop at red traffic lights. We pulled off again and soon the shops dropped away, leaving just one or two houses to pass before we left the town behind.

I turned to Drew. “Where are we—”

My head slammed against the glass as the car flipped over, rolling across the road and sliding down into a roadside ditch. Upside down, I hung from my seatbelt, unable to hold in my terrified scream.

Drew snarled and growled, ripping through his belt. I watched in shock as he lowered himself down onto the roof of the car and reached up to help me.

With the crunching of metal, the driver's door was ripped off, and his entire body was dragged through the hole and out onto the road.

I couldn't breathe. Panic was fully setting in. They had found us, the Horsemen had found us again, and there were only two of us against three of them – that is providing Death had shown up. Best case; there'd still be two of them. *No*, I reminded myself. Trev and Machidiel would be coming. They were meeting us here. They'd be here in minutes.

I struck out at the belt, gasping as it remained firmly locked. I pulled at the straps, trying to stretch them in some way, trying to slide out between them. I remembered the knife Machidiel had given me and pushed my hands deep into my waistband where I thought I had stuck it after the fight in the motel. It wasn't there.

I craned my neck to search the roof of the car. The knife had to be here. It had to have fallen somewhere. I could only pray it hadn't fallen out of the car as we had rolled.

My eyes blurred. Freaked, I lifted to my hand to my temple and pulled it away with fresh blood dripping down my fingers.

Do not pass out. Do not pass out, I repeated to myself as the pressure in my head increased, pain pulsating through me.

I could hear snarls and growls outside, and I struggled harder, knowing Drew was out there alone.

A flash of metal gleamed at me. I pushed my feet against the dashboard and pushed, trying to slide through the belt. I reached out, stretching with my fingertips skimming the roof of the car towards where the knife lay, covered in shattered glass. With one last push, I was able to flick it back towards me. Ignoring the slice of the broken glass, I palmed the blade and started cutting through the material of the belt in vicious strokes.

When the straps gave way I fell onto the roof, landing heavily on the glass. I kicked at the window of the passenger door and booted the glass through, crawling backwards once there was a gap wide enough. I screamed as a hand grabbed my foot, dragging me out into the dirt.

I immediately used my go-to defense and lit myself on fire, kicking out at the person holding onto me. I slammed them squarely in the chest, and staggered up to my feet when they fell back. Though it was dark, I could still make out the fangs of the vampire lunging at me. In the split second afforded to me, I wondered at the attack. Vampires, working with the Horsemen? It had happened before, obviously, but the vampires had been working with Asmodeus, and Haamiah and Machidiel had seemed to think that now, the Horsemen would be coming after us solo. What had happened to make them attack us together?

The vampire was dressed in distressed jeans and a designer T-shirt which was now covered in mud. With a shaved head, glinting silver earrings and a snarl on his face, he looked like a thug—a rich, well-dressed one.

He ran for me, arms outstretched. I neatly evaded him and spun around, kicking him in the back. He fell to his knees and I struck him in the face. I was about to go in for the kill, when I was laid into from behind. I fell forward, sliding across the ground. I spun on my back and flipped up to my feet, fists held up. I swung a punch and missed, but landed a second blow. I blew my fire towards my assailant, catching his clothing with sparks. He screamed as flames rippled up his body. Turning and running into the field by the road, I was left with only one.

Using the car as leverage, I ran up the side and flipped off the top. As I arched over the vampire, I whipped my knife around and slit his throat, pulling hard on his head so that it ripped off amidst blood and sparks.

I landed heavily, twisting my knee, but ran around the car, jumping up from the slanted ditch onto the road just in time to see the lycan finish off his vampire. I skidded to a halt, panting for breath, and stared in astonishment.

I had seen lycan fight before—I knew their bodies grew larger, their muscles intensifying in size and strength, and that their minds seemed to turn feral, but as I watched Drew's mouth expanded, sharp white teeth shredding the vampire's head and neck. When the vampire dropped to the floor, he turned to face me his lycan self very much evident. It was like looking into the jaws of a shark; one about to attack.

I couldn't have cared less. The vampire had been killed, and somehow we were still alive. I ran for him, jumping up and wrapping my arms and legs around his wrist. It took a second before he returned the squeeze, and I knew it'd taken him by surprise.

God, this guy, he was a true friend. He was someone I could rely on, someone capable of reveling in battle and in comforting me. He didn't ask for anything, was just happy to be a part of this. Maybe it was because he knew I used to be an archangel or maybe he had something to prove but I just didn't feel like that was it. I felt like he genuinely wanted to kill the bad guys, and that was definitely what I was about. They could keep coming at us, they could attack us at every damn stop, but as long as I knew I had Drew, Trev, and even Machidiel, I knew we would be okay. I only hoped I wouldn't let myself down. I did have something to prove. I wanted to prove that I wasn't the angry, violent bitch I used to be, and was now worthy of friends as wonderful as I had, and worthy of winning back my soul mate.

18

'Love me when I least deserve it because that's when I really need it.'

Unknown.

"Don't go soft on me," Drew murmured with a smile in his voice. "I adore you for your bad-ass hybrid attitude."

I laughed. "I'm having a moment here. Don't worry; I'll get over it."

With the revving of a car nearing us, I dropped to my feet and turned so Drew and I were standing side by side. I raised my blade and gritted my teeth. This had to be the Horsemen coming. I glanced up at Drew and grinned; we were ready.

As a black hatchback pulled up beside us I breathed a sigh of relief. How had I forgotten Machidiel and Trev were coming for us? Idiot!

They leaped out of the car as soon as it came to a stop and immediately scanned the area for a threat. They crossed the distance to us, mouths dropping open in surprise.

Machidiel whistled as he spotted the trashed car in the ditch. "I'd ask what happened . . .?"

Drew pushed past them and jogged towards the new car. "We'll tell you on the way. Let's go."

Trev and I took the backseat again, and Drew took the passenger seat this time. Driving off, we headed north and soon left the town behind.

"Can't believe you had fun without us." Trev sniggered.

I rolled my eyes. "Yeah, because getting our car knocked off the road by vampires was *so* much fun."

"Vampires?" Machidiel asked, surprised.

Drew nodded. "There were five of them."

"No Horsemen?"

"Nope."

Machidiel was silent for a moment. "That's weird."

I made a face at Trev. "Crawling out of an upside-down car was weird, being attacked by vampires—not so much."

Trev grinned, and I heard Drew snort in the front seat.

"What's weird," Machidiel continued, "is that the battle we were in was constructed by Lucifer. He orchestrated the whole thing; when Lilith failed to find the dagger and the Falchion, Mnemosyne found them, and the Horsemen were brought in to kill everyone protecting them. The vampires were only involved because Asmodeus united them and the fallen in order to get Jasmine to open a portal to the Heavens where he could hide."

"So, Asmodeus has found us." I hesitated and reached behind my head to pull my hair back into a ponytail.

"He wouldn't send vampires; he would come himself, or at the very least he'd send the fallen," Machidiel said.

"So, who sent them?" Trev asked.

"I have no idea. It doesn't make sense to me. Now they have the Falchion, and the Heavenly gates will be wide open, they only need the Dagger—*Sam*—to open Hell's gates. So to put it simply, the Horsemen and Mnemosyne want Sam, and Asmodeus wants Jasmine. The vampires have no reason to be here on their own."

"God, how do ye have so many enemies?" Drew moaned.

I glared at the back of his head. "It's not my fault I was reincarnated, or that Sam was born who he was."

Drew swiveled in his seat. "That's not what I meant. I mean, we need to take some of them out already."

That idea immediately pricked at my interest. "Who?"

He turned back to face the front and ran a hand down his face tiredly. "Can't we send some of our allies after Mnemosyne for a start?"

"She would just use her magic on them," Machidiel argued.

"Not if they used some sort of protective charm or spell, something that stopped her powers from working. Then, she should be an easy kill."

My eyes widened in astonishment. Why hadn't we thought of this before? It seemed so simple. "Witches," I said. I leaned forward, tugging on my seatbelt to allow me to move more freely. "The witches will be able to cast a spell to protect themselves."

Machidiel grinned at me in the rear-view mirror. "It's a good job that's where we're headed then, isn't it?"

Machidiel sped up, pushing the speed limit, and as we drove with a more refined goal in mind, I knew we were each wondering where the next threat would come from.

We drove without talking, listening to the radio for traffic updates. We stopped only once, filling up with petrol at a gas station halfway to Portland. When Machidiel paid, he returned to the car with food and a handy pack of wet wipes. I felt a thousand times better once I'd rubbed the dirt and blood off my face, and thankfully we didn't encounter any other demons or vampires at that stop. Within a few hours we were soon passing a sign welcoming us to Portland, Oregon.

Machidiel knew where he was going and pulled off the motorway to head north along the riverside. Turning onto Oak Street, we took a right towards a park, and pulled up outside a multistory building, which looked over bushy grounds lined with cars.

I peered out of the window up at the tall buildings. It stood at four stories, and looked modern with double glass doors at the entrance, and a white foyer just inside. The outside of the building was well cared for with immaculate brickwork, lights on either side of the doors to illuminate the entry, a clean, swept sidewalk, and even a small, silver cigarette bin attached to the wall. With it being the middle of the day, humans walked by briskly, going about their business, I doubted even considering for a second that powerful beings lived here. Basically, it looked the complete opposite to where I imagined a witches coven to live.

“Are you sure we're in the right place?” I asked, opening the car door.

I stepped out onto the pavement and ignored the way I was stared at. With the blood patch on my thigh, my face and arms scratched, and the aroma of burned flesh, I was surprised no one called the police there and then.

We hurried towards the door and pushed at the glass. It swung open easily and we entered the foyer. We crossed the white marble floors and stopped at the elevator at the back. Machidiel tapped at a small communications box against the side of the lift doors and waited.

"Yes?" a female voice asked over the intercom.

"The house of Haamiah calls on warriors to fight for its cause," Machidiel's voice boomed into the speaker.

There was a pause. "Oh, crap."

There was a high-pitched beeping, and the lift doors opened. Machidiel entered solemnly, and we cautiously filed in behind him, Trev and I exchanging an anxiety-filled look. What were the odds that there would be something waiting to kill us? Had we walked straight into danger? Probably.

The lift was probably only designed to fit a couple of people in at a time. It was modern, with mirrored walls and blue flashing lights around the buttons, but despite the illusion of space I found myself a little closer to Machidiel than I would have liked. I pressed my arms across my chest and held my breath, uncomfortable in the closet-like space.

Machidiel pressed floor four and we sailed upwards, gravity sucking at our feet. We travelled the few seconds in silence and when the doors opened, to my surprise, there was no one waiting for us, no weapons pointed at our bodies.

"No welcome party?" I asked, raising my eyebrows at Machidiel.

He shrugged. "That's witches for you."

The angel and Drew exited the lift first, Trev and I trailing behind, still unsure if we were going to be attacked. Were the witches *peeved* at our arrival or angry at it? That thought dropped away as my mouth dropped open stunned at our surroundings. The lift had opened straight into what seemed to be an apartment, wooden floors underfoot, and soft cream and muted grey colored walls decorated with what appeared to be expensive artwork—not that I was an expert, or in fact knew anything at all about art. These pictures were abstract flashes of color; pinks and blues twisting across canvas. Seeming to be a collection, there were four or five separate paintings all differing in pattern but with the exact same colors and style.

I stared up at them, drawn to the bright hues. I almost reached up to touch them before Trev nudged me, and we hurried to catch up to the others.

We had walked through what seemed to be a reception room; a small, hard bench was pushed against the wall with a narrow table beside it, a tray of keys sitting on top.

Looking around furtively, Trev and I stopped behind Machidiel and Drew when they paused by a glass doorway leading onto an outside terrace. I peered between the gap in their shoulders, seeing figures sitting on chairs and a sofa in the large outside space.

We passed the glass screen and stepped down onto the dark, tiled flooring, mutually deciding to fan out in case we were attacked. I stared, surprised at who I presumed were the witches we had come to see. I admit, my knowledge of witches was limited and based solely on the evil witch who had tried to kill me in the Werewolf plane and on Emily, a good-ish witch who, despite initially being a vengeful bitch was actually a pretty cool girl. See; I had grown as a person.

These witches just looked like ordinary people. Of course, I didn't actually know any ordinary people, but they were dressed in very average looking clothes—jeans, casual tops, and maxi dresses. Unlike in the nephilim house, there were no weapons strapped to them, no wings forced under T-shirts by nephilim unable to control their abilities. There were no headdresses or metal armor like the sorceresses liked to wear, or even eccentric hair colors, piercings or tattoos like the valkyrie. They looked completely normal.

"Ladies." Machidiel inclined his head. "Who is your in-charge?"

One woman stood up and planted her hands on her hips. "I am. What do you want?"

Machidiel gave her a charming grin. "Don't I get to know your name? Don't you wish to know mine?"

I rolled my eyes.

She flashed angry blue eyes at him and tossed her curly, auburn hair across her shoulder. "I don't care who you are; I want to know why you're here."

"I'm Machidiel, of the House of Haamiah." Machidiel ignored her comment and introduced himself anyway.

The woman paled and took an involuntary step back. My heart sped up, and I turned to face the angel beside me, worried.

"You're not from the House of Haamiah. I know who you are," she said, her voice wavering.

He flashed his teeth in a mimic of a smile. “You know who I am, yet I still do not know who you are.”

She stiffened her spine, and lifted her chin to glare at him angrily. “I’m Karen of the Witch Guard.”

Machidiel bestowed a smile on her. “You’re aware of the apocalypse?”

“Of course we are,” she snapped. “Even a fool would know of our impending doom. The auras are black and red, fire shooting from the gates as the malevolent spirits force their way through. Even the youngest witch can feel Hell’s heat reaching for them with gripping fingers.”

I shivered. That sounded pretty gloomy.

Machidiel seemed to expect that answer, and for some reason was pleased by it. “Have you chosen your side?”

Karen stood tall. The group of witches, ten, when I quickly counted—stood up behind her. “The Witch Guard have stood against evil for centuries. Your games are useless here, warrior. State your business.”

Machidiel seemed to relax, turning away to look out across the terrace railing. There was a slightly obscured view of the park, but it was pretty, nonetheless. “We’ve travelled far and fast to be here. May we trouble you for a glass of water?”

One of the witches glared at him and moved at silent bidding, filling three glasses with water and sliding them across the small glass table towards us.

Machidiel took one and returned to look out over the railing, while Trev, Drew and I remained where we were. I thought it was kind of rude they only put out three glasses, but then maybe they thought vampires only drunk blood. It was a common theory.

It was beginning to get awkward when Machidiel spoke again. "We have an archangel among us; Jophiel."

I flinched, not expecting him to out me like that.

Karen snorted. "You and your people have been telling us that for years. What makes your words any different now?"

"She's standing right in front of you."

19

'I look for you everywhere.'

Unknown.

Ten pairs of eyes turned to me. I tried not to cringe from the attention, but was sure I failed miserably when Trev stepped closer to shield me.

"You're Jophiel?" the witch asked doubtfully.

I was about to protest and say, actually, no, I was Jasmine, before realizing how pointless that would be. I shrugged and replied, "Yep."

Karen seemed to be struggling with an inner conflict. Expressions crossed her face rapidly, her brows working and her mouth tensing.

"Look at the others," Drew whispered in my ear.

I let my eyes glide past her to the women standing behind her. They had similar facial movements.

"They're communicating with each other." I realized.

"Can you hear what they're saying?"

I tensed, my eyes flicking from Drew to the witches. I pulled on my power, feeling the mass of churning, swirling magic rise up through my abdomen to my chest. I focused on one of the witches at the back of the group, a petite, brown-haired girl who looked younger than the rest. I presumed she would be weaker than the others, giving me easier access.

She was harder to read than a human but definitely easier to read than the angels, but what I found was confusing. Instead of just her thoughts I found one voice, one thought, then another, and another, until hundreds of individual whispers were echoing through my mind. It was as though I had tapped into a huge tree, roots delving deep across the world; one giant conversation with connections to voices across the universe.

I kept waiting for pain or pressure or some kind of explosion in my brain from an onslaught of voices, but it didn't come. Instead my mind was massaged by soft pattering rain. There were too many voices and too many trails of thought to fully comprehend the conversation, but the general consensus seemed to be, "yay for the archangel," which I figured was a good sign.

I pulled out of the witch's mind and looked up at Drew.

"I think we're okay," I muttered.

After two or three minutes of eerie silence, Karen relaxed and took a deep breath.

"Fine," she said.

"Fine?" Drew echoed. "Just like that?"

She shrugged. "What?"

"You don't want proof?"

I had wondered that too. When our world was built of proof, trials and prophecies, wouldn't they expect Machidiel to prove his claim?

“We had proof,” she answered with a smug expression.

“When?”

“She tapped into the witches minds and heard their true voices.” Machidiel turned around and leaned against the railing.

Trev frowned. “She did? You did?”

I gave him a small smile. “Yeah. Kind of.”

Drew raised his eyebrows. “Can’t any telepath do that?”

“No, they’d be driven mad if they actually managed to tap into us,” the witch answered. She sighed and crossed her arms. “You’ve got our attention, angel, what do you want?”

I waited for Machidiel to outline our demands only he never spoke. I frowned at him, only to see him grin.

Oh. “We’re looking for some escaped spirits; two zombies and a werewolf. We were hoping you would do a locating spell.”

The vacant look crossed her face again as she conversed with her coven silently. A weird feeling that pressed on my brain made me flick my eyes to Machidiel. He was scowling at me, insisting on something. I focused, and pushed my way through into his thoughts.

Do not tell them we’re raising Zach afterwards. Witches are incredibly fussy about the natural order of the world. They don’t believe in acknowledging the dead, so if they even agree to find the spirits it’ll be a miracle, he said. *The only thing we have going for us is that we’re going to rid the human world of them, sending them back where they should have remained.*

I glanced at Trev. *But . . .*

Have you seen any of them speak to him? I could hear the grin in his voice.

I bit my lip. Witches didn't acknowledge the dead? Was that why we only got three glasses of water? I so didn't know what to do with that information, aside from being offended on Trev's behalf.

"We'll do the spell," Karen spoke, jolting me into awareness.

"In exchange for what?"

She paused. "In exchange for an alliance."

I smiled. I hadn't expected this to be so easy.

"You'll have your alliance," Machidiel agreed.

"We're asking the archangel, not you," she snapped. She turned back to me, locking me with her eyes. "I mean it; we would appreciate an alliance with you, but be warned; when you ally yourself with witches, you don't get to double-cross us. We don't want empty promises from the warrior. He is one of *them,* but you we can use in our fight."

I bit my lip and shot a worried look at Machidiel. "Machidiel's good. He's on our side."

"He won't choose us when the time comes," Karen replied.

I shook my head. I honestly didn't know what she was talking about. When the time comes? When was that? When the apocalypse came? Because as far as I was aware we were already standing right at the beginning of it.

Did I really have a choice? To get to Zach I needed the zombies and the werewolf and if I needed to make an alliance with the witches, then so be it.

I nodded firmly. “You have my alliance.”

“The witches will never forget your promise.” Karen stepped closer and edged passed me, stepping up off the terrace through the glass doors. “Don’t let us down, Jophiel.”

At Trev’s look I bit my lip hard. That sounded ominous.

Never one to flinch away from getting myself into even more trouble, I nodded.

“Okay; I won’t.”

Karen shrugged. “Okay. Let’s get started then.”

The witches pushed us back into the apartment, and nudged us towards the sofa where Trev and I sat awkwardly, with Drew and Machidiel lurking to the side. They gathered ingredients, knives and a large sheet of cream material, and spread out around the room.

One witch spread the material out on the floor and knelt by the corner, while two others lit candles around the room. Soon, the smell of rosemary and sage was wafting in front of my face, sinking into my skin.

Karen and a long, blond-haired witch spread their ingredients, mostly consisting of herbs, stones and crystals, and what appeared to be a small collection of twigs, into small piles at the edge of the material. Simultaneously, the witches knelt and began to chant. It sounded very much like what I had heard when I had tapped into their minds during their meld, only this time the words were archaic. They weren't speaking English or Latin, or Angelic. Their words didn't sound like they came from any language I had ever heard.

Karen picked up stones and placed them carefully in a semi-circle on the material before sprinkling herbs across them. One of the other witches took one single twig and lit it in a candle before passing it to her. Karen leaned over the material, careful not to touch any part of it, and blew on the flames, letting sparks and little pieces of ash drop onto the collection of stones and herbs, while the chanting grew in volume.

I was mesmerized, completely entranced in the magic dancing in the air in front of me. It was tangible; I could feel it singeing my skin, sense the powerful pulses of energy vibing. I held myself stiffly, afraid somehow I would draw it into my body or that it would simply take over me like I had experienced too many times before.

"I need your blood," Karen said, her eyes on me.

"Mine?" I gulped and at her scathing look, and quickly scrambled forward, ignoring Trev's outstretched hand.

I knelt beside her and held out my arm, gritting my teeth. The witch smiled grimly and before I could ask what she was going to do, she had slid her knife across the inside of my arm, red-hot blood running down my hand and dripping off the end of my fingers in rivers. I gasped at the pain and scowled. Surely she hadn't needed to cut so deeply?

I held still until she had deemed my blood loss adequate then knocked my arm aside. I crawled backwards, trying not to look at Trev, imagining the blood hunger on his face. I pulled up my power and sent it through my own flesh to heal the gash, all the while keeping my eyes on the material where my blood had pooled.

When the blood began to bubble and move across the stones, creating a map of sorts, my mouth dropped open. The little lines traced all across the sheet, some joining up, others ending abruptly. The herbs were dragged away by the drops of blood, carried down the roads in waves until they clogged in various locations. Four specific piles were dotted across the sheet, three relatively close together, and one right in the far corner.

The witches stopped chanting and turned to eye me. "You told us there were only two zombies and one werewolf."

I nodded. "Right."

"Then why are you so desperate to find *four* locations?"

I knew why. I flushed, my face burning hot. I couldn't tell them the fourth location. Or at least, I couldn't tell them *why* I needed the fourth location. Another terrible idea of course, was to lie.

"The fourth location is the Pool of Kali. It's where the spirits escaped," I said, telling the truth.

"Why are you so interested in getting there?" She narrowed her eyes suspiciously.

I bit my lip. "I don't know why it showed up, really; I already know where it is."

She tilted her head, studying the material again. "The spell shows us where the objects that we desperately want are; where our mind is demanding us to go." She looked at me again, her blue eyes fixing mine with mistrust. “I guess you must *really* want to prevent any other escapes.”

I nodded quickly. “I do.” I took in a deep shaky breath. “I guess I, *we*, need to restore the guard there, so no more spirits escape. Does it show you where the spirits are?”

She nodded. “Two are in this world, and one has moved on.”

“Move on?” I asked, alarmed.

She shrugged. “To another realm.”

Shit. “Which one?”

“Who do you want to return to the dead first? The zombies or the werewolf?” she countered.

I thought for a second. I guessed the zombies sounded like more of a threat. “I’ll start with the zombies.”

She nodded. “They’ve crossed the border into Canada. Zombies avoid heavily populated places; they’re hiding out in the mountains of Revelstoke.”

“Where?” I scowled.

“North,” she answered glibly. “Your werewolf, shockingly, is now in the werewolf plane.”

My heart sank. I had presumed the werewolf would be the easiest of the kills. I did *not* want to take on Damian’s pack again.

I pressed my thumb and forefinger to my temple before running my palm back across my hair, flattening it. With the witches staring at me in silence I dropped my face into my hands for a second, rubbing my tired eyes.

"So now we know," I said.

Karen nodded slowly. "So now you know."

"Thank you." I stood and turned slightly to Trev, Drew and Machidiel who waited expectantly. "We should go."

The witches stood up, the candles extinguished with a strong breeze that suddenly rushed through the apartment. We edged out of the living room and edged towards the lift.

I felt the witches move, their conversation teasing at my senses. I quickly turned around to face them. "I won't forget."

20

'Alice: How long is forever?

White Rabbit: Sometimes, just one second.'

Lewis Carrol.

As we exited the lift and pushed through the doors back out onto the street, my body seemed wearier than it had ever been. Though technically, I had spent most of the previous twenty-four hours sitting in the car, I ached all over. We had all been so wired, so on edge since the Horsemen and then the vampire had attacked us, we had expended a huge amount of energy simply expecting something to happen.

Drew offered to drive and we each dived into our seats again, the air in the car filled with both relief and exhaustion.

"They could have offered us a place to crash, if only for a couple of hours," Trev grumbled.

I turned away to look out of the window. If they weren't willing to offer him a glass of water, they sure as hell weren't going to offer him a bed to sleep in.

"It doesn't matter, we're better off keeping going anyway." I rested my forehead against the glass. "Less chance of the Horsemen catching up with us."

"Maybe they already know where we're going, and are lying in wait. Maybe having a few hours sleep would be the difference between having our throats slit and living to find these zombies."

"Maybe," I agreed. "How many hours' drive, Drew?"

"Maybe fourteen, fifteen hours," he said. "Depends on traffic, and getting across the border too, I guess."

"So, we could be there by tonight?"

He shrugged. "Maybe; depends who else is on the road."

With that glum thought I fell silent, staring as Portland dropped away and we headed north.

We spent most of the daylight hours driving, following the motorway through smaller towns until we reached Seattle. Despite the fact we hadn't eaten since the night before, Machidiel refused to allow us to stop when we drove through Emerald City. My mouth watered as we passed by diners, cafes and restaurants, and even when we filled up at the petrol station, Drew only picked up one bag of Doritos and threw them back to Trev and I.

"Seriously? Do angels and lycans never get hungry?" I grumbled.

Drew snorted. "I'm no' eating anything from a cheap petrol station. I'll wait until we stop somewhere."

"Never known a guy to be fussy with food." I smirked.

"We'll stop in a couple of hours," Machidiel spoke up.

I rolled my eyes and stuffed a handful of Doritos in my mouth, crunching them loudly. I pulled my knees up to my chest, and eyed Trev.

"These satisfying any urges you might be having?" I quipped, popping another one into my mouth.

He gave me a sly look. "Not exactly, but you're safe for now, unless you're offering."

"No!" Drew growled from the front seat.

I chuckled then grimaced as Trev huffed out a breath.

"He was joking, Drew," I chastised, feeling guilty for goading Trev.

Drew kept silent, and Trev turned to glare out of the window. This was going to be a *long* journey.

The towns continued to drop by and I eventually dropped off to sleep, resting on my arm against the window. When I woke, the first thing I did was check I hadn't drooled on my arm, then check the time.

"Is that all?" I groaned, as I caught a glimpse of the clock in the dashboard. Little over two hours had passed since we had left Seattle, which meant I'd only spent an hour of that time sleeping, and though the light had dimmed slightly it was probably due to the heavy cloud overhead, rather than the time passing.

Machidiel turned to look at me. "What do you mean?"

"I've been asleep for what—an hour?" I yawned, covering my mouth with both hands.

He smiled. "We're near the border though. We'll stop for food once we cross."

That perked me up. "Really? Cool."

I sat up straight and leaned forward, peering between the front seats, waiting for my first glimpse of Canadian soil.

Of course the first thing I spotted as we began to slow down with the building traffic was a sign warning drivers to have their passports and car registration details ready to hand over to officers.

"Machidiel . . ." I began, trying not to panic. "Tell me that in those ten minutes you had, you actually bought this car legally?"

He laughed. "We'll be fine."

"How? *Exactly* how will we be okay crossing the border dirty, with torn and bloody clothes, a stolen car, and no passports?"

"A glamour," he replied.

"Sorry, what?"

Machidiel grinned at me. "The witches have promised to be our allies, and they know we're crossing the border into Canada; they're going to help us get through."

I shook my head, tired of men and their weird assumptions. "Did you think to mention to them that we'd need actual documents? Are they just going to appear in our hands the moment we need them? Did you tell them we stole this car?"

"Jasmine, Jasmine!" he exclaimed. "I thought you were the rebel! I thought you were all about throwing caution to the wind, and jumping in feet first; what's with the inquisition?"

I didn't want to tell him that I still didn't fully trust him, because really, that was rude after everything we'd been through together. Hadn't he proven himself over and over? He'd fought off the Horsemen, taken me to the witches, joined this entire damn zombie hunt on a whim—recently he hadn't given me any reason not to trust him. Selfishly, I also didn't want him to back out now; I still needed his help.

I sat back, and rested my head against the hard headrest. "Fine; no more questions."

The car fell silent as we crawled up the road, in the third of five lanes waiting to approach the immigration booth. When we were just one car away, I nudged Trev awake, flinching when he shot upright.

I jerked my head towards the officer approaching the window. Drew pressed the button below the window and waited for the glass to roll down fully in the front and the back. The man, a thin, balding guy who looked close to retirement, looked through the windows at us and jotted something down on his clipboard. I imagined he was writing, *possible suspects involved in a hit and run*. I wouldn't blame him, judging by the state of us. Unable to help myself, I began to chew on my fingernail, anxiously waiting for a heap of men to come and either arrest us or, if the demons had arrived before us, murder us.

"Passports, proof of address, and car registration papers," the man said.

I felt Trev tense beside me, and my own muscles locked in place, my magic running freely through my body. I looked down at my knees, praying Machidiel was right, and that the witches would have anticipated this.

"Are you bringing any alcohol or cigarettes over the border?" the officer continued.

I looked up, startled. Had he just brushed over our lack of papers? I tried to hold back the relief that flooded through me, worried it would jinx us, but as Drew replied that we hadn't brought any banned substances with us, I couldn't help the elation heating me up. Drew pressed a button letting the boot lift up and the officer crossed behind the car, checking for dead bodies or something.

The moment he waved us onwards, Drew wound up the windows and carefully drove away from the booth, pulling onto the motorway again. We remained silent for a moment, Trev and I constantly looking behind us, waiting for what was surely an inevitable car chase when they realized we hadn't given any of our papers over. When the minutes dragged by, we turned to face each other in astonishment.

Whooping loudly, we high-fived, and laughed hysterically.

"Jesus! I was waiting for him to call us out," Drew cried.

"Have you seen the state of us?" I screeched. "I've got blood on my knees, my jeans are torn and singed, and Drew you're just as bad."

"How the hell did we get through in a stolen car, man?" Trev shook his head, laughing.

Machidiel turned back to raise his eyebrows at me expectantly.

I shrugged, grinning. "I was wrong. Somehow, you keep surprising me."

"Is that an apology?" he asked in wry voice.

I nodded. "Yeah, I *am* sorry for second guessing you but there's still more to you than meets the eye."

"Hey." Trev leaned forward. "That reminds me of something that's been annoying me since we left Portland. What did the witch mean when she said you're not from the House of Haamiah?"

I stared passed Machidiel at his reflection in the mirror when he didn't answer. He looked . . . sad, maybe reverent.

"Mach," I whispered. I wanted desperately to read his mind. It would be so easy to know what he was thinking about, but I couldn't, not when I had just apologized for giving him the third degree. I smiled inwardly. Maybe my Jasmine side wanted to stoop that low, but archangel Jophiel just wouldn't let me.

"I'm from a much older division," he answered hesitantly after a long pause.

Trev and I flicked a glance at each other. Would he continue? Would he leave us with that irritating half answer?

"As you know, I'm allied with Jophiel—*Jasmine*," he added apologetically, "and of course everyone involved in that situation. I also have loyalties to Haamiah, Maion and Elijah."

I flinched, sorrow biting a hole in my chest when he didn't say Zach's name.

He sighed. "But there is another soul I am loyal to, and it is to her house that I am bound."

"A *soul*?" I whispered. A soul mate? Machidiel had a soul mate? I shouldn't have been so stunned, especially as he had hinted at this before but I had pushed it aside in my mind. Despite his jaw-dropping appearance and sexy-as tattoos I had always thought of him as kind of *asexual*, which of course now sounded ridiculous.

Just because someone doesn't talk about being in love with someone all of the time doesn't mean they aren't, or haven't been.

I wanted to ask who. I wanted to know his story. I had known he had something painful, some dark secrets he was hiding, and now he had shown me a glimpse I wanted to pry right inside and learn everything I could. I wished I could convince myself it was because he seemed sad, and I suppose in part it was, but the largest part was that if he could convince me he knew love, then I could believe that he was actually going to help me bring *my* love back to life.

I had been wondering for a while how to ditch him when the time came. I didn't think for a second he would actually help me bring one of his best friends back from the dead. Angels were stiff and unbending. They were the type of people who always obeyed the rules; there's no way they would allow me to do what I was planning on doing. If I succeeded, wasn't I defiling everything they stood for? What was the point in an afterlife if someone kept dragging you back? Yes, it had happened before with Zanaria, but that hadn't been my fault; that was Lilith's doing. The fact that I was being sent after these three escaped spirits in the middle of the apocalypse was proof enough that the angels took this matter very seriously.

No I hadn't expected Machidiel to actually help me. I'd thought he would ensure I got the job done with this mission and then maybe knock me out and lock me up in the Heavens, or leave me here for the demons. If it were true that he had a soul mate, could I persuade him to actually help me bring Zach's soul back?

Thankfully, Drew decided he wanted to know more. "You got a girl waiting for you?" he asked.

"Something like that," Machidiel answered.

Don't let that be the end of the conversation. Keep asking! I mentally begged the lycan.

"Sharing is caring," he said with a smile.

Machidiel snorted with laughter. "My girl's in a bit of trouble. Hell, my girl *is* trouble."

"Sounds familiar." Drew looked at me pointedly through the rear-view mirror. I glared in return. "So why are you sitting in a car with us, and not wherever she is?"

Ugh. Trust Drew to say something that could encourage him to leave us when we needed him—although it was a valid point.

"This is the only way I can think of helping her," he said.

I paused, my mind ticking over. It all made sense. He had said before that he was the only angel who could help me, the only one who would truly believe in me. I was the Archangel of Miracles. I'd bought Zanaria back from the dead, and I was going to do the same to Zach. He was helping me complete my mission and get to the Pool of Kali because he wanted something too. I wasn't the only one with a lost soul mate. He wanted me to bring his own back with Zach.

21

‘Let’s be nothing; I heard it lasts forever.’

Unknown.

I kept my mouth shut and sat back, my mind racing at a millions miles an hour. I couldn’t let him know that I knew. He hadn’t asked for my help yet, so I needed to wait. It was hard, knowing there was someone sitting next to me, okay, *in front* of me, who was going through the same devastating heartbreak as me. Someone surely just as conflicted, yet determined to see this through. I now saw him in an entirely new light. He was heartbroken, lost, and alone. I could feel my compassion soaring through me, my healing ability begging to be let loose to soothe the ache I knew he would feel.

“Rein it in, Jas!” Drew hollered.

I blinked . . .then blinked again. Mist clouded my eyes; a sparkling, glimmering mass swirling around inside the car. I took a deep breath, squashing my emotions and sucking my magic back inside like a vortex.

When the car was clear, I bit my lip sheepishly. “Sorry.”

Drew laughed good-naturedly, which was sweet, considering I could have made us crash. Still feeling emotional, I reasoned with myself that this was what friends and family did; forgave each other for almost causing a car crash, draining the blood out of them, almost getting them shot or murdered, or kicked out of an airplane a few thousand feet up. Even going psycho and killing a few hundred demons on a whim, or accidentally setting someone on fire was no cause for alarm. *Yeah*, I thought; family forgave things like that.

"Okay, you promised us food," I said once I felt my emotions were back under control.

"Agassiz is right up here, just a few minutes more," Machidiel said.

He was right; within five minutes we welcomed by a sign for Agassiz, the district of Kent, and we turned off the highway into a small, quiet town. Tourist information signs told us we were entering a farming community with a population of six thousand. I grimaced; would that make it easier for the Horsemen to lie in wait for us, or harder?

I stared out of the window at the small houses and businesses we passed, much hidden by thick vegetation, trying to spot anything that looked suspicious. Of course, being out here in the middle of nowhere it was probably us that would look out of place. I turned my head and pulled up my knees to rest my chin on them, trying to contain my anxiety as the car followed the signs for Agassiz-Rosedale Highway. We soon pulled over into an almost empty car park and turned the engine off.

Hunger riding each of us, we bolted out of the car and headed for the street, finding a Mexican restaurant called El Sombrero. We silently agreed to go there; whether it was because it was the first place we had seen or because of the gaudy yet attractive yellow and green exterior promising hot food and cocktails. My heart gave a pang as my mind took me back four years ago, images flashing across my mind of Zach and I when we had run away together, small pockets of emotion popping into my head as I recalled the way I had felt, the things I had done, back then, including eating

Mexican with my lover. It was silly to well up at the sight of a stupid restaurant. I hadn't even known Zach properly then; I'd thought he was crazy at the time . . . until he'd saved my life *again*.

Oblivious to my argument with my inner mopey self, the boys pulled me along and we sat at a table at the back, near to the fire exit so we had a clear run if we'd been followed.

Flicking open the menu, I could barely read a thing, still caught up in my torment as I was. When Trev nudged me I looked up, realizing the waitress was frowning, and waiting for my order. I flushed with embarrassment, unsure how long she had been standing. How many times had she asked me what I wanted?

"Burrito, please," I said quickly, picking the first thing I saw.

"Which filling?"

"Umm, beef."

I handed over my menu, and the waitress hurried off behind the counter. Picking up the jug of water on the table, I briefly wondered how long it had been sitting there before deciding I didn't actually care. I scanned the rest of the menu and stared at the other customers while the boys stared at the news flashing up on the screen behind the bar.

"Jesus."

I turned my attention to Drew. "What?"

He nodded at the television. I narrowed my eyes at the scenes unfolding; a fire had enveloped a building in flames, grey billowing smoke filling the air and partially obscuring the view of the ground crew videoing. The camera zoomed in on figures jumping from the top of the two-story building into nets firemen had spread out. In the darkness, the camera picked up retreating figures behind the building . . . figures much bigger than humans.

I leaned forward, balancing on the edge of my seat with my legs tensed, adrenaline rushing through my body. From what I could make out, the figures were close to a story high, maybe around fifteen feet. As one swung around, a wide tail swept into view. The reporter carried on babbling about the possible cause of the fire, and the efforts the firemen were going to in order to rescue those inside, completely oblivious to the creatures in the background.

As the screen cut away, focusing on the presenters in the newsroom, I forced my eyes away from the television and looked to Machidiel for help.

"What were they? I've never seen anything like them," I said breathlessly.

He sat still, silent for a moment, his face expressionless. "Demons; they've come through Hell's gates."

The four of us were frozen in place, surely thinking the same thing: *How could we close the gates before any more of those creatures escaped?* How could we go up against beings so huge and survive? What were their weaknesses and their strengths?

"We aren't ready," Machidiel said softly.

"What do ye mean?" Drew huffed. "They're demons, the same as any other; we can take them."

"They're stronger than anything you've ever faced before," he replied, rolling his eyes.

Drew grunted and threw his hands up. “Stronger than the Horsemen? Stronger than the Queen of the Damned?”

Trev snorted in agreement.

“Yes, they are,” Machidiel said with a sharp grin. “There are more of them. Double the number; double the strength.”

Drew shook his head, his black shoulder-length hair falling in front of his face. “They’re still demons.”

“Demons that can potentially eviscerate you on sight, trap you in your dreams, or set you on fire.”

He pointed at me. “*She* can set people on fire.”

I rolled my eyes and looked at Trev.

He smirked. “Yeah, but she’s just as likely to set *us* on fire at the same time.”

Maybe there was a time when I’d have been upset by that, but right now I thought it was hilarious. I sniggered and pointed at him. “And *you* would just drink us!”

He broke into a grin. “Too right.”

We chuckled under the unamused glare of Machidiel and Drew, then simmered down.

“The truth is,” I took a breath, “you’re right.”

“Who?” Drew scowled.

“Not you,” I said. I shook my head. “We’re not ready. Drew, you fight best as a pack; you’ve said that before. Here, you’re packless. Machidiel—you’re an angel, but one with a sardonic sense of humor. In order to teach me a lesson you let me plummet from the sky and almost die. I hold my hands up, it worked, it taught me, but now I constantly second guess you, wondering if you have an ulterior motive. Trev isn't confident in his abilities, and neither am I. I worry he's going to go psycho and kill us all as soon as he gets hungry, and he can't reassure any of us that that's not going to happen because he doesn't know how to control the thirst.

"I don't know what I can do. I know some things, and they scare the crap out of me. I've almost killed all of you at some point because I can't control the fallen angel rage that spreads through me. I'm terrified I'll accidentally open a portal and send one of you or myself to a Hell dimension so I'm always holding back, trying to hold on." I sighed. "We're not ready to take on demons that have escaped from Hell . . . but we don't have a choice. We all know what we're going to do—we just don't know how we're going to do it. We'll start with finding the zombies and then the werewolf."

Trev slid his hand across the table slowly and pressed his down on top of mine in a show of solidarity. "Then we'll get Zach."

Drew leaned forward and clapped his hand on top of ours. "Kill Asmodeus."

"And Mnemosyne," Machidiel immediately added, joining his hand to our fist pile.

I smiled. "Break out Gabriel."

"Hunt down and kill the Horsemen," Drew snarled with a show of teeth.

"Close the gates." Machidiel said.

"And save the world," Trev finished.

One by one, they pulled their hands back from mine, and I sat back in the stiff chair, regarding them seriously.

“It sounds do-able,” I said, hiding a laugh.

Drew grinned. “After we’ve eaten.”

22

'If it's both terrifying and amazing then you should definitely pursue it.'

Erada.

"I don't know if I dare ask how much longer this journey will take. Are we going to be driving through the night?" Trev asked as he sat back in his chair, stretching his arms up over his head.

Machidiel grimaced. "I guess it's up for discussion. We're looking at another six or seven hours."

I groaned, and rested my forehead on the table. "Really? It's already late; it's pretty dark out there already."

I wasn't exaggerating; it had been getting late when we had crossed the border, and now, after driving, eating and sitting, the sun had gone down outside, and I didn't like the idea of carrying on the journey in the dark. It wasn't that I was scared of the dark—more I was scared of meeting the Horsemen by the side of the road up here in the middle of nowhere. We had already clarified that our team sucked, and we'd be lucky to get out of this alive, so why invite more trouble?

"Just to make things a little more difficult, this food was great and all, but I'm still . . . hungry," Trev said quietly.

I sat up immediately and eyed him. "How hungry?"

He shrugged, one fang popping out over his lip.

"So we find something . . . *someone* for you to eat, fill up the car and head off," Drew suggested. "No fun in hunting zombies in daylight anyway. If we head off soon, we'll be in Revelstoke by two or three in the morning."

"Yeah, and exhausted! What use will we be in a fight if we're wrecked from traveling two days straight?" I exclaimed.

"If we get there and we're too tired, we can find a motel and go hunting the next night," Machidiel offered.

"Fine," I agreed.

I didn't really know why I was stalling; I wanted this mission over. I needed to finish this so we could get to the Pool of Kali, and Zach. I should be cheering Machidiel along, rushing the boys out of the restaurant, but something told me we were heading into more trouble than we were expecting. My nerve endings were tingling in anticipation of the coming fight, my heart pounding a fighter's rhythm. I was sure something else would be there; the question was, which one of our enemies knew we were heading for Revelstoke, and *how* did they know it?

I wasn't a coward; I wouldn't act like one now.

"Let's go," I said.

I pushed my chair back, scraping the legs across the floor, and headed for the counter. Machidiel handed over his credit card, grinning at me. He knew what I'd been thinking.

I rolled my eyes and stomped across the restaurant to the door, pushing it open. I stood outside, Trev appearing beside me.

"Sam is gonna be so mad," he said.

Surprised, I turned and looked up at him. "Huh?"

He looked down at me, his dreadlocks falling over his shoulder. "Are you serious? He got left with Grandpa Haamiah, and is likely sitting on a cloud somewhere learning about history while we've driven halfway up the U.S., crossed the border and are heading into the wilderness on a zombie hunt. We're bad ass."

I smirked. "Yeah, happily running or *driving* off to our deaths is way cooler than sitting on a cloud . . . playing a harp."

He laughed, bending over to clutch at his stomach. "Dude, I hope he's playing a harp. That would be awesome!"

I laughed and leaned back against the wall, looking out at the dark street. Images of Sam dressed in white robes with a huge golden harp danced in my mind.

Slowly the image faded, leaving the familiar feeling of my magic swirling around my abdomen. I stood up straight and took a step out, scanning the area.

"What is it?" Trev hissed.

"Something's here. Something's out here. Get back inside." I pushed him through the door, sending a hasty look back over my shoulder.

We walked straight into Machidiel and Drew. Without needing to say a word, as a group we ran to the back of the restaurant and threw the fire exit open, running into the alleyway behind. We spread out and ran, sprinting past the garbage bins towards the opening of the alleyway.

Five vampires rounded the corner, stalking towards us.

"Back up!" Machidiel bellowed.

I skidded to a halt and ran back. Spinning around, I realized we were trapped. Two vampires stood on the other side, blocking the way back to the restaurant. I lifted my fists and crouched, ready for them.

"Weren't you going to try to persuade the vamps to join our cause?" I hissed at Trev.

He stepped past me and held his hands up toward the two Vampires who had exited the restaurant, closing in on them. "I'm one of you," he called, flashing his fangs.

Both of them snarled in response.

"Try harder!" I cried.

He looked at me, his eyes wild with panic and frustration. "What do I say?"

"I don't know, just do something!"

He turned back to them. One vampire reached him first, throwing Trev into the brick wall. He smashed through it and landed on the ground.

I shrieked and jumped forward, kicking away one vampire that edged too close to Trev's body. I picked up a brick and smacked the other across the face, scraping off a layer of skin. I hit again and again until the vampire fell to his knees. I spun, kicking out and snapping his neck. That wouldn't kill it, but it would keep him down for a while.

Machidiel and Drew stepped backwards towards me, creating a loose semi-circle around Trev where he lay, unconscious. I reached into pocket for a knife, panic setting in when I realized I'd left it in the car. Machidiel looked over and read the situation correctly. He threw me a knife and I reached up, picking it out of the air. I tackled another vampire, throwing him over my shoulder. He attacked me from behind, his arm wrapping around my throat, cutting off my oxygen supply. I gripped the knife and hacked into his arm, cutting deep, sawing the flesh apart.

Pain seared through my neck; a pain I had felt recently. The vampire had dug his fangs in deep, drawing on my blood. I threw my head back, catching him in the face and loosening his grip. I ripped his arm off, smiling as the vampire screamed in agony.

I spun around, booting the vampire in the chest and sending him through the wall into the building next door. I took a huge breath, my lungs expanding as magic soared through me, ripping through my fiber. I glared angrily at the remaining vampires. Machidiel had taken out one, leaving five still attacking.

"I'm going to enjoy ripping you open," one hissed at me, creeping around me sideways.

I opened my mouth, mirth spreading through me from my widening lips to eyes. I quirked one eyebrow at him.

"I think that pleasure will be mine," I jeered.

I lifted my palm and blew a kiss across my fingers, laughing as flames roared to life, licking up his clothing. The screams were delicious; I could almost taste the fear and panic that echoed through the air. Rage poured through me, filling my skin with heat and pain.

"A little help here, please!" Drew grunted.

I flicked my eyes to him, and to the vampire he was fighting. Sparks flew and the vampire backed away in horror, looking down at his hands. Fire billowed from his skin, scorching him from the inside out. My flames jumped from him to the others, and soon the vampires either lay dead or screaming.

"Fuck!" Drew shouted.

I spun around, my attention pulling back from my anger. My mouth dropped open, terror pushing through all other motions.

Two demons, similar to those we'd seen on the news report, stood facing us at the end of the alleyway. Up close, they looked even taller than they had seemed. Their skin was reptilian, grey, lumpy, and covered in battle scars. Their tails twitched behind their huge bodies, the only outward sign of agitation. Tusks protruded from thick black lips, red eyes staring straight at us.

I stepped backwards, and reached down to touch Trev. I sent healing power through my fingertips, along with adrenaline and pure rage. It worked, jolting him into awareness. He snarled, growling low in his throat. Risking him biting off my hand, I stretched back and pulled Trev to his feet, praying the rage I had sent into him wouldn't tip him over the edge.

As he pulled away from me, I grimaced and turned slightly to see what he was doing. His fangs were out and he was glaring at me, crouched over threateningly.

"Back off," I warned. I reached out with my mist, sending a trail of it to him, sucking out the tendrils of rage I had imparted.

He drooped, energy leaving him.

“Sorry,” I said, wincing. He needed energy, but I couldn’t have him attacking me.

I turned back to the demons and began to back away. With a loud bang, they began to stomp forward, slowly at first, then running.

“Run!” I screamed.

We sprinted toward the wire fence. The heavy footfalls of the demons got closer and closer. I focused on keeping Trev with me, dragging him along when he stumbled.

The fence loomed up and I shrieked, magic exploding through me as I leaped, flying through the air with Trev in my grip. We landed against the fence, our fingers gripping through the wire to pull our bodies close.

Almost at the top, it wasn’t hard to flip over it and drop to the ground. We staggered off, Machidiel and Drew landing beside us, their vault over the fence much smoother than Trev and mine’s. I glanced back then picked up speed, passing the others in my urge to get away.

“What are they doing?” Drew hollered.

“They cut straight through the metal!” I screamed.

We slid around the corner and headed onto the street, running in the direction of the car park. I saw movement and looked up, spotting vampires running across the top of the buildings lining the road.

“Incoming!” I shouted to warn the boys.

I sent my fire up to reach them, their bodies lighting up quickly. We raced across the road, spotting our car, now on its own in the car park.

Drew unlocked it electronically and we piled in. The car roared to life, and we screeched out onto the road. We slewed across the concrete, Trev and I bashing into each other in the backseat. He caught me as I almost fell to the floor and dragged me up against him.

Something landed on top of the car, the roof bending inwards. Trev covered me with his body, protecting me from the glass of the back window that shattered across us. Drew spun the car in a full circle, and we heard the demon fly off the vehicle, landing heavily on the concrete and smashing it into ripples as it slid across the road, the tarmac breaking into pieces. Drew slammed his foot down and sped through the streets and onto the highway, leaving the town and the demons behind.

23

'Someone I loved once gave me a box of darkness. It took me years to understand that this too, was a gift.'

Mary Oliver.

We entered Revelstoke at precisely two forty-five a.m. For the past two hours, the road had wound upwards through the mountains, each side coated with thick trees, ponds, and rivers diverting heavy rainfall away from the less-than-intact highway. At the edges, the tarmac crumbled into the mud while potholes shook us as we raced over them. Though the dark shielded them, I knew from what Machidiel had told us that the Selkirk and Monashee Mountain ranges rose up around us on all sides.

We followed the Trans-Canada Highway over the bridge across the Columbia River. I flinched as a sign popped up by the side of the road. Drew slowed the car slightly.

Revelstoke. Close to Heaven, down to earth, I read.

Signs for the golf course, hot springs and museums sprung out of the darkness, highlighting the fun and exciting things to do up here in this small mountainside town. If only we were here under different circumstances; if only we were here with people who *should* be here.

Despite driving through the town center, the shops were spread out, the streets clean, and the houses large and well-built. Drew pushed the car on through the town until we reached the outskirts on the far edge. We pulled off the road, and parked behind a cheap and tacky looking motel.

I slid out of the backseat and shut the door quietly, standing with Trev behind the car. The car park was covered in shadows; small, crooked ones from the cars lined up, and larger flickering black shadows the motel cast on us. Anything could be hiding here . . . *anything*.

"Are we staying here?" Trev asked.

I turned my head, reading him; he was hungry for blood.

"Maybe," Machidiel said, joining us. "Though, if anyone's up for it, I'm going hunting for zombies."

I nodded. "I'm up for it."

Drew laughed, and winked at me. "I'm in."

We stalked off through the shadows, heading back through the streets, winding up thin lanes and alleyways behind houses. We jogged off the main streets, avoiding passing cars.

Trev stopped, tensing and breathing deeply.

"What is it?" I asked.

He lifted his eyes to mine. "I can smell humans."

Drew hefted his sword into his hands, narrowing his eyes at him. Machidiel sighed and stared at me, seemingly expecting me to say something.

“What?” I hissed. “He needs to feed; he’s a vampire. It doesn’t mean he has to kill.”

“I don’t know if I can stop myself,” Trev bit out, dropping his head into his hands.

His body began to shake, his shoulders trembling as he groaned.

I bit my lip and marched off. Differently to Trev, yet still just as accurate, I could sense the same humans nearby. I followed the path we were on, running behind a block of houses. Traditional wooden backyard picket fences were interspersed with wire mesh, garden furniture, trampolines and manicured gardens, mixed with gardens filled with rubbish and grass so high the house windows were obscured.

I paused behind one, hearing whispered voices. I knelt and peered around the corner, spying a teenage boy and girl sitting on a back porch, kissing. Trev knelt beside me, staring at his prey. He leaned close, his face near to mine. As we watched the boy pushing the girl back gently, our spying turning into voyeurism. I felt Trev take in a deep breath.

Drew shoved him out of the way, snarling as Trev fell to his knees.

“What’s going on?” I hissed.

“Jasmine’s blood stays where it is, vamp.” Drew ignored me, focusing his deathly glare on Trev.

I rolled my eyes. “Trev, get going. You want blood? There are two completely oblivious people right over there.”

Trev rose to his feet and skirted around the lycan, jumping high over the mesh fence. He landed in a crouch, and began to stalk up through the garden towards his victims. I leaped over after him, and followed the path he made, staying hidden in the shadows.

My mind raced, guilt, fear, and anxiety rushing through me in rivets. Was this right? No, clearly not. Two innocent, or maybe not-so-innocent kids necking on in the back garden at three a.m. were about to get their blood sucked out. If we could prevent Trev from hurting them too badly this could still work out okay. Trev was on *my* team, and I was on his; I wouldn't let him down, no matter how scared I was.

Trev zoned in, inches away from the unsuspecting couple. He grabbed the guy by his hair and pulled his head back, exposing his throat. Sinking his teeth in, he guzzled the blood, a trail running down his face. I pounced on the girl, catching her eyes with mine. Her mouth opened slowly, about to scream for help. I unleashed my magic, holding her in a trance. Mist poured out around me, holding her still, freezing her in place. Her eyes were held open—dazed, tinged with horror. She was stuck, caught in the moment Trev had pulled her boyfriend away from her. I didn't know what I was doing; how could I keep her trapped like this?

Movement and noise behind me made me turn. Machidiel had loosened Trev's grip on the boy and thrown him into the grass. Trev snarled angrily, threatening the angel. Drew appeared beside me and grabbed hold of my arms, pulling me to the side. We fell into the grass together as Trev lunged over us, sinking his fangs into the girl's neck, leaning over her.

The sound of gulping filled my ears, wet and sloppy. Pushing Drew off me, I crawled over to where Machidiel had dropped the boy on the porch. He lay face-down on the wood, his shirt saturated with blood. I scrambled over to him and pressed my hand to his neck, sending in my power to heal him. The wound was only small and quickly disappeared, but boosting his blood supply was a little more difficult.

Thankfully there was no need to pry Trev's fangs away from the girl; Trev pulled away and put her down gently. He looked to me, guilt filling his eyes.

"It's okay," I whispered.

I crawled across the porch to him and put my hand on arm, sending a flood of reassurance. I pushed past him and put my hand on the girl, healing her from the inside out. I sat back and looked up at the boys as they crowded around me. Drew held out his hand and pulled me up to my feet. I staggered and leaned against him.

"You okay?" he asked, concerned.

I nodded. "Just a little weak. I'll be fine."

Machidiel swung me around, looking down into my eyes. He frowned, his eyes glaring into my soul.

He shook his head. "We need to get somewhere safe and rest."

"I'm fine!" I protested. I pulled back, standing up straight. "You're not hunting zombies without me."

He smiled and looked around, encompassing Drew and Trev. "We're *all* going to rest. We've travelled far over the past two days, and we're all tired. The vamp is rehydrated but now our secret weapon needs to gather her strength."

"Your secret weapon?" I rolled my eyes. "Hardly *secret*."

Drew put his arm around me. "Let's go."

We climbed over the mesh fence, leaving the two teens lying on the porch. I had a moment of regret and worry for them, before Machidiel knocked loudly on the back door. As lights inside flickered on and we heard footsteps walking towards us, we scampered off the porch and climbed over the mesh fence Out of sight, we walked back to the motel just as furtively as we had left, keeping to the shadows.

Drew pushed me into the backseat of the car as Trev and Machidiel jumped in.

"What happened to resting?" I complained.

Drew flashed a grin at me as we reversed out onto the street. "Not here. We'll go somewhere else."

I dropped my head back against the seat and closed my eyes, feeling my power still churning inside my abdomen, unwilling to settle back down. My heart pulsed with every churn, shooting anxiety and adrenaline through me. Though we were in the car and technically safe, I still felt on edge. The zombies; they were here. I could sense it. Having our mission *this* close to us was too head-trippy for me to just relax and let it go. What if they moved on? If I could sense them, could they sense me? Did they know how close they were to being returned?

"We need to hunt them down. We shouldn't give up now," I muttered.

Machidiel glanced at me. "We're not giving up, we're just regrouping."

"You don't think they'll run?"

He shook his head. "No, they won't. It's nearly dawn; they'll be stuck here until tonight. We'll start tracking before the sun goes down."

I sniffed, and ran my hand back over my hair. "Yeah, I suppose."

"Trust me," Machidiel said, turning away. "We're close to winning. We're not going to miss this opportunity."

"Are you sure?"

I saw his body tense. "You're forgetting that I have someone at stake too."

I bit my lip and flicked my eyes over to Trev. "Yeah, I know; just as long as we're on the same page."

Five minutes later, we had pulled up outside a hotel that looked significantly higher class than the tacky motel we had parked outside of the last time. The parking lot was half empty, clean, and there was only a short walk to the brightly lit entrance.

We stumbled across to the glass doorway and pushed through into the foyer. We approached the desk and a suited man quickly stood up from where he had been leaning forward onto the counter. He pasted a smile onto his face, even as he frowned at our dirty clothing.

Machidiel pushed Trev and me behind Drew. "Greetings," he said with a cordial smile.

"Indeed," the man said, frowning.

Thankfully Machidiel managed to talk the man into giving us two rooms. If I had been the one behind the desk, I was pretty sure I wouldn't have allowed four dirty, blood-soaked fiends into my hotel. Maybe he was planning on calling the police as soon as we left his sight.

If he *had* been planning that, the huge tip Machidiel pushed towards him seemed to help our cause. He quickly led us to two rooms, side by side, and handed over the swipe cards to unlock the doors.

I pushed open the first one, number twenty-four, and searched the room for anything evil. The room was posher than the last; a large flat-screen television on the wall, big soft beds and a beautiful ensuite with white towels piled up.

Drew searched the cupboards, even looking under the bed.

"Anything evil?" I asked.

When he shook his head, looking miffed that he hadn't found anything he could kill, I smiled and threw myself onto one of the beds, letting my arms fall to the side as I bounced. I opened my eyes a crack, watching as Drew, Trev and Machidiel had a silent conversation as to who stayed in which room.

"I don't like this," Drew grumbled as he and Trev left, pulling the door closed.

"I guess it's you and me, big guy," I murmured.

Machidiel snorted, flicked off the light and threw himself onto the other bed. We lay there in silence for a while, simply breathing and recovering.

I rolled onto my side. "How did she die?"

The air was tense. "Who?"

"I'm not stupid. An angel would never help me bring another angel's soul back without good reason. And by good reason, I mean an *amazing* reason! You said you had someone in trouble, someone you needed to help. It makes sense that you're going to bring her soul back too. What other reason would you go against everything angels stand for? Am I wrong?"

He sat up and stared at me across the room. "Not entirely. Things aren't as straightforward in the angelic world. Haamiah might have taught you that angels are all on the same side, fighting evil, guiding and guarding humans while fighting vampires and demons, but there are other factors."

"Like?"

"The principalities, for a start. They predict the future and try to move important figures around to get them into the right place at the right time. Only some angels don't like their strings to be pulled, and some simply don't agree with the principality's game plan. That's where things get tricky."

I sat up, still able to see him in the dark. I bit my lip. This seemed way over my head. Angels fighting angels? Was that possible?

I thought hard, racking my brain. It *was* possible; I'd seen it as Jophiel, I just hadn't remembered that I'd seen it.

"I remember," I whispered. "Raphael and Gabriel hated each other."

"They don't *hate* each other," he said sharply. "Gabriel doesn't hate anyone. She's a principality in archangel form; she has a game plan, and Raphael doesn't agree with it."

"What's her game plan?" I asked.

Machidiel sniggered. "Think, Jophiel. You know her game plan. You're part of her game plan."

I scowled. I didn't like *that*; the fact that he'd used my other name, or that he'd told me I was just part of a game. "How am I part of a game plan?"

I felt his eyes on me and I lay back.

"You agreed to it," he said simply.

"Oh." I sighed, remembering. "Good point."

Gabriel's game plan: uniting the factions to form one super army to take out the ultimate evil. That was Gabriel's game plan—mine had been to save Zach at any cost. It still was. Gabriel's was so much more selfless than mine. She was the good one; she'd always been purer and sweeter and better than me.

"I need to get her out," I said.

Machidiel took a deep breath. "When?"

"Soon." I shook my head. "If she's even still there."

"The dungeons?" he asked. "She will be."

"For this long? She would still be imprisoned after more than a quarter of a century? How could they do that to her? She's one of them!"

"Time is different there. Time moves different and feels different." He shrugged. "And to be honest, they don't care that she's been imprisoned for so long."

"She didn't do anything wrong. She was trying to help us," I objected.

"Raphael is a force to contend with. He has his reasons for what he did."

"He loved me," I said, sitting up again. "I know he loved me, like a sister."

"He did. He misses you every day."

My eyes opened sharply. "Really? How do you know? Doesn't he know I'm here?"

Machidiel snorted. "No! If he thought his angelic little sister had been reincarnated into the body of a half valkyrie-half fallen angel hybrid, he'd track you down and kill you to save you from yourself."

"Are you serious?" I gasped.

He nodded. "He thinks you're dead. You jumped through the Heavenly gates and disappeared. The prophecy was foretold that the Archangel Jophiel would be reincarnated, but no one really knew if it was going to happen. Angels don't usually have anything to do with prophecies; they leave that business to the lower beings. Raphael thinks you're dead, just like Michael and the others. Only Gabriel knows you're down here somewhere."

I gulped. I could still feel love for my brothers though I wasn't there anymore, though I wasn't the same person anymore, I could still despair that my brothers thought I was dead, and that one of them would kill me on sight. Tears welled with hopelessness inside of me.

"We've gone off topic a little bit," I said, trying to pull my emotions back. "I still don't understand why you're helping. I only agreed to Gabriel's plan because I saw what would happen to Zach in a vision, and I thought I could save him. I *will* save him."

"Everything always happens for a reason, even if it doesn't seem like it at the time," Machidiel said.

"But you said that by helping me you would be helping her, or something to that effect. You said you were the only angel who would believe in me, who could help me. I thought you wanted me to save your girlfriend when I saved Zach."

"I do. I do want you to save her, and you will."

I pulled the sheets back on the bed and slid under the covers fully clothed, mulling over his words and the dark emotion I could sense behind them. "I will, Machidiel. I promise."

"Where does that fit in with your revenge plans?"

I frowned, darkness filling my soul. "I still have them. They're just building up." I rolled over. "Give me time."

24

'And what might seem to be a series of unfortunate events may, in fact, be the first steps of a journey.'

Unknown.

Unsurprisingly we slept until the afternoon. The light had come and was almost about to set when I woke. The world had gone about its business, oblivious to the fact that here in this hotel were four beings determined to bring about their ultimate revenge and were starting with kicking some zombie ass.

When I stirred, the boys were in the room. Trev had moved into my room and fallen asleep on the bed next to me while Drew kept watch. Machidiel had been shopping, again buying clothes for us so that we would blend in.

A long shower later, I was clean and clothed, and ready to fight again, all weakness gone, all fear and anxiety replaced by a renewed sense of purpose. I was ready.

We ate, and as soon as the sun began to set we headed off on a zombie hunt with some weapons Machidiel had bought for us; a mixture of daggers and even two swords.

We left the hotel on foot and crept into the town via back lanes and quiet streets. We stalked the pathways, our feelers out for any disturbance or evil vibes, but there was nothing. I didn't get the slightest tingle of my senses alerting me to danger or threat.

We left the town and headed into the surrounding forests, trekking through the mud, searching for zombies that were apparently not there.

"I thought it would be easier than this," I moaned after we had been hunting for a couple of hours. "It's almost midnight. What if they've already left?"

"No, we just need to think about this differently," Machidiel replied, sounding just as irritated as me that we hadn't found them. "Zombies without masters hunt weakened humans to eat their flesh. So if you were a zombie, where would you go?"

I looked up at the stars, marveling again at how clear the sky was out here. Without light pollution to hide them, they were as clear as sparkling diamonds. I stared at them, thinking, my mouth pulling into a grin as the solution came to me.

"If I were looking for weakened humans in the dead of night, I'd either head to a hospital or wait outside a night club at closing time."

Drew laughed, and slapped me on the back. "Damn right! They won't want diseased or ill humans though, so night club it is. Come on; let's head back into the town."

We discovered that there were a number of clubs and pubs in the small town, and unfortunately they were all spread out. Machidiel and Trev agreed to stake out the ones at the far end closest to the bridge, while Drew and I would remain up where a particularly rowdy club met the surrounding forests. Trev tried to argue at first, wanting to switch locations, but I had a feeling this would be the one the zombies headed to. There was ample darkness for hiding and plenty of creepy, narrow streets to follow their prey to as they drunkenly made their way home.

Fifteen minutes later we were standing next to each other with our backs against the brick wall of the nightclub, hiding in the shadows. Music pounded through the walls, pulses of bass reaching us where we stood. A group of young men and women were standing a little closer to the front door, a halo of white smoke pirouetting above and around them as they puffed on their cigarettes. More people came and went, some leaving in cars and others on foot. A few times I went to follow someone, only to be pulled back by Drew.

"I'm freezing," I grumbled after an hour with no action.

I rolled my eyes as Drew pulled his jumper over his head and handed it to me with a grin.

"Really?"

He smirked. "Really? You don't like being treated like a lady?"

I coughed a laugh. "I think you're the only person in this world who would call me a lady . . . or treat me like one." I wasn't joking, and I wasn't even bothered by it. When you were a bad-ass hybrid who could kill pretty much anything, it wasn't often someone offered you their jacket in case you got cold. By laughing at Drew's incredibly sweet gesture I hadn't meant to be rude, it was just weird; saving my life from a vampire or a demon was one thing; saving me from having cold arms was just trivial.

"I've told you before that I think you're amazing. You know it's true; what other archangels do you know who have been reincarnated?"

"Yet you offer me your jumper?"

“Because you’re amazing, not because you can’t handle yourself.”

“What about you? You must be pretty amazing to be leader of a lycan pack?”

He snorted. “Who told you I was the leader?”

I paused, frowning. “I thought you did? You mean you’re not? Your lycans sent a *commoner* to protect me?” I winked. “You must still be pretty special if they sent you on this insane hunt with me.”

He laughed. “Or maybe I’m a readily available sacrifice.”

I punched him lightly on the arm. “Hey, I thought you said you had faith in me.”

“You know I do,” he replied.

We lapsed into silence as I pulled his jumper on over my own. I immediately felt warmer but kind of guilty that Drew was now in just a T-shirt.

A group of middle-aged men piled out of the club, laughing and fist pumping. They stalked across the road away from us and disappeared into the darkness.

“So, why *did* they pick you?” I asked, dropping my head back against the wall.

Drew shrugged. “It’s my destiny.”

I rolled my eyes. “Destiny?” I asked with distaste. Destiny and fate were just words to say that someone else got to make important decisions about your life.

"I've known since I was a young lycan that I'd be sent to you. There's been an agreement between our species for a long time that it would come to this."

"This?" I laughed, gesturing around us. "Hiding in the dark in the cold, in the Canadian wilderness? That was their agreement?"

He tipped his head back and roared with laughter. "You know, I really should have verified the specs."

We were interrupted by another rowdy group of men staggering past, one vomiting on the ground a few meters away. My good mood immediately dissipated.

"This is stupid. What are we supposed to do; wait until there's no one left in there?" I hissed. "What if we miss them, or if Machidiel and Trev get them? As much as killing zombies isn't at the top of my list of favorite things to do I'd feel better if we handled it."

"Trying to protect everyone?" Drew looked down at me with a knowing smile. "Sometimes you have to let your friends go their own way and do their own thing. Trev can handle himself."

I grimaced. "I know, I guess. I can't help it; Sam was betrayed and tortured by Lil, Gwen and Trev were kidnapped when I wasn't there to help, then we lost Gwen and I didn't even see it coming. Aidan left us to join the Human Resistance, and if that wasn't enough of a shock I wasn't there for Zach when I should have been." I sighed and ran my hand through my hair. "I can't let anything happen to Trev. Are you sure there's nothing we can do except just wait here?"

"It's either that or follow everyone home," Drew answered with an annoying smile. "I guess we can only hope they're out here, waiting for someone weaker. These people might be able to fight back . . .

whereas someone like *that* will probably look just the right amount of weak and tasty." Drew narrowed his eyes on a girl stumbling past us.

The blond-haired girl was dressed in jeans and a sleeveless black top, with a golden pattern splashed across the front. She staggered forward, and slid down the side of a parked blue pick-up truck. She laughed hysterically and pulled herself to her feet. I lunged forward to help her, only to be pulled back by Drew, and thrown rather roughly into the wall.

"What are you doing?" I growled.

"We're on a zombie hunt, remember?" he whispered. "We wait and watch."

I looked past him to where the girl had moved on, laughing to herself as she toppled off the curb and tripped over her own feet trying to make her way across the road. My senses were warring with each other. I wanted to help her, to protect her from the zombies that would undoubtedly be tracking her at any moment, but another part of me knew this could be our only chance at killing them. Could I do both? Could I kill the zombies *and* save the helpless girl?

I took a deep breath, anxiety shooting through me. I bit the inside of my cheek hard, tasting blood as I forced myself to stand still behind Drew.

A greasy, turbulent emotion crept stealthily into my abdomen setting off my power. Mist slid out, delicate tendrils circulating around my wrists, rising up to coat the skin on my face with glittering powder. Something was here. I could feel it—it was the same feeling I'd felt earlier; something was here. . . *Zombies*.

Out of the black shadows two slender shapes slithered forward, tracing the girl's footsteps, keeping a distance to stalk her slyly. I sucked in a breath, my eyes focusing in on them. When they had moved past us and followed the girl down the road, we moved off in pursuit.

Keeping close to the walls of the buildings that lined the street, we jogged down the street following the girl's haphazard direction. She turned a corner, the zombies following out of sight, and I took the opportunity to sprint across the street and close in.

"How do you kill a zombie?" Drew asked, close behind me.

I flinched at his question. I hadn't even thought to clarify that. "Beheading or fire," I answered, knowing I hadn't given a stupid answer; just about everything could be killed by beheading or fire.

With my back against the brick, I slid my head around the sharp corner, my eyes piercing the darkness. I couldn't see anything; the space between the buildings hid its interior from me, no moonlight or streetlight penetrating the gloom, but I could hear something. I could hear sloppy eating, drinking, feeding, and the wet sound of blood being sucked from someone.

I exploded into action and ran into the alleyway, aiming for the zombies feasting on the drunken girl. Looking up, I spotted a thin metal pole reaching across between the buildings. I jumped and grasped hold of it, using the leverage to barrel into the zombies feet first. I kicked one hard, sending him crashing into the wall, coughing as the bricks crumbled into dust beneath it. I landed softly and spun again, knocking the girl and the remaining zombie onto the ground.

Talons dug into my shoulders, sinking deep into the flesh, tearing and ripping my muscle. I dropped to my knees to get away, screaming as the zombie dropped with me, crushing my body to his. I threw my head back, hearing a satisfying crunch of bone and I used my power to spin my whole body around, knocking the zombie free. With relief, I saw the girl running away.

Even in the darkness I could make out the white, slimy glow of the zombie's skin, the grey rims around its red eyes. It wore ripped, dirty, blood- and mud-covered clothes, its hair and skin in tatters, hanging in shreds around its bones. I pulled out the knife Machidiel had given me and lunged forward, attempting to stab deep. The zombie moved before I made contact, sliding through the air as though it had never been there. I was thrown forward, landing heavily against a large, metal dumpster.

I reached up and pulled my legs under me, standing shakily. These zombies, they were nothing like how I had imagined. I had thought they would be weak, slow moving and dim-witted half-dead creatures, but instead they were as fast as the wind and just as invisible when they wanted to be, deadly strong, and dominant in battle. I had no idea how I was going to defeat them because they were much, *much* stronger than I was.

A blow to my face bent me over double. I spat out blood, and what I was almost sure was half of my tongue as pain spread down my jaw into my neck. Another blow pounded into my stomach, again and again, before the agonizing pulverization changed into a sharp stab. I gasped, staring down in horror as the sharp blade was pulled free of my abdomen.

My mouth open, unable to breathe, I stared up in horror at the zombie's face as it stared down blankly, completely expressionless, seeming only to be evaluating the life draining from me and how much more he needed to do to kill me.

The blade dropped onto the concrete with a clatter, and the hand that had been grasping it was suddenly around my throat, dead fingers digging, closing my windpipe. I heard noises from Drew; war cries. *Come on, I can do this.* I lit myself up, fire soaring through my skin, melting the zombie in front of me. I fired it hotter and hotter, stoking the embers in my power center. Why wasn't he dying? How did he still have strength in the arm that I was literally melting? His flesh was dripping from the arm still holding me, skin running onto the floor as fluid.

With my last remaining energy I opened a portal behind us, gravity dipping and tilting, spinning and whirring us around. The zombie threw me away from him. I flew through the air, landing heavily, further down the alleyway, on my back.

My head span, the black of the night making way for a sparkling, glittering mass . . . and it wasn't of my own making. I was losing consciousness—and fast.

I screamed in anger and rolled onto my stomach. I looked up, only to see the legs of one ragged zombie standing in front of me. My body was lifted and hurled against the opposite wall. My bones crunched, snapping as I slid to the ground. I gasped for breath, spluttering out blood as it gurgled up through my chest. As the zombie ran for me again, Drew launched himself in my way, knocking him aside.

"Jasmine, get up!" he bellowed.

"I can't!" I coughed, feeling the wetness of my blood running down my face. "I think I'm dying."

The words sounded foreign, surreal. What was happening to me? How could this be true? I had a goal, a mission, and I was failing. I was losing. I wasn't going to save Zach. I wasn't going to be able to keep my promise to Machidiel and bring back his soul mate. I knew I shouldn't even think it, but the thought that I had so much revenge planned, so many people who still needed to pay . . . and that I wouldn't be there to make them was almost as devastating as losing Zach.

I smiled to myself grimly. What would they think of me now, their glorious miracle angel? I was nothing but revenge. I contained nothing inside of me but revenge, and I never would. I wasn't the Archangel of Miracles, I was the Archangel of Death, Regret and Misery. I couldn't fulfill my promises, and all I had achieved was to drag my friends into this sad mess with me.

No, I wouldn't. I wouldn't let my friends die because of me; not if there was a single breath left in my body.

Drew screamed as the knife dug deep into his chest, and my attention pulled away from my selfish thoughts and now firmly fixed on him. I burrowed my fingers into the wall behind me and straightened my legs. I willed Drew to move to the side to give me a clear shot.

I knew what I needed to do; I needed to open a portal and send the zombies away. But I wouldn't be able to go up to the Heavens if I didn't complete my task, and if I sent them through a portal I would probably never find them again. Haamiah would be furious, and I would be beyond devastated, but there was no way Drew and I could defeat the zombies while holding back. No, I needed to give up my only chance at getting Zach back if we were going to come out of this alive.

25

'Just because I am strong enough to handle pain doesn't mean I deserve it.'

Unknown.

I built my power up, sending my flames, strength, love and hate into a vortex of my own creation. My hair was whipped around me in a storm, blood still dripping down my face as I held onto the wall behind me. The dumpster squealed as the metal was dragged along the ground, sucked towards the portal swirling behind the zombies and Drew. Cardboard flew through the air, vanishing into the portal and narrowly missing Drew. I cringed as a deafening crash blasted past me, window glass shattering into pieces and flying through the air into the vortex.

I screamed as shards fell around me, cutting my skin on their passage to the alternate dimension I had opened. Drew spun, punching the zombie hard, knocking him backwards. It fell to the floor, the whirling portal sucking it backwards, dragging it across the ground towards its greedy depths. Drew panted, bending over to rest his palms on his knees as he panted for air.

I let the portal dim slightly, relief pouring through me at the thought that we were almost one zombie down. I sunk down to my bottom, leaning my back against the wall. My head throbbed with pain, lethargy sweeping up through me as I realized how depleted of energy I was. From where I sat I could see the concern in Drew's eyes as he plodded towards me, his hand outstretched. He turned his face to check for the second zombie, his eyes hardening in panic as he began to run towards me.

I frowned, uncertain what had caused the alarm. I stiffened as Drew jerked, stopping where he stood, his mouth opening in shock. I shrieked as I saw a ghostly white body rise up behind the lycan. My heart stopped, and my brain scrambled in terror as blood began to spew from his mouth. I sobbed, open-mouthed, as Drew was stabbed again and again. He lurched towards me, his eyes open in horror as he stared, still trying to reach me.

"Jasmine, run!" He gasped around a mouthful of frothy blood.

I crawled onto my knees and stood, taking a step away from the wall, edging towards him, needing to help him, needing to *heal* him. I shrieked when my body hit the floor, my head smacking heavily onto the concrete.

The world slowed further, spinning, rotating, and nausea ripped through me. My breathing was heavy in my own ears, seeming to echo though my entire body. Pain bit down on my arm, flesh severing amidst wet blood flow. The second zombie we had lost sight of was now gnawing on my arm, then was ripped away, its head torn free as Drew slid next to me, falling onto his knees.

"God, Jasmine, this isn't what's supposed to happen. Not like this. They don't know where we are! They haven't found us yet," he rambled, spitting blood out onto the ground.

I didn't know what he was talking about; he wasn't making sense. Who didn't know what? Machidiel and Trev knew where we were; surely they had felt the portal's disturbance in the atmosphere by now and would be sprinting for us. They'd be here at any moment.

Drew gathered me up, lifting me in his arms as he staggered forward with lycan strength, running out of the alleyway. We were stopped at the end by the second zombie; the only one remaining. Drew dropped me to my feet, letting me slide onto the floor in a heap. He roared fiercely, snapping his teeth at the zombie. In a haze of fangs and blood I dropped off, losing consciousness. I opened my eyes moments, minutes, or maybe hours later to see a zombie head on the ground beside me.

I breathed; it was all I could do. I felt a hand touch my face as a heavy body lay down beside me. Drops fell; rain beginning to drip and then pour. It was cold . . . freezing cold, maybe because of the blood loss, or maybe because it was the middle of the night and we were wet. Drew's face came into focus.

"I don't regret it," he whispered hoarsely.

"What?" I breathed.

"This. It's what I promised to do. I believe in you, and I don't regret any of it."

With those words his lips stilled, his eyes lost focus and before me, his lycan spirit let out a sigh and disappeared.

26

'Never let an old flame burn you twice.'

Unknown.

The ground was soft and warm beneath me. I yawned and rolled over onto my back, bouncing slightly. I opened my eyes, wincing at the pain in my arm. I moaned softly and tried to sit up, gasping as I realized I wasn't alone.

A man sat beside me, studying my face. He was beautiful; masculine, clean-shaven with a chiseled jaw and dark eyes that stared at me with interest, as though he were trying to read me.

"You're awake," he said quietly.

I frowned. "I guess so."

I relaxed back into the pillows, unable to summon the energy to be at all bothered that a stranger was sitting next to me.

"You look different," he said after a moment.

I bit my lip and crooked my neck to see him properly. "I look . . ." It dawned on me; he looked so familiar, and clearly he felt comfortable enough to be sitting on my bed. "Raphael."

He dropped his head forward a couple of inches and gave me a sad smile. "Jophie."

As I stared at him feeling overwhelmed with emotion, pain and love and guilt all intermingling in my body, black and white flashed in my eyes. I shut them tightly, opening again quickly to make sure Raphael hadn't left me alone. He hadn't; there were others here.

I tensed, my eyes searching the faces peering down at me. Men and women stared at me sadly, some rigid with anger, and some shaking as they cried. I looked at Raphael, flinching when he dropped his head into his hands.

"What's going on, Raph?"

He lifted his head and stared at me, not answering my question. I grimaced and forced myself to sit up, gasping when I looked down at the bed. I was covered with pure white sheets from the bottom of the bed right up to my neck. It would have been nice if it hadn't been for the giant patch of blood seeping through the sheet across my body. The material was thirstily soaking it up, soaking me up.

Panicked, I looked up again at Raphael, pulling back as his image flickered. Was he even here? Were any of them here?

"What's happening?" I asked again. "Where am I? What's happening to me?"

Raphael slid his hand across the sheet to touch his fingers to mine. I looked down to where our skin met, surprised when I saw that the sheet was once again clean.

"Nothing's happening; it's already happened," Raphael's voice washed over me.

I barely heard his words; I felt so nauseous, waves of it flowing over and through me, making me press my lips together tightly. The flashing increased, faces, eyes and lips appearing so close and then vanishing into a white haze and then black.

"Make it stop," I protested, snapping my hand back to cover my eyes. My stomach rolled.

"It's already happened. You took a chance—you listened to them instead of me, and it didn't pay off." His words were soft and gentle but the more I played them over in my mind, the more aggressive and insulting they sounded. "You lost, Jophie and you know what the price is."

I scowled. "The price?"

"You were an archangel and you gave it up! You gave it up for what? The beasts on the human plane? Soul mates?" He shook his head. "You should have listened to me."

"I haven't lost," I denied. "I can still win."

"You left the Heavenly realm to save Zacharael, and you failed."

"I . . ." I froze. What could I say? I had failed. But I had a back-up plan.

"You don't."

I met his eyes, shocked. He'd read my mind.

I'm your brother; of course I can read your mind.

I glared at him, refusing to speak telepathically. "I have a back-up plan."

He shook his head. "Not any more."

I sat up again, and slid sideways through the sheets away from the mountainous archangel who was trying to prove his point by hurting me.

"I'm not trying to hurt you."

I sat up on the edge of the bed and paused. There was no floor, only white smoke. I was afraid, too afraid to put my feet down. What if there was nothing else there? What if I fell?

"Relax, Jophie, it won't be long now," Raphael said, attempting to soothe me.

"What . . .?" I turned sharply to face him, catching his eyes as they looked at me with pity. "What won't be long?"

He bit his lip, staring at me.

"I'm not dead." I shook my head. "I'm not dead yet; there's still a chance. I can still pull this off. I can still win."

"Please don't do this." Raphael pleaded. "I can't watch you hurt any more; you have no idea what Michael and I are going through up here watching you fail, watching you torture yourself. Come back to us. You won't be as you were before, but you'll be safe."

"There are people depending on me," I said, willing him to understand.

"Michael wants you to come back," he said.

I narrowed my eyes angrily. "That's a low blow. I'll come back when it's time. It's not time."

It had to be now. I had to do it before I lost all of my courage. It would be so easy to stay here and just wait it out safely with my brothers. I could close my eyes against the flashes and pretend I wasn't bleeding out, sailing rapidly towards my death, but I had made promises, and I didn't mean my promises of revenge—though I would still follow through on those. Trev and Machidiel were back there, Gwen was somewhere hurting and alone, the apocalypse had started, I still had to bring Machidiel's soul mate back from the dead, and I had a werewolf to hunt. I needed to make the world safer; Asmodeus, the Horsemen, Mnemosyne, Lucifer . . . there was too much still to be done.

I closed my eyes and sniffed, the pain in my body rippling up my body. "Don't hate me, but I'm not ready."

I turned and slipped over the edge of the bed.

27

"You're all geniuses, and you're all beautiful. You don't need anyone to tell you who you are. You are what you are."

John Lennon.

Someone was calling my name. I blinked, tears and rain coating my face. God, the pain was excruciating. Even the blood loss itself was agonizing. My arm felt as though it were on fire, shooting sparks up my shoulder. My head throbbed, a cut on my forehead stinging with each pelt of rain. My bones felt pulverized, and though my power trickled through my veins, trying desperately to heal, it wasn't enough.

I let out the breath I had been holding, and let my eyes focus on a shape beside me; it was Drew. His eyes were open and unseeing. His face was pale and clammy, blood the only splash of color I could see. A trail of it still remained running from the corner of his mouth to the concrete, despite the rain's attempt to wash it away.

Where I lay on my front, with my left cheek pressed to the ground, I could see him, and past him I could see a zombie head, or what remained of it. It would appear that zombies didn't disintegrate the same way fallen angels and vampires did, nor did they remain preserved in their goriness like demons; they seemed to shrivel, losing all fluid, to turn into stone.

Drew had saved me, and he had said he didn't regret it, but I did. He was a thousand times more worthy of life than me. Everywhere I went destruction followed, as was proven by this. He didn't deserve this. He wasn't meant to be lying here in the rain, dead.

I screamed as my body was moved, my head dropping back against my neck. I could make out Trev's face, his dark eyes as he ran his hand over me. His mouth moved, shouting something at me, shouting something at Machidiel who miraculously appeared in my line of vision too. Between them, I was hoisted up and cradled, and I felt my body move in a jolting rhythm as they bolted out of the alleyway.

They couldn't leave Drew there; they couldn't just leave him. What about his family? His friends? They'd want to know what had happened to him . . . just like Emily. I hadn't told the witches what had happened to her either. It was all my fault.

"Shh. It's okay. It's going to be okay." Machidiel's voice reached down to me, coating me in warmth despite the ice in my veins. Maybe that was his talent—giving hope when there was none.

"You have to go back for him," I murmured. It didn't matter that the words were barely spoken, he could hear me.

"We'll send someone to clean up," he replied harshly.

I flinched, or at least I would have if I'd had the ability to move my body.

He must have sensed it as he sent another wave of tranquility towards me. "He's gone, Jasmine. He's in a better place now."

"I was there. I was gone too," I muttered absently.

"No!" He shook me, all peace and tranquility gone. "You're not going anywhere. There are still things we have to do."

I let the pain wash over me, both mental and physical, and soon we were climbing up the fire escape into the hotel and I had been deposited gently onto the bed. Trev took hold of my jumper and began to slide it up over my stomach. Machidiel stopped him and took hold of the neck, ripping straight through the material again and again until I lay there in just a bra and knickers, with folds of material either side of me.

I saw their horror-struck expressions and could only imagine the damage the zombies had done. I had been so foolish to think they would be so easily taken care of, to think that I, the great Jophiel, could easily dispatch them, and then we could head off on our next mission.

As Trev took in the savage bite wound on my arm, the air around him seemed to still.

"Oh my God, is she . . .?"

I also wanted to know the answer that unspoken question. Was I going to turn into a zombie?

"She'll be fine. It works the same as vampires; she'll only turn into a zombie if she dies with the zombie bite."

That made everything crystal clear. Whatever hidden vestige of power still remained inside me was dragged out by my will and pushed around my body with each faltered pulse of my heart. I was not turning into a zombie; that wasn't the way I was going out.

Painstakingly slowly, my body began to knit itself back together. Whether it took minutes or hours, I could feel every internal stitch like a fresh stab wound. I could also feel the influence of Machidiel as he sent his own strength into me to patch me up. Although angels had varying talents, one thing they could all do so some degree was heal—luckily for me I had one right next to me. No . . . I could feel the influence of *two* angels. I cracked open my eyelids out of curiosity, and was stunned by what I saw.

Maion's pale skin contrasted sharply to Machidiel's bronzed hue. He was dressed in black, as all of the warrior angels preferred, and I could see the edge of his tattoos peeking out from under the short sleeves. I could also see the tops of the blades he had slung across his back. I shivered; I didn't doubt for a second that he wouldn't hesitate to chop my head off if I became a zombie. He'd probably like that.

I coughed as one of them had moved up to my chest, beginning to heal the wounds there. I could feel them working on my ribcage together. I regained focus and got my own healing energy back on the job. My arm had to be healed first; it needed to be *completely* healed . . . just in case.

What seemed like hours later, I woke up again. I had passed out after finishing the work on my arm, and as Machidiel and Maion were standing up, arguing across the room, it would appear that they had finished with me.

I sighed and rolled onto my side, thankful when no pain accompanied me with the movement.

"She's awake."

I looked up at Trev, and gave him a slight smile. "I am," I whispered.

He paused. "I don't even know what to say."

I shook my head, biting my lip hard. "There's nothing to say."

"You know that Drew . . ."

I held my hand up. "I know." I remembered something I had been worried about. "You didn't leave him there, did you?"

He quickly shook his head, reassuring me. "No, of course not. Machidiel called someone . . . some 'cleaners' and they took him away. The zombies too." Before I could ask, he continued, "They'll return his body to his people."

I nodded. "Good." I winced. "Not *good,* I mean—"

"I know," he whispered.

My eyes welled up, my heart aching. "It's my fault. I should have been stronger, or faster."

"It's not your fault; we didn't realize just how strong they were. If we're going to play the blame game, then we should have stuck together instead of separating, or we should have gotten here quicker, or found another way to catch them. It happened and it's awful, but it's not your fault."

"You weren't there . . . you didn't see it. He died saving me—like everyone does. Everyone dies because of me."

Trev leaned in close, stroking my hair back away from my face. "Everyone dies, period. It's life; it's what happens."

I wiped my tears away and sat up, pulling back from him. "There's so much to do," I said tiredly.

"You need to restore your energy," Machidiel said, handing me a box of cold pizza.

Cold pizza wasn't what I usually salivated over, but in this instance, the moment the scent of it reached my nose I couldn't shove it in my mouth quick enough. I was ravenous, my strength so completely depleted that I would refill my stores with anything going—cold pizza included.

Over the top of the slice of pepperoni, I tried to feel out Maion's vibe. What was he doing here? He didn't even like me. Actually, when Zach was around he hadn't liked me; once Zach was gone, he'd hated me. I had seen him once since it had happened, and he'd tried to snap my neck. I didn't blame him, but I did want to know why he had just helped to heal me.

"What are you doing here?" I asked, in between bites.

Maion knew I had directed the question at him. He scowled. "Don't you mean 'Thank you Maion, for saving my life?'"

I swallowed a mouthful of pizza. "Thank you. What are you doing here?"

He shrugged. "Looked like you were about to be zombie meat; I just wanted to make sure no one let you go."

I paused. That sounded about right.

Machidiel sniggered from where he had resumed his favorite place—looking out of the window. "Yeah right."

I glanced up at him thoughtfully, tilting my head to Maion. If there was another more complicated answer then I didn't want to know it.

"We don't want to drag up painful memories," Trev began with a worried expression. "But you killed the zombie—"

"Drew killed one and I sent another through a portal," I corrected.

Trev nodded. "What do you want to do now?"

I knew what he meant. He meant, 'Are you so traumatized that you can't continue?' The answer was that I was traumatized, but I *had* to continue, because there was nothing left of my old life to go back to. I had committed myself to this so fully that I hadn't considered failing as a possibility.

I took a deep breath and reluctantly put down the slice of pizza I was holding. My mantra of *'Zombies, Pool of Kali, Zach'*, no longer applied. This wasn't about me, and I couldn't be selfish anymore. "We still have a werewolf to hunt, then we need to destroy Asmodeus, Mnemosyne and the Horsemen. Providing Sam's still safe with Haamiah, we don't need to worry about Lucifer at the moment. Heaven's gates are open wide, so we need to take out anyone aiming for them. Am I right?"

Trev nodded. "I'm with you."

"For the first time, it would appear we are in agreement," Maion muttered sarcastically.

Machidiel stirred. "What about—"

"It doesn't matter anymore," I cut in. I didn't want Maion to know what I had been planning, and I didn't even want to think about what I wasn't going to do anymore. That way led to hurt and pain, and all sorts of horrible things; I needed to concentrate on what I could and would do. I met his eyes. "I'll still help you with your problem, as I promised, but after this, my own priorities have . . . shifted."

He nodded, thoughtfully rubbing his chin between his thumb and forefinger. “You need to eat and rest, then we’ll go hunting for werewolves.”

28

'It's better to walk alone than with a crowd going in the wrong direction.'

Diane Grant.

I slept for almost two entire days and when I woke up, I still felt tired . . . and bursting for the bathroom. I left the boys in the bedroom where they had apparently camped out to watch over me, and I showered, scrubbed my teeth, blow-dried my hair, and put on more new clothes that Machidiel had purchased for me. This time we were out with the jeans, and back in more comfortable and familiar black combat pants and a top, as well as a navy-colored jumper with a hood. I could bet my mystery shopper had been Trev this time. He knew I lived in dark colors and comfortable fighting gear back home.

I slathered complimentary moisturizer across my face, screwing up my nose at my dry skin. When healing my broken bones I should have considered adding a top layer of skin to my face.

I stepped out of the bathroom and picked up a bottle of Gatorade from the desk, downing a good amount. Machidiel remained by the window, Maion was sitting stiffly in a chair, and Trev lounged on top of the second bed in the room.

I had been able to block any dark thoughts as I busily washed and dressed, distracting myself with mundane tasks, but now, standing here and looking at the guys in the room, missing the person who should have been us . . . an all-consuming ache began to gnaw through me. It would never be the same. I would never be the same; too much loss, too much horror and terror. It ate away at me from the inside, and though no one could see it, I knew I was losing myself, losing my soul and my being. Everything I stood for, my dreams and hopes were all ripped away with each kill I made, and each death I was responsible for. I wasn't self-obsessed enough to really believe that I was directly responsible for Drew's death, but no one could deny that *indirectly* I was. Life really was a Hell that no one would escape alive.

"Are we going to have to fight our way out?" I directed my question to Machidiel.

He turned and shrugged. "We could open a portal right here, but I wouldn't advise it in case we suck anyone in the adjoining rooms through too." He hefted a backpack over his shoulder and threw a long, curved blade across the room towards me. I picked it out of the air before it struck the wall. "If we make it to the car park, we can open one, so long as there are no humans there."

I nodded, and waited for Maion to march out of the room. I followed him, with Trev and Machidiel closing in behind me.

We stepped out into the hotel hallway and turned left, heading for the reception. A young girl was on duty, sitting upright stiffly on her stool. She yelped as she saw us striding past holding up weapons, and jumped off her stool, knocking it over with a clatter.

Machidiel approached her with a stiff smile. He dropped the keys onto the counter along with a handful of crinkled notes. "We're checking out." He didn't wait for a response and stormed out through the glass doors behind us.

It was daylight, probably morning—I hadn't bothered to check the clock in the hotel room—but it didn't matter where we were going. What was the point in knowing the time in one realm when you were travelling to another?

We moved away from the door, looking for somewhere quiet where no one would see a huge portal opening, ripping through the fabric of this world, and four people brandishing weapons, disappearing in plain view. There were a few people in the car park so we moved further on, following Machidiel's directions. The car park seemed endless, wrapping right around the back of the hotel and behind a neighboring property. Fewer cars were parked back here, maybe just employees'.

With a roar, a demon landed in front of us, splitting the tarmac. It lashed out, knocking Machidiel into the side of a car, the metal crunching inwards around him. He shook it off and strode forward, narrowing his eyes.

The demon swung towards us, focusing on Maion; possibly what it thought of as the only other threat. Maion's eyes boggled at the sight of it. It was identical to those we had encountered before . . . encountered and *fled* from. The reptilian creature covered in scars shot its huge tail out behind it, slamming it down on the ground, shooting cracks and quakes through the ground towards us. It opened its huge black mouth and roared, showing yellowing tusks.

Maion seemed transfixed, unmoving as the demon barreled down on him. I leaped into action, shooting flames as I threw my entire weight into it. I managed to knock it off balance and dodge the punch it sent my way, scampering over the top of a car and sliding down to the ground. Maion had woken up, and was attacking it from one side while Machidiel attacked from the other.

What did it want? Why was it attacking us? I let my mind relax and slipped into the demon's head, trying to see what it wanted so badly that it would follow us. I drew out a moment later, my heart pattering in panic.

We had something they wanted. They could smell it on us. They didn't want to kill us—they wanted to return us to their mistress so we could be tortured into giving up what she wanted. Mnemosyne had broken the demons out of Hell, and they had been sent to find Sam so she could open the gate wider and free Lucifer.

Something wet splattered across my face, knocking me off-guard. I lifted my hand to my cheek, wiping off the black blood that had gooped on my skin. Trev reached my side and wrapped his arm around my shoulders, supporting me. He stared at my face for a second before we turned our bodies, and together we gawked in astonishment as Maion cleaned off his swords, grinning sadistically.

While I had been in the demon's mind searching for answers, Maion had scissored its head off. I reached up to touch my own neck, feeling my frantically beating pulse as I realized that potentially I could have been mystically decapitated. If I were in someone else's mind at the same time that they were killed, would I be killed too? I would really need to clarify that.

"Let's go," I said weakly.

Maion sauntered over smugly, tilting his head to the side as if expecting me to say something. He took in my expression, and presumably realized how little control I had on my reality; his face dropped, the grim mask he usually wore slipped back in place, and he bit his lip. Machidiel joined us, breathing heavily, and gripped my arm with one hand. Trev wrapped his arms around my waist while Maion took hold of my other arm, grunting loudly to show his displeasure in my portal travel. I didn't blame him; my hold on reality was tenuous at best; the way I was feeling now could have endless repercussions on where we landed.

Drawing strength and comfort from the strong warriors crowding me, I concentrated on my power and let my mist free to coat us in a sparkling haze. A second later the ground tilted, and we were falling.

29

'There is meaning in every journey that is unknown to the traveler.'

Dietrich Bonhoeffer.

To my surprise, we landed well; upright, with only minimal staggering. Maion leaped away from us with his swords held up, as though he were expecting an army waiting to ambush us. Which, to be honest, was fair enough.

I had been to the werewolf plane before, and after being tricked, lied to, and then betrayed by a pack of wolves, I had leaped through a portal with Valentina as arrows were shot into us. Valentina's brother, Damian, was leader of one pack, while Gregory, Ronald, and Vernon were leaders of their own packs. Together, the four men were steeped in treachery, allying their packs with a witch who had captured two angels in the hope she would draw in more. The werewolves sneakily arranged a fight between the witch and I, hoping their betrayal would never be discovered, and that I would kill the witch and release them from their agreement with her—then *they* would conveniently free the captured angels. I *had* killed the witch, and I freed the angels, denying them their redemption. They had never meant for me to know how deep their lies went, but thankfully I had a talented telepath on my side to relay all of their nasty secrets.

It wasn't the entire pack's fault; most of them didn't know anything about it, but I had hoped never to see their leaders again. Only, here I was—hunting down an escaped werewolf in their territory. Correction; here *we* were. This time I hadn't come on my own, and I wasn't trying to find myself, or work out whom I belonged to. Thinking of my love triangle between Zach and Aidan seemed ridiculous now; I would do anything to get back the time with Zach I had lost.

Enough. I shook my head and pushed my shoulders back, stepping away from the guys.

"Which way?" Machidiel asked me, seeming to sense my inner conflict.

I took a deep breath and blew it out loudly. As the werewolf plane was largely made up of forestation, we had—surprise, surprise—landed in one. I peered through the trees and shrugged.

"Maybe you can fly up and look around for us?" I suggested.

Machidiel nodded, but before he had a moment to jump Maion had already taken off, torpedoing through the canopy until he was out of view. Within seconds he had landed again with a thud, the leaves, twigs and dirt on the ground rippling in a wave from his impact.

He pointed with one blade. "We go south. Smoke rises in the distance."

"Far?" Machidiel asked.

Maion shrugged. "Too far to walk in this damn forest. I want this wrapped up quickly; I have somewhere else to be."

I rolled my eyes. "We didn't ask you to come. You kind of just imposed yourself on us . . . Feel free to leave."

Maion stalked towards me, stopping only when Machidiel stuck his arm forward to block him from closing in. He growled at Machidiel before sneering at me, "I keep *my* promises."

I frowned. "What's that supposed to mean?"

He batted Machidiel out of the way. "You leave your responsibilities to come here on a noble cause; to unite the armies and save the life of our friend, yet you do neither. Zacharael lies in the ground, his sister, my soul mate, *devastated* because you failed, because you didn't keep your promise. The only reason Machidiel is on this hunt with you is because you have promised him to save his soul mate, yet you've shown no sign of fulfilling *that* promise yet.

"While you hid, cowering from us after the last battle, you swore and ranted that you would exact revenge for our loss, yet Asmodeus, Mnemosyne, Lucifer and the Horsemen still stand, mocking us! I gave my promise to Zacharael that I would protect his soul mate if anything should happen to him—"

"As did we all, Maion," Machidiel interrupted angrily, his eyes glaring at the bulky Russian.

Maion snarled at him, "Yet we hunt for werewolves instead of seeking revenge! Our brother is lost to us forever because of you."

In a flash of movement, Trev attacked, slamming his fist into Maion's jaw, knocking him aside. The angel warrior spun and struck back, getting one good blow in before Trev leaped away to land before me protectively.

"I've not forgotten my promises," I said, forcing my body in front of Maion's as Machidiel also cut between the fighting pair. "But who are you to say which promises should be dealt with first?"

"You don't think avenging your soul mate should be your top priority? The fact that you can still function just days after his passing tells me you never loved him," he hissed, his dark eyes flashing with menace.

I exploded, fire rippling over me, leaping onto the branches and into the debris around my feet. The ground fell and spun, knocking Maion over. I grinned evilly as he scrambled back away from me as I approached. With my portals zapping open all around, he stayed low, hesitant to attack me or even say a thing. "You think I didn't love him because I haven't had my revenge yet? Just wait." I laughed. "You'll get yours when I'm ready for you."

I stormed away, my eyes hazed over. I was barely able to see. Trev took my arm gingerly, avoiding the flames that still danced on my skin. I felt claustrophobic, too trapped here, too closeted. I began to jog, channeling my power into my legs so that I could sprint, covering mile after mile with little effort, aware of the others following. I leaped over fallen trees and rivers, then weaved out of the thicker patches of trees, following a little worn path south to where I presumed I would find a wolf pack.

As I ran, the sun began to set, shadows lengthening around us, strengthened by the already dark interior of the forest. Insects fell silent, birds darting out of trees as I passed, fleeing the madness of my soul.

By the time I had calmed my inner beast and felt less likely to decapitate the first person I saw, I noticed a flash of moving shadow running parallel to me. It grew, joined by another and another. I opened my mind, feeling for the beings that ran with me, finding . . . wolves.

Werewolves escorted us to their pack, running with us, supervising our descent as we deepened our forage into the werewolf plane. Only when I smelt the first hint of smoke did they approach us, seeming to herd us in a particular direction.

I refused to slow my pace, knowing only that the werewolf I was hunting would head straight for the pack. Rarely, if ever, did wolves strike out alone; this werewolf would be no different. He or she would have found sanctuary among their people. I had no choice but to find and destroy it, even if it meant taking out the entire pack, and honestly, tackling Damian again would be no chore.

The camp came into view in the upcoming clearing; beige- and cream-colored tents peeked out, and torches with flames billowing upwards sent warm air through the trees towards me, beckoning me onwards. I could hear voices now, and I braced myself for what I remembered took place here; an orgy of bizarre proportions, werewolves falling on each other everywhere, drinking, dancing and fighting. Only as I stepped out of the trees, flanked by werewolves now in naked human form, the voices were definitely not animalistic in passion and hysteria; arguing, shouting and raw conflict met my ears.

“Careful,” Trev warned, following behind me.

I glanced at the werewolves as they narrowed their eyes at us, some snapping their teeth together. We wound our way into the camp, following the sound of angry voices while making sure we weren’t attacked. We each held up a blade, Trev flashing his fangs to warn off anyone approaching while I sent sparks of fire in the direction of those blocking our path.

We reached a crowd of people, all bellowing for attention, shouting, screaming, and some even crying hysterically. At the back of the group, I stood on my tiptoes, my eyes widening in shock. I spun around, catching Machidiel's eye.

"Go and get Valentina," I hissed urgently.

I opened a portal directly behind him. He scowled and looked past me before his face dropped. He stepped into the portal and disappeared, leaving us with only Maion as our back-up.

"Is that . . .?" Trev asked, aghast.

I nodded. "It is."

Up on a wooden platform, Damian's head was displayed on a spike as a tall, black-haired man embraced a young female werewolf. Her black hair trailed down her back to her waist, her skin, a molten caramel color, flashed around the dark wrap she had pulled over her shoulders. I knew her. I knew her scent, the feel of her soul in my mind—she even felt familiar. I knew who she was, and I knew she was the werewolf I had to kill.

Our wayward soul, the being I had let escape, was Sofia—Valentina's ex-lover.

30

'No one is born with religion. Everyone is born with spirituality.'

Anthony Douglas Williams.

The longer we stared, the more it became apparent that the dark-haired man on the wooden platform was not embracing Valentina, but trying to restrain her. With messy plaits, half undone around his shoulders, and wearing only a dark brown loin cloth, it was hard not to be transfixed. Muscles bulged across his body as he gripped Sofia's wrists tightly, and pulled them up over her head so that another, fairer werewolf could come behind and fasten her with rope to a wooden beam erected on the platform.

The fairer wolf glared at her, recoiling in disgust once his job was done. Straps holding swords and knives close to his body were crisscrossed across his chest, his back, and even around his thighs. He took one now, and held it out towards her as he hastily stepped backwards.

My eyes flicked to Damian, or what was left of him. His golden hair was dirty and matted with blood, his mouth open in what seemed to be pain, which could have been due to having his head hacked off. I hated him for what he did to me; his betrayal, lies and scheming ran deep. I hated him more for what he had done to Valentina, but I couldn't help the sickness that slithered through my stomach as my eyes were glued to what remained of him, his head protruding up as a warning or some kind of primal ritual. I didn't want to feel sorry for him; I didn't want to feel anything for him. I wanted to feel pleasure in his slaying, and relief that I didn't have to off him myself.

How could I focus on revenge, on the just killing of so many people who had wronged me when I felt guilt and sadness for someone I hated—who I didn't even kill? Knowing how I felt now, could I go through with my plans? Could I get revenge for Zach's death like this?

Was it too ordinary, too predictable to want to be the bad-ass slayer finally defeating her enemies? Why did I feel like I owed something? Zach was there for me when I'd had nothing, and my enemies had taken it and thrown it all away with shady dealings, betrayal, lies, and cheating. So many times had I ignored my intuition and passed it off as suspicion, thinking I was wrong, thinking there was something fundamentally wrong with me that made me unable to trust anyone. What if the person who I really needed revenge on, the person who was to blame for all of this, was me? I couldn't kill myself—I wouldn't kill myself, but how else could I make up for the part *I* played in Zach's death, and Drew's?

Trev nudged me out of my inner conflict. "We need to get out of here. Any moment now and our heads are going to be up there with his."

I shivered. "We can't leave without her."

He frowned. "It's not worth it; you don't even know her. She could have done anything. She was probably plotting with Damian or something. We came here for the spirit, so let's just keep looking."

"I do know her." I fixed my eyes on him. "That's Val's ex-girlfriend; we're not leaving her here."

"Val's . . ." He trailed off, quickly turning to look up at the stage. "Oh my God."

I swallowed and put my hand on his shoulder, making him turn towards me again. "And Trev . . . even if it wasn't, I wouldn't be leaving her here to be murdered."

He flinched, grimacing. "Yeah, you're right, but seriously, look around; there's got to be two hundred wolves here. How are we going to take them out?"

I stepped back, pushing up against the material of a tent, Trev and Maion sliding closer to me. I glanced around over their shoulders; the wolves were so fixated on whatever was going on in front of them they didn't even question us being there. Yes, I had seen more than a few looks of acknowledgement, and they knew we were here; they just didn't care right now. The wolves tracking us in the forest had disappeared, either blending in to the others in human form, or remaining hidden away.

"I know these past few months have been hard. We've just gone from fight to fight, losing important people and friends along the way. Our entire existence has turned into one long battle, and sometimes I feel like it's never going to end." I took a deep, fear-filled breath. "I just need to be completely honest with you; I can't kill her. I know she's the re-embodied spirit that we came her for, but she's not evil and she didn't deserve to die."

"How do you know?" Maion growled.

I shook my head. "I know her, or at least I know *of* her. I'm not killing her. As for the wolves . . . they betrayed us, and they allowed two angels to be captured and tortured."

Maion rolled his eyes. "Spare me the lecture, I got it firsthand."

I shrugged. "Fine. Then you know what I'm going to do."

"Kill the wolves, save the girl?" Trev asked with a grim smile.

I nodded. That was exactly what I was going to do. Slowly, all of these loose ends were coming together one way or another.

"I understand if either of you don't want any part in this. I honestly do," I said hesitantly.

"Fuck you," Maion snarled, spinning away.

Exchanging a look with Trev, I pushed past them both and kept my back to the tent as I circled the platform. Three others had joined the dark-haired wolf. My mouth dropped, my whole body tensing as dark fury rolled through my skin. I knew them—the other wolves up there. They had been Damian's allies—Gregory, Ronald and Vernon. They were each dressed exactly how I had seen them last—fur knee-high boots, minimal coverage across their waists, and weapons strapped to every limb.

Wrath froze my skin, and focused my mind. I wanted them dead.

As my eyes narrowed, glittering mist began to seep from me, pooling around my feet before tentatively spreading across the grass. Oblivious, Ronald picked up a fiery torch and laughed as he set alight the platform, jumping off and retreating to a safe distance within the cheering crowd.

Sofia began to scream as the flames licked closer to her, sparks dancing across the wood, racing towards her legs as she kicked and struggled to free herself. It was now or never.

I sent one prayer off for Trev's safety and exploded into action. My power detonated, visible purple ripples rushing through the air like waves in the sea, knocking into everything in their path. I shrieked, vehemence and passion splitting the sky into lightning strikes again and again. Werewolves spun to face me with horror on their faces. Most ran, while some shifted into their wolf form. Screams and shouts echoed around me as I stormed through the wolves, killing any in my path to the platform. I leaped up on top of it in a crouch among the flames.

The fire hissed and spat at me, catching a hold of my clothes, trying to take me over. I didn't care; all fire belonged to *me*. I breathed in deeply, the black smoke curling in my lungs, trying to suffocate me. I breathed out pure mist, glittering, stinging. The flames didn't hurt; I could feel them but they became me, backing off from where Sofia was strapped. I smiled at the carnage around the campsite; arrows were shot towards me, and were incinerated into dust by the flames rushing to defend their mistress.

I smirked as a werewolf dropped onto the platform, and rushed at me with a sword held high. I ducked and side-stepped, kicking him in the back amongst the flames, increasing the temperature to an inferno, singeing him to a crisp as he screamed death threats at me.

I turned my attention to Sofia, seeing that the flames had caused enough chaos among the wolves to afford me a moment. I reached above her, biting my lip at the terrified look in her dark brown eyes as she cowered away. I sliced my knife through the rope and helped her to stand.

"Who are you?" she whispered in fear.

Was I really that scary? "I'm a friend of Valentina's," I answered simply. The full answer would have taken more time to get out than I had spare.

Her face immediately relaxed and she smiled, while her eyes filled with tears, taking on a red tinge. "I trust you," she said.

I baulked at her words, scowling at her before turning my face away. Why would she trust me? I had come here to kill her. No one should trust me, not until I had proven myself, and I was a long way off from that.

She took my arm, her fingers gripping painfully as she stared at the wood beginning to cave in at the far end of the stage. I forced the flames to part and dragged her through the gap, jumping down to the grass. I was immediately rushed by a , its jaws snapping, brown fur flashing before me as I slid my knife in deep. I struck again and again, spinning around, trying to keep Sofia behind me. It wasn't until I almost turned on her that I realized she had taken on her wolf form too. She was black like coal, with shining amber eyes.

I nodded to her and turned back, noting the absence of new attackers. Then I came face to face with the three werewolf leaders. This is what I had wanted. This was what I had been waiting for.

I crouched and waited for them to approach. It took a moment's hesitation, then they rushed me, swinging swords at my neck. I ducked, and lifted my leg high to knock one sword away, catching another on my bicep. I spun in a circle, with one right behind me, and threw my head back to catch him in the face. I rolled my body around so that I was now behind him and I reached forward, yanking hard on his own blade, completely decapitating one . . . Vernon.

Gregory and Ronald roared in anger and shifted to wolf form. They knocked me back, teeth biting at my face as I forced my legs up to my chest and kicked one off. They shifted back to human form and took hold of one of my arms each, launching me up against the burning platform and holding me there.

Before I knew what was happening, the dark-haired wolf I had seen restraining Sofia rushed towards me with a blade clenched in his hand and a maddened look in his eyes. I flared my nostrils, sucking in my power, and detonated it like a grenade, shooting straight for him.

In the seconds that followed, he lit up, luminous with neon yellow and orange colors as the flames ate him from the inside. He dropped to the ground before he had a chance to scream.

The wolves holding me took their opportunity while I was focused on their deceased pack member and bit me from each side, one catching me on the shoulder, and the other around the ribs that had only recently healed. I shrieked in pain, lightning striking the wood behind me. A flash of color passed over me and I was released, dropping to the ground in agony. I held my hand to my ribs, pulling it away covered in blood.

As the wood behind me rumbled, threatening further collapse, I scrambled away, skidding to a stop when I clapped my eyes on Sofia and four other wolves ripping Gregory and Ronald to shreds. A bleeding hand was flung towards me, slapping onto the grass beside my legs, tendons, bone and cartilage exposed from the gaping wrist wound.

I gave only a cursory glance at the hand, completely bewildered by what was going on around me. Wolves were attacking each other, mutilating their own kind. Snarls, growls and howls filled the air while the smoke from the fire cast an haze across the entire camp site. Bodies would appear in the smoke then disappear again. I'd see flashes of amber eyes before they melted into the mist.

I felt rather than heard another's approach and jumped to my feet groaning at the pain in my shoulder and ribs. A giant werewolf approached me, naked, covered in blood—someone else's—carrying an axe. Bald headed, with black eyes, he stood at least two feet over me. I threw myself out of the way of his axe swing, and kicked him hard in the abdomen, knocking him to the ground. I dropped on top of him, bringing my knife down towards his face.

He caught my arm with his and wrestled with me. My arm shook, my power pressuring for release. I sent fire onto his skin but he just roared—there was no give in his strength. He overpowered me, throwing me to the ground, and striking me in the stomach hard enough for me to flip over.

I coughed and scrambled away, picking up the first thing that came to my fingers. I turned my head. The smoke had begun to dissipate, bodies littering the ground coming into view slowly. I turned back as the ground shook with the force of the wolf bearing down on me. I threw my arm forward, letting loose the weapon in my hand, praying it would find its mark.

The giant wolf gave a bellow and swung his axe. From up in the air where he held his weapon, he opened his hand and dropped it, gasping as blood pooled out of his mouth, running down his chin. He clutched his chest and the tip of the spear that was protruding from it, and fell face down.

My chest gave a deep ache, pain shooting up my neck. I dropped my head back onto the grass for a moment, trying not to pass out.

I heard more footfalls. My breaths came in pants as I waited to see who would emerge from the mist. Friend or foe?

31

'What we find in a soul mate is not something wild to tame but something wild to run with.'

Robert Brault.

Machidiel jogged towards me, grinning. "Isn't this amazing?" He laughed.

I let out a nervous, disbelieving laugh. *Amazing?* Not really what I would call it. Chaotic, insane and frenzied? Yes. Confusing with wolves attacking wolves? Yes. Traumatic and painful? Triple yes.

"Did you bring Val?" I gasped.

He didn't answer, but instead turned his grin into a grimace. "You're injured. I knew I took too long to get back."

"Too long?" I frowned. "You've been gone, like, thirty minutes!"

He frowned, his confusion evident before relaxing. "Time difference between realms. I've actually been gone three hours. It took a while to find and then get to Val, plus getting back here was tricky."

"Shit," I swore. "How did you even get back? I didn't even think of that. Did you fly here?"

He paused, guarding his expression for a moment. "No. Portal."

I scowled. As far as I knew, there were only a couple of us in existence who had the rare ability to open portals. "How did you get a portal? Did the angels help? Or the witches?"

He nodded. "Yeah."

He leaped away from me as another wolf rushed out of the smoke. Machidiel batted it away, slicing and dicing while I turned to my own assailant. I set the wolf alight, burning as hot and as quick as I could, knowing it wouldn't be long before I ran out of energy due to the blood I was still losing from my puncture wounds. I fired over and over, the whimpering screams of werewolves becoming music to my ears.

A smaller grey and white wolf shot out of the smoke cover and trotted towards me, amber eyes glowing. I relaxed; this was one wolf I *wasn't* going to burn.

Valentina shifted forms and stood before me, her hands running over my body as if to assure herself that I was unharmed. She cried in dismay when she found the bloody mess of my shoulder and ribs. "You're hurt!"

"I'll be fine. I can heal myself once this is over; I can't waste energy on it right now though."

She tilted her head and smiled sadly, showing a glimpse of her white teeth. "It's over; we won. It's all going to change now."

"How?" I demanded. Had Machidiel brought angel warriors back with him? How on earth could he, Val, Trev, Maion, Sofia and I defeat a two hundred strong pack of werewolves?

"The Unworthy are back." She grinned, her eyes glowing.

"What?" I asked, raising my eyebrows.

"For years, Damian and the other pack leaders have forced the weakest of the wolves out of the pack to live alone in the woods. Anyone who disobeyed or fought for what they believed in was sent away. We knew they were out there somewhere, but I never would have guessed they had joined together to take down Vernon, Gregory and Ronald. One told me just now that after we left more of the pack were forced away, leading to the uprising."

I shook my head. "So I really did see wolves attacking wolves."

"You're the one who set them off. They were waiting for the right time, but you led them into battle."

"Unintentionally," I added with a look. I was sick of being made out to be a martyr. When would people around me realize I was making this up as I went along? I didn't want credit for things out of my control.

She grinned, then sobered quickly. "Did you see Damian? He probably ran as soon as the battle started."

I froze. My expression must have given me away.

"What is it? You saw him . . .?" Her breath caught.

I shook my head, unsure what to say. "He was already . . . dead when we got here. I'm sorry. If I'd gotten here sooner maybe he'd still be alive." I bit the inside of my cheek, searching her face for any sign of what she was feeling.

She seemed to be locked in place, expressionless. I linked my fingers with hers, squeezing slightly.

"Val, I'm so sorry."

She shook her head repeatedly, tears flooding free to stream down her face. She was wordless, devastated. Part of me could understand; she too had lost a lot of people close to her. She must have felt like she had no one left. She gripped tightly to my hand for a few minutes, only releasing me when Trev, Maion, and Machidiel surrounded us.

"What's wrong?" Maion asked, scowling. Though he wasn't a fan of werewolves, he could see Valentina was overwhelmed.

"Damian," I said her brother's name, knowing that would explain everything.

Maion, being the arrogant prick he was, rolled his eyes and snorted. "The bastard deserved what he got."

Valentina nodded in response.

"Don't listen to him," I said quickly, scowling angrily at the Russian angel.

"He's right," she whispered between sobs.

She let go of my hand and stepped back, brushing tears away from her face, trying desperately to compose herself while werewolves surrounded us.

At first I readied myself for a fight, my power churning around my abdomen, ready to be unleashed. A male werewolf, not much taller than me, stepped forward with his hands outstretched.

"My lady," he began. "Thank you for coming back to us."

Maion snorted his disgust and stomped away, shoving Trev aside to stand behind us. I cringed in embarrassment both for his behavior, and for what I knew was coming.

The werewolf spun in a circle, addressing the pack that was listening eagerly. "There was a prophecy that an angel would come among our pack and befriend our wolves. They would lead us into to a victorious battle against evil. We would gain forgiveness, and once again be under the protection of the angels." He paused as the wolves cheered. "That day has come! The Unworthy have been led into battle by our angel, and we have been triumphant!"

"Are you kidding me?" I hissed at Machidiel. He shrugged, and smirked in response. As the wolf continued to wax lyrical about me—their supposed angel miracle—I turned to Val for help. "You know it's not true! The witch confessed to making up that prophecy!"

She ran a hand down her face, and took hold of mine again. "Yet it came true. Yes, she said she made it up, but it happened. The wolves were waiting for a signal or a sign, and you gave it. You were here when they defeated our oppressors, and you were here to free the angels and kill the witch. You can deny the prophecy all you want, but the facts still stand. You will always be our angel."

I shook my head, frustrated. I didn't *want* to be anyone's angel. "Stop!" I shouted.

Trev and Machidiel turned to me in shock. Machidiel gave me a warning frown which I ignored.

"I'm not your angel. This prophecy isn't even real; the witch confessed to making it up as part of her plan so that any angels coming here would be brought straight to her." I took a deep breath. "I didn't come here to lead you into battle; I didn't even know what was going on. I came here hunting a spirit that I let escape from a pool of souls. I followed a werewolf spirit here to kill it."

The wolves fell silent, gazing at me in shock. Machidiel was furious; I could tell from the vibes his brain was sending out. Trev looked in awe of what I was doing while fighting the urge to get his psycho on and drain the blood from everyone around him; he'd taken a few hits too, and would need to replace his blood soon.

"I can't do it," I said, biting my lip. "I can't even follow through on my promise to return the escaped soul."

"A werewolf soul?" Valentina breathed.

The wolves began to mutter, turning to look at each other and around the campsite as though expecting a ghostly figure to loom up at them.

"It's me," a clear voice called out from the back of the crowd. "I'm the soul that came back."

Valentina turned, her hair swinging around her body like a curtain. She knew that voice. She ran, sprinting through the wolves, and fell into Sofia's arms in a tangled mess of crying and laughing. My heart clenched, palpitations hammering at my throat. Is this what it would have been like if I had managed to bring Zach back, if I hadn't given up? Is this what it would be like for Machidiel? If I had returned Sofia to the pool and fought my way in there to bring Zach back, would I cry, and laugh, and wrap my arms and legs around him, and never let him go? Would we tell each other how much we loved one another, and how much we'd missed each other, just like Val and Sofia were doing? Would I apologize for everything I ever did wrong, and swear to spend the rest of my life making it up to him if only he would stay with me? Would I beg him to stop me from falling? I could feel it rising inside of me, threatening to make me evil, to take away all the good in me. Would he save me? Would he promise to always save me?

I turned to Machidiel, my eyes so wide they stung. "I have to go. We have to go, *right now*."

Whether he could sense something broiling inside of me or just because he was feeling the same emotions I was, he immediately knew what I wanted. He grabbed hold of me just a second before Trev and Maion, and together we fell through a portal.

32

'A wolf does not concern himself with the opinions of sheep.'

Unknown.

I pulled away from the boys and stormed over to the remains of our house. I stomped through the burned grass to the steps and sat down, resting my face in my hands.

"Why are we here?" Maion shouted.

"Because this is my go-to place," I mumbled into my palms.

Trev sat next to me, leaning forward to rest his elbows on his knees. Long shadows touched my feet as Maion and Machidiel approached, Maion no doubt scowling at me as usual.

"So, are you telling Haamiah you couldn't complete your mission or am I?"

I looked up at Maion, pursing my lips at his smug expression. He was such an arse.

"By leaving her alive, we've guaranteed an alliance with the werewolves. Valentina is the natural successor to lead them, and if we'd killed her mate we would have been declaring war." Machidiel tilted his head to Maion, sharing his own smug expression.

To my pleasure, Maion muttered a few words in Russian and leaped into the sky, his wings taking him up through the dark-grey lurking clouds.

"Ding-dong, the witch is dead." I scowled, sitting upright with a sigh.

Machidiel snorted. "He's not that bad. He's a good guy."

"Hmm. That's still up for debate," I said. "What *are* we going to do?"

Machidiel looked up past me at the ruins that remained of our house, the only real home I'd ever had, and definitely the only place I'd ever felt safe. He took a deep, loud breath.

"I guess that's up to you. What was your plan before?"

I bit my lip miserably. "Zombies, Pool of Kali, Zach."

"Is that still your plan?" Trev asked with an air of expectancy.

I turned my head to him, seeing the tense look on his face, his drawn eyebrows and worried mouth. His dreadlocks had fallen over his shoulder messily, unsurprising, since we'd been in numerous battles and only escaped with our lives by the skin of our teeth.

I shook my head in response to his question. "No, that's not my plan anymore."

Trev's face dropped. "Why? Jasmine, if you think you can get him back then why aren't you going to try? *It's Zach!*"

I stood up, and spun around angrily. "I *know* it's Zach! You don't think that I would do *anything* to get him back? You don't think that I miss him every day, every second of every day?" I raised my hands, running it through my hair. "In order to get to the Pool of

Kali I'd have to take out dozens of angels standing guard. I can't do that on my own."

"You don't have to do it on your own!"

"I'm not asking my friends to risk their lives just because I don't want to be alone!"

"You're not asking—I'm offering! *We're* offering." Trev nodded to Machidiel, who quirked his eyebrow at me with a smile. "And this isn't about you not wanting to be alone; an apocalypse is here on our doorstop. We need our greatest warrior."

Tempting as his argument was, I wasn't going to give in. "Zach told me if he was going to die, he wanted to go in the heat battle with glory, in defense of innocent people. He *told* me that; so, who am I to force him back here?"

"So you're just giving up?"

"Who's giving up? I'm still here, fighting every day. I'm still willing to do what has to be done," I shouted.

"Which is . . .?" Machidiel asked.

"Mnemosyne." I stood up and fisted my hands onto my hips. "We're going to go after Mnemosyne, because she's the most acute threat at the moment."

"More so than Asmodeus, who's probably winging his way through Heaven's unlocked doors right now?" Trev questioned.

I nodded. "There are a thousand warrior angels in the Heavens just dying to pick him apart. Mnemosyne is trying to find Sam to fully open Hell's gates. She's also working alongside the Horsemen, probably sharing information. So, to protect Sam, we're going after Mnemosyne."

Trev laughed, leaning back to roar.

I frowned. "What?"

"You don't want to risk our lives against angels to get to the Pool of Kali, yet you want us to go up against the Goddess of Memory and kill her." He hooted. He toned it down as he saw my expression. "Don't get me wrong, I am right there with you, but you are awesome."

"I wouldn't blame you if you didn't want to do this," I said solemnly, pushing my hair behind my ear. I rubbed my hands up and down my arms, shivering at the cold gust of wind that rustled over me.

Trev lifted his eyebrows, giving me the *look*. "I'm doing this with you—can't think of anything else I'd rather be doing."

"I'm in too," Machidiel agreed.

I looked up at him, taking in the glorious bronzed skin and dominating tattoos running across every visible piece of it. I was lucky to have him on my side. "I haven't gotten your girl back for you yet."

He grinned. "She's not going anywhere; she'll be there when we get back from killing that dumb bitch."

I grinned and pushed past him to gaze down at the garden. This place used to be so peaceful. There were so many memories here. "Are angels supposed to swear?"

"Are valkyrie supposed to try to kill Goddesses?" he countered.

I laughed. "Are you kidding? That's the *only* thing we're supposed to do."

Trev stood up and clapped his hands together. "Okay, how do we do this?"

I had no idea. I looked up at Machidiel.

He winced. "I see how I'd be your best bet but I haven't got a clue." He dug his hands into his pockets. "I know a few people who *would* know how to find a psychotic Goddess."

I had a feeling I wasn't going to like his suggestion. I waited, my muscles tensed.

He bit down on his lower lip, staring at me, almost daring at me to refuse to do whatever he was going to say. "Let's head up to the Heavenly realm, where Maion and Haamiah will know where to find her."

I grimaced and turned to Trev, seeing his face drop. "We can't go up there."

"Why?" Machidiel asked.

Trev turned away and took a few steps down the garden with his hands in his back pockets. "You have to. Don't stay here because of me."

I sent a scowl towards Machidiel. "I'm not going up there and leaving Trev here. We stay together."

The angel shrugged. "Then how are you going to find her? My suspicion is that wherever Sam is, she'll not be far behind."

I froze. *Shit.* What was I supposed to do now? Sam was up in the Heavens, surrounded by a thousand angels, completely safe, except for the psychotic, murderous bitch who wanted to drag him into the pits of Hell to let Lucifer free, while Trev was stuck down here not allowed to go with us because he was half vampire. If he got hungry and had to feed from a human while we were gone, how would he stop without help? Never mind the fact that there seemed to be demons and fallen angels everywhere we went.

I pressed my palm to my forehead, recognizing the beginning of a headache. I moaned in indecision.

"We can leave Trev with someone," Machidiel suggested.

Trev swirled around and growled, his fangs very much evident over his bottom lip. "I don't need a babysitter."

"Who?" I demanded, ignoring him.

"Aidan?"

I rolled my eyes. "Yeah, because we actually know where he is."

"Don't you?"

I flinched. "He's with the human rebellion . . . if he's even still alive."

"You haven't heard from him since . . .?"

"What? You thought as soon as Zach was murdered I'd go running to him?" I shrieked.

"Whoa! Not what I meant." Machidiel held his hands up with a laugh. "I thought he'd come running to you."

I punched him hard on the arm. "Shut it. I'm not in the mood, and this doesn't help our situation."

Trev shook his head. "There is no situation. I can handle myself."

"Yeah? With the nephilim all tucked up safely in their cloudy beds, where are you going to go?"

He scowled at me.

"Exactly." The perfect solution came to me. "We'll leave you with Caleb. You'll be safe, I'm sure they can supply you with blood, and they won't be scared of you or try to kill you."

"You're getting the valkyrie to mind me?" he snarled.

I shrugged nonchalantly. "Fine, if you don't want to spend a day or so with beautiful, tattooed babes while drinking a ridiculous amount of tequila and playing video games, I'm sure we can come up with some other arrangement."

Trev's eyes flicked towards me, narrowing for a second. "On second thoughts, maybe I didn't think that through fully."

I laughed as he stomped closer and wrapped his arms around me and squeezed me, lifting me up off the floor.

"So we have a deal? We've got a plan?" I squealed.

"I'm in, just . . ." He trailed off, scrunching up his face.

"What?" I turned in his arms and gazed up.

"Don't leave me here," he whispered.

My heart melted. As if I would leave him. Gwen left us all, Sam was hidden away in another realm, Haamiah was watching over Sam, Maion was a dick and had nicked off who-cares-where, Zach and Drew were dead, and Aidan had thrown his lot in with humans.

"I'll never leave you." I shrugged. "Not for any length of time, anyway."

He nudged me, grinning.

"Best friends?" I teased.

He nodded. "Best friends. Now come on, there are some half-naked warrior women waiting to get me drunk."

I rolled my eyes and held out my arms to Trev and Machidiel, summoning up a portal. I looked over at our home one last time before we fell.

33

'When we honor our true path, we come face to face with who we really are.'

Jeff Brown.

After reluctantly leaving Trev with Caleb and Shmaz, Machidiel closed his arms tightly around his waist and hefted me up against his body as I squeezed my own arms around his neck and rested my head on his shoulder. He spread his wings out behind him, and we shot up into the sky. My stomach dropped away, and I closed my eyes against the wet clouds we soared through. I hated this bit.

We sped faster and faster until the valkyrie house was just a dot below us. I peeked over Machidiel's shoulder, watching the thickly coated wings smashing through the atmosphere so rapidly it appeared that they weren't moving. Gold sparks flashed around us, growing brighter, almost blinding me. The sparks turned into streaks of light, then we were through, flying through huge bronzed double doors, one of which was open a fraction, allowing us to sail in.

We landed on the white marble floors and skidded to a halt. I jumped down out of Machidiel's arms, and gasped as I spun in a circle, taking in the magnificence of the room.

"The Heavenly reception hall." I breathed, looking up at the ceiling.

It was otherworldly. Two rows of gigantic, golden pillars were lined up, reaching up to the ceiling. They were thicker at the bottom then skinnied in, tapering at the top, splitting into threads of gold touching and fading into the white of the ceiling. Images of clouds swirled across the ceiling, surrounding beautiful angelic figures.

The room gave off a gold, glowing luminescence. Strangely, it was a peaceful place, making me feel instantly relaxed and kind of sleepy.

“I remember this place,” I whispered.

“Of course you do. It’s home,” Machidiel said, with a strange tone in his voice.

I turned around to frown at him. He was striding off down the hall, so I had one last glance around and jogged after him.

“Not now.” I heard Machidiel groan.

I looked past him, seeing a man . . . an angel . . . Raphael.

He was even more beautiful than he had been in my dream; he had a chiseled jaw that would make Prince Charming jealous, and his eyes weren’t just dark, they were molten chocolate. He was rakishly good looking, much more slender than Zach, and at least a foot taller than Maion or Machidiel. He was being blocked by Machidiel, but as I stepped closer, my feet drawing me towards him step after step, he shoved him aside and took two steps towards me before stopping. His eyes were wide and clear, his expression one of shock and reverence. There weren’t many people who looked at me like that now, or back when I was Jophiel.

“Jophiel,” he said, shaking his head slightly. A grin broke out on his face and he closed the distance between us with one giant leap, swooping me up in his arms, squashing me so tightly I almost couldn't breathe.

"I can't believe you're still alive," he said.

I pulled back and dropped to my feet, smiling up at him. "You know, I'm just going by Jasmine now."

He frowned. "You are Jophiel. You'll come back to us."

I gave him an uneasy smile, trying to look reassuring and confident. I stepped back to look around him to Machidiel, hoping he would remedy this situation with a sarcastic comment, my heart pounding in fear.

Machidiel was scowling, a look of murderous rage coating his face in a dusky red glow.

"Oh my God." I gasped.

Raphael stepped in front of me, protecting me as he turned around to view Machidiel. "What?"

I attempted to push him aside, not wanting them to fight. I froze when Raphael turned back to me. Machidiel was relaxed and smiling, his eyebrows peaked in a query.

"What's up?" he asked.

I looked from him to Raphael. They were both staring at me with a confused expression now.

I shrugged my shoulders, pursing my lips. "Nothing; I'm just excited to be here."

Raphael smiled and nodded. "Let me take you to your rooms."

"Rooms? As in, plural?" I echoed. They had kept Jophiel's chambers intact for almost twenty seven years?

"Getting a little off track here," Machidiel said.

Oh yeah. "Okay, umm, actually I need to find Haamiah," I said. At Machidiel's look, I added, "And Maion."

"Your family haven't seen you in such a long time, yet you want to find *them*?" Raph asked incredulously, raising his eyebrows.

I put my hand on his arm. The sane part of me wanted to sugarcoat my answer. I wanted to smile and say, "I can't wait to see everyone; roll them on out," but that required a finesse I was inherently missing. Instead, without thinking, I said, "I'm not here for a family reunion. We think Mnemosyne's here, and I'm going to kill her."

He tensed, his eyes boggling. "Mnemosyne?" He shook his head, and cleared his throat. "No, you must be mistaken; she's not here."

"How do you know?" I asked.

He made a face. "We would know if evil broached our doors."

I rolled my eyes. "Your gates are wide open, and Mnemosyne is the Goddess of Memory—she already fooled us by erasing our memory of her and implanting her own version. She could have strolled in here, and you never would have known."

Raphael's face clouded over in anger, and he glared at me. "There is no other god! If you have such little faith and belief in the Heavens then maybe you should have stayed on the human plane with the beasts." He sniffed and took a step away from me, shaking his head in disappointment. "Maybe you should go. Michael would be devastated to see what you've become."

That was it! What did I have to do to get some respect? Saying that Michael would be disappointed in me was the equivalent of doing poorly in an exam, and your parents saying they weren't mad, they were *disappointed*—for normal kids, anyway. Clearly, Raphael preferred me to be a yes-girl, following my big brothers around and doing anything anyone asked me to do. Now that I had a thought in my brain, and could follow through with my own initiative, he thought he could bully me with snide comments, and physically intimidate me? I hadn't been through so much to go all gooey-eyed at Raphael, and roll over like a dog. He had no idea who I was.

I held my hands up. I was so over this. "Enough. Raph, I'll catch up with you later; I've got things to do."

He stood back, aghast, staring at me as though I had two heads. Maybe it was the fallen angel side of me, or maybe my inner valkyrie was crowing over this small yet important victory, but I smugly shoved past him and strode forward purposely, collecting Machidiel along the way. A few seconds later I leaned closer and hissed out the corner of my mouth, "I don't know where I'm going."

Machidiel smirked and wrapped his arms around with me, his wings throwing us into the air. I held back the shriek trying to escape as my stomach dropped, and closed my eyes tightly. Machidiel weaved us through the pillars and we sailed through a wide rectangular gap close to the ceiling.

After the initial anxiety-filled float, we dropped to the ground in a huge garden that spread as far as I could see in all directions. There didn't seem to be any particular order to it; in fact, it seemed as though someone had picked up a landscaping magazine and created one of everything. We were standing in thick, light green, dewy grass, while a stone fountain spewed water high up in front of us, sparkling in the sunlight. Further away, angels sat on a bench under a trellis covered in roses, and I could see other heads bobbing above bushes, and hear the laughter of angels talking amongst each other. Towering golden architecture surrounded us on all sides, some low one-story buildings, while some rose to a great height with reaching spires. One even had a huge golden bell tower at the very top. White sky above us shone with the sun's heat.

I gazed at the sky in amazement. I had forgotten that there was no *sky* as such here; everything was so different, and so beautiful. Everything was so pristine, from the perfectly-cut grass to the blooming roses; it almost seemed unreal. How had I ever forgotten this place?

Machidiel was standing beside me silently.

He'd be in for a long wait.

"Where will Haamiah be?" I asked breathlessly. I felt so out of my depth right now.

Machidiel took my arm and pulled me to my left, towards a tall building with perhaps fifty wide steps leading up to open doors. Up on the rooftop, four huge golden spires rose up to meet the clouds above us. I wanted to run up the stairs to find my friends, desperately needing to feel some kind of normalcy, the kind I imagined I would gain with seeing Haamiah, Maion and Sam. Machidiel gave me a warning look to slow down and we took the steps together one at a time, ascending at a steady pace until finally we passed through the doors into a hall with a number of doors closed to us. Machidiel opened one, and held it open for me to pass by him.

I took two steps into the room and stopped, emotion rolling over me. I remembered this place. It was like picking up a piece of your past, something you had forgotten now fresh and real.

We were in the Library of Choices, a room designated for the pondering of hard decisions, schemes and universe-changing judgments. Even now, as I looked around the vast chamber, I could remember the many nerve-wracking conversations Gabriel and I had had . . . especially the one leading up to her arrest and my new life. Here, there were hundreds of books from ceiling to floor, there to assist the angels in their plots.

I stepped further into the room, skirting around a pile of tombs left open on the floor beside a pool of water. Angels, sitting at the edges of many of the pools with their feet dangling in, looked up then away again, unconcerned by our entry. Machidiel smirked as he passed me, pushing on towards the back of the room.

I ran my hand across the material at the back of an empty armchair and absently trailed behind him. A few moments later and I had bumped into the back of him after he'd stopped. I smiled sheepishly and peered around his body, endorphins flooding through me as Sam grinned up at me from where he was sitting.

I crouched by him and threw my arms around him, squeezing him tighter than could have been comfortable. I felt I was home. I could *feel* the love and comfort coming from him.

"God, you have no idea how much I've missed you," I whispered in his ear.

"I'm pretty sure I've missed you more." He laughed.

I refused to let go, only unwrapping my arms when Haamiah forcibly pulled me away. I fell into his arms, hugging him before returning to sit down beside Sam. I sat on the edge of the pool and pulled my mud-covered shoes off, grimacing as I thought of the mud I'd probably tracked in. I rolled up my pants and stuck my feet in the water, sucking a huge breath into my lungs, holding it for a moment, then letting it go. I reached out and tangled my fingers with Sam's, closing my eyes for a moment to relax.

I'm okay. I'm okay, I chanted to myself.

You are. I won't let anything happen to you, Sam chimed in telepathically.

I opened my eyes and smiled at him, tears stinging my eyes.

Haamiah was talking to Machidiel. "Are the spirits returned?" he asked in his gravelly voice.

Machidiel coughed into his fist, glancing at me. "Slight change of plan."

Haamiah glowered. "What kind of change?"

I shrugged. "We got the zombies. They're definitely staying dead now."

"And the wolf?"

I pursed my lips. "There was a werewolf revolt. Damian and the other leaders are dead, Valentina has gone back to the wolf plane and is the most obvious choice to lead the pack."

"And?"

"The werewolf spirit was Valentina's ex-girlfriend. Keeping her alive will also mean that the werewolves become our allies," I said in a rush, tensing for his response.

He tilted his head, his black dreadlocks falling over his shoulders as he thought about what I had just confessed. I was more than a little bit nervous; he'd sent me on a mission and I'd only finished half of it, making my own decisions and excuses, and now here I was. What would he say? Would he be angry, and send me back to finish the job? What were the rules regarding escaped souls anyway?

He slowly nodded, finally giving me a grin. "Good call."

Relief poured through me, as well as some querying confusion from Sam.

I'm going to need a way more details. You do realize that, right?

I nodded and looked up at Machidiel. I wasn't sure what to say, or even if we should tell them that we were here hunting Mnemosyne. What if she were one of them?

Haamiah eyed us apprehensively; he seemed to feel whatever vibe we were giving off. "So, you've decided to seek shelter here while the apocalypse reigns?"

Machidiel lost his usual smirk. He glanced at me worriedly. "We think Mnemosyne's here."

Sam paled and balled his hands up, turning to look around the room. "*Here*?"

I joined him in casting my eyes around the room. "She's after *you* Sam . . . Where else would she be?"

He turned to Haamiah. "Can she get in?"

Haamiah snorted his denial at the same time as Machidiel said, "Of course."

While they glared at each other, I nudged Sam. "You know they found the Falchion and opened the Heaven's gates. She could have waltzed right in here, not because the warriors aren't any good, but because you know what she can do. She can make us think we're seeing anyone," I added at Haamiah's scowl.

He acknowledged that with a glower.

"So, let me get this right; the woman who wants to kill me is probably in this room right now," Sam said.

I grimaced. "Actually, she wants to drag you to Hell first and get you to open the gates to let Lucifer out."

He glared at me.

"That's why we're here," I said, trying to soothe him. I guess I wouldn't have felt particularly reassured either if our roles had been reversed. "We're here with a thousand warrior angels; nothing's going to happen to you."

"Where's Trev?" Sam asked suddenly.

"He's with the valkyrie, probably drinking tequila right about now." I laughed. What I wouldn't give to be doing that instead.

Apparently my answer wasn't quite good enough. "Why didn't he come with you?"

I pursed my lips, and looked to Machidiel.

He shrugged. "Vampires aren't exactly on the guest list for the Heavens."

I looked down at the water, peering up at Sam when the silence grew too long.

“You left him?” he asked in disbelief. “How could you just leave him there? It’s Trev!”

Anger rolled through me. I was here to save his arse and he was angry I’d left our half vampire-half nephilim friend, who could totally take care of himself, with my family?

“I’m here to kill Mnemosyne,” I said, standing up in the water. “I’m not a nanny or a nurse maid; Trev can handle himself. You have no idea what Trev, Machidiel and I have been through in the past few days while you’ve been sitting up here in your pools of water. It’s a war zone down there, and we’ve been stuck in the middle of it. I’m taking Mnemosyne out, and then I’m going back down to take out the rest of our enemies or die trying. Either support me or shut the hell up; you’ve got no right to judge.”

“My, my, I seem to have interrupted something.”

34

'When you walk up to opportunity's door, don't knock on it . . . kick that bitch in, smile, and introduce yourself.'

Dwayne Johnson.

I looked up, raising my clenched fists, pausing when I saw the classically beautiful woman standing beside the pool. She wore an almost see-through floor-length dress, her wings folded against her back. She picked the bottom of her dress up and pointed one bare foot towards the water, sinking down into the lukewarm pool, sitting on the edge.

She looked so familiar, with long brown hair, the ends of which were trailing in the water around her knees. A small brown mole beside her lip moved as she flashed her white teeth at me. It all came flooding back to me; Bëyander, soul mate of the murdered Tabbris, whose weapon had been used to open the gates. She was a principality and good friends with Haamiah . . . and I had never really liked her. Maybe it was because Haamiah had had something I didn't—a soul mate who adored her. Well, we were both in the same boat now. I wondered how she'd had her revenge for the death of Tabbris? What had she done to enable herself to keep on living without him? I could barely see beyond my next revenge task; once I'd finished them all I had no idea what I would do.

"Bëyander," I said in greeting. I tried to smile, succeeding in more of a grimace.

She lifted her hand, and gave me a little wave across the pool. "You've come to find Mnemosyne, then?"

I flinched. How much had she heard?

She smiled, smugness oozing out, raising her eyebrow in challenge at Haamiah. "I'm a principality; this move would be in keeping with the natural order of the game. Well," she amended, "this, or hunting down the rest of the Horsemen."

Haamiah grunted in acquiescence, clearly unhappy she had beaten him with her prediction.

"So who's out?" She pushed on, oozing satisfaction. "The vampire?"

"No, he's fine," I muttered. She was grating on me already, I'd forgotten how irritating she was. Maybe Tabbris had killed himself just to get away from her.

"You're grasping, Bëyander. No one's *out*," Haamiah said crossly.

"Actually . . ." Machidiel trailed off, glancing at me.

I shook my head, rage roiling through my stomach. I turned away and stepped up out of the pool, needing to leave before I exploded in some kind of emotion-filled bomb. "This isn't a game. Why don't you just carry on siting up here making your predictions on your master game while we fight for our lives?"

I almost ran from the room, skidding on the wet floor out into the corridor, pulling the door closed beside me. I couldn't think, couldn't think about everything and everyone who I'd lost. I needed to find Mnemosyne, and two people who could have helped were too busy scheming and gloating about being one up on each other. I couldn't think of anything worse than enlisting Maion's help, and Raphael had annoyed me too much already. Who could I turn to? Was there anyone up here I could really call my friend?

Yes, there was, I realized. *Gabriel.*

I started towards the doors, trying to remember the way to her chambers, when Sam edged around me, stopping me in my tracks.

"What do you want?" I asked with a scowl.

He held his hands up. "I'm sorry about what I said." He took a deep breath. "And I'm sorry about Drew; I didn't know." *You'll not find Gabriel in her rooms.*

I flinched, not expecting to be having a double conversation. I turned slightly, Machidiel, Bëyander, and Haamiah coming into view behind me.

Nerves trickled through me. "That's okay. I know you haven't really seen Trev in action, but he's really strong, and Caleb will take care of him. I'm sorry about Drew, too. He was a good friend," I said outwardly. *Where is she? And why are we talking like this?*

"I wish I could have been there to help you." *We can't mention her in front of the others; she did something bad and is being punished.*

I shook my head. It took all of my willpower to concentrate on the two separate conversations and answer accordingly. "No you don't; I've never been so scared in my life. We took out one Horseman, two zombies, and demons unlike any other that we've seen before. I don't know how any of us made it here alive." *Punished for what?*

"I believe you. Come on, let's go for a walk," he suggested.

I waited for the telepathic response to accompany his words, but it didn't come.

"Okay." I nodded and forced a smile towards the angels, following Sam out of the door.

He jogged down the steps and sauntered across the grass.

Gabriel's still imprisoned in the dungeons.

What? Why?

How am I supposed to know? No one talks about her; no one even mentions her name. I've only found out tiny bits of information telepathically.

What have you found out?

Not much at all. From what I can make out, she was put in the dungeons for plotting against the other archangels and hasn't been released. She's still alive, but hasn't been out of there since—

Since I left to be reborn as Jasmine.

I think so. This isn't your fault though.

How do you know?

He gave me a wry look. *I don't, I'm just being supportive.*

I huffed out my breath and held back my smile. *We need to get her out; she's the only one who can really help us. She is involved in everything. She was supposed to be Jasmine. This whole mission to gain allies for the angels was her idea only Raphael locked her up before she could leave, so she persuaded me to do it instead.*

Seriously, how haven't you ended up on Oprah?

I rolled my eyes. *Show me the way to the dungeons.*

We'll not be able to get in there.

Why?

Well . . . they're dungeons! Don't they have prison guards?

We're not on the human plane. Who's going to be game to break out prisoners in Heaven?

I nodded and smiled at an angel who walked past, staring at me curiously. She could probably tell I was 'other' and was wondering how I'd gotten in. The angels all seemed so relaxed...were they even aware that the gates were open and that there was an apocalypse going on, or did they just have so much faith *in their warriors* that they *didn't care?*

Don't you remember the way there?

My memories are still a little fuzzy. Do you not know the way there, or are you stalling?

I'm pretty sure it's the building with the bell tower.

I squinted my eyes at the building in the distance. That felt right. *I think you're right.*

For fifteen minutes we jogged and walked alternatively, depending on if there were any angels in the vicinity. We didn't want to look like we were up to something and draw unwanted attention, yet a sense of urgency was in me, and I wanted to be there *now*. How had Raph kept Gabriel locked up for so many years? Why hadn't anyone broken her out yet?

We entered the building through an open alcove and headed along a dark corridor. A wide, spiraling staircase stood near to the entrance, and Sam gestured to it in question. I shook my head and kept walking, passing a number of doors, and pausing in front of them before shaking my head and continuing.

Finally I felt a pull towards a wooden door near the back. I reached for the black, iron handle and turned it, pulling it back. It opened smoothly and quietly.

Sam hissed in a breath. Darkness greeted us. Pitch black led the way down steps, and I knew from memory that it was a long way to the bottom.

I turned to Sam and linked my fingers with his. When he was going to leave the door open I told him to close it behind us and reassured him we could open it again from the inside . . . I hoped that hadn't changed since I'd been gone.

I tugged Sam towards me and together we descended slowly, stumbling on occasion. I kept my free hand against the wall, and told Sam to do the same to help with the dizziness and disorientation of walking down stairs in darkness.

Eventually, after what seemed like forever, the steps stopped, and we almost fell on top of each other. It was lighter now, shadows dancing around us, cast off from the lit torches held up on sconces around the dungeon.

Light flickered, the fire reflecting on the metal bars of the cages, shiny eyes peering out at us. Beside our steps and the gently hissing and spitting of the torches, the dungeon was completely silent.

I knew the way now. I pulled Sam off to the left and we tiptoed past the cages through an opening. Following the path to the very end, I began to run, dragging Sam with me, seeing as he refused to let go of my hand.

I skidded to a stop outside a cage at the far end and gripped the bars tightly in my fists, staring through at shapes in the darkness.

"Gabriel?" I hissed.

A slender figure moved in the shadows, accompanied by a rustle of fabric.

"Who is it?" Her voice reached me.

My heart began to ache, each pound sending slivers of pain through my veins. "It's . . . Jophiel."

Immediately fingers wrapped around the bars in front of me, touching my skin. Sharp green eyes looked out as her breath hissed in and out.

"Is it really you?" she asked in a shocked voice.

"I can't see you properly," I whispered.

"Here, try this." Sam held up a torch beside me.

I flinched away from the heat then looked eagerly into the depths of the cage. It *was* Gabriel. She was short and thin, with golden hair loose down her back and around her arms. She wore a dark grey dress and a grey wrap tied across her chest. All around her, piles of blankets and cushions were stacked up over the floor and around the bar edges. It almost looked as though she had herself a nice hamster cage.

Gabriel reached through the bars and touched my face. "It's really you."

I hadn't thought I would feel like this. I honestly had mixed feelings about Gabriel; as Jophiel, I remember feeling protective of my sweet, loving sister, yet irritated by her incessant need to plot and scheme. I loved her with all my heart and now, I realized how much I'd missed her.

I hadn't given her any such reason to miss me. As Jophiel, I had constantly run after Michael into the middle of battle, coming home wounded and dirty to be nursed back to health by Gabriel, and then run right back to battle again without a word of thanks. Even when she had been locked away, I had only agreed to take her place in the human world when I had found out Zacharael was involved. I wouldn't have done it just for her.

I could make it up to her now. I *would* make it up to her.

I clenched hold of the bars and jerked them, looking up to see where they were joined. Her hands reached out to mine and rested on them.

"Be at ease Jophie," she whispered, her eyes glowing green with emotion. "I knew you would come back for me."

I frowned. "Did you?"

She smiled softly. "I have faith in you, but I've wished many times over that I could go back and stop you from leaving. I've thought about you every day, wondering where you were and if you were safe."

"And if I'd accomplished what you wanted me to do?" I guessed, trying not to scowl at the turn of my thoughts.

She tilted her head. "You're still angry with me."

I shook my head in denial. “I’m not; I’m just still trying to work through all of this. You have no idea what I’ve gone through, not knowing who I was for so many years, then eventually finding things out piece by piece.” I winced. “Although, I guess you’ve been stuck in a cage for twenty-seven years, so I don’t really have a lot to complain about, do I?”

She grinned. “You haven’t changed.”

“I have,” I said. I glanced at Sam. “I’ve changed a thousand times, and I’m still changing.”

Gabriel dropped her grin and frowned in concern. “What happened to you?”

I bit my lip and let out a short laugh. “A lot! And I really missed you.”

She smiled, and gripped my hand in hers. “I really missed you too.”

I leaned forward, resting my forehead against the bars, and wrapped my arms around her. This felt right, it felt familiar, and comfortable, and more real than anything else in the Heavens. If only the people I loved could be here too.

Tears began to fall, and that was the end of me. I sobbed against the bars, railing against the construction that held me away from my sister.

“I’m so sorry,” she whispered into my ear.

I pulled back. “There’s nothing to apologize for. It wasn’t your fault; it was mine. I spent so long obsessing over things that didn’t matter instead of just living. I had everything, and then I lost it all.”

“What do you mean? What did you lose?”

My chin trembled as I tilted my face, trying to rein in the tears. "I lost Zach."

Her jaw dropped. "Oh my God, Jophie."

Anger and resentment got the best of me. "I'm not Jophiel!" I shouted. "I'm Jasmine! I've spent my entire life trying to find my path and learn who I am, only to find that I'm already on the that path, and I'm already the person I'm supposed to be! Jophiel was no one. No personality, no fire, nothing. I'm Jasmine, and I had nothing, then everything, and then nothing again. I'm here for revenge, and that's all."

"Jo—Jasmine, don't be like that," Gabriel said, pleading with me.

I shook my head. "You don't understand. I did this to save him, and I failed. I lost him, then when I was trying to kill the zombies for Haamiah I got Drew killed."

"Who's Drew?" She asked, a confused look on her face.

I closed my eyes against the tears threatening to flood out. "My friend . . . a lycan."

She pulled back. "A lycan? He died saving you?"

I nodded, eyeing her with caution.

"Drew accepted his destiny a long time ago. He knew what he was doing, and he would have been proud to complete his task," She said with a reassuring tone.

I froze. She *knew* about this? She knew about Drew?

"You knew he was going to die saving me?" I asked with a chill running through my voice.

She hesitated, biting her lip. “There was a deal.”

“A deal!” I laughed. “Of course there was. What kind of deal?”

She sniffed, and anxiously looked from me to Sam. “An alliance was brokered as long as they would provide a lycan soldier to defend you.”

“To *die* defending me?”

She nodded. “Yes.”

“If one lycan would agree to die saving my life then the angels would ally themselves with the lycan?” I clarified.

“It wasn’t exactly like that.”

I shook my head. “It was exactly like that. I’ve lost Zach and Drew because they tried to defend me.”

“They didn’t *try*; they succeeded,” she said.

Anger and stress made my power churn through my stomach and up through my throat, choking me. “And for what? Nothing!” I screamed. The ground rolled slightly under my feet.

Sam pulled me away. “Don’t! Come on, let’s go.”

Gabriel reached through the bars. “No! Don’t go! They didn’t die for nothing, so don’t tarnish their memory.”

I turned back with anger in my gaze. “You didn’t even know them—you have no right to talk about their memory.”

“Who are our allies now? You went to the human realm for a reason, so tell me, who are our allies?”

I rolled my eyes. "The witches, valkyrie, werewolves and lycan."

Gabriel lifted her arms. "Then it wasn't for nothing, was it? You've never wanted to look at the bigger picture, but maybe you need to. I've remained here, locked up for over a quarter of a century, giving up my freedom and rights for the bigger picture. I would have given everything to be the one to go, but it had to be you."

I bit the inside of my cheek hard, tasting blood, needing to ground myself on the coppery taste. I'd had this conversation with myself over and over again about losing Zach, but hearing that Drew was also just a pawn in the big game Gabriel and her allies were playing was hard to hear, because that's what I was too. I was a pawn to be sacrificed when the time was right.

"This isn't how I'm going out. This isn't how my story ends," I whispered.

"No, it's not," Gabriel agreed. "Jasmine . . . Jophiel, whoever you are now; I love you, and I'm sorry if what I've done has caused you pain, but you are going to be the driving force in the apocalypse. This is your job. You're the Angel of Miracles, so do your thing. I'm behind you."

I shook my head. "No, it's too late. I can't do this. You're just like the others; you sit here ruling people's lives. People think that they have free will, but you're here making decisions and dooming them to death, when you don't even know them! You don't know the people you're planning on killing, and you don't even care."

She recoiled from me. "I do care!"

"How can you, when you're up here and they're down there? You don't know them; you don't know their hopes, dreams and fears. You don't know if they deserve to live or not. As it turns out, Drew was a kind and wonderful guy, and didn't deserve what you did to him. He deserved a chance to live, but you took that away. I'm not nearly as decent as he was, and I would have given up my life for his in a heartbeat. You have no idea what he was like."

"But I wanted to. I wanted to go to the human realm—it was never supposed to be you."

"Well, it was me. You have no idea what it's like; you'll never understand the loss . . ." I trailed off, emotion getting the better of me. My skin seemed to crawl with anxiety and stress. My heart contracted painfully.

"I understand."

"No, you don't," I snapped. Sam put his hand on my shoulder, trying to calm me. "How can you understand loss when you've never lost anything, except maybe your freedom—which you deserve, for plotting the death of people you don't know."

"I do understand loss," she insisted.

Impossible. "What have you ever lost?"

She bit her lip and peered through the bars at me. "I lost you."

35

'Own who you are. Be the bitch if you have to, but never accept less than you deserve.'

Unknown.

I shrugged off Sam's hand, hesitantly looking into Gabriel's eyes. How bizarre that an archangel was telling me she had missed me. If I could take a step back from my life I would swear I was actually in a mental institution in an imaginary world. How could this be happening? How could I *feel* like this? How could I feel so topsy-turvy?

What were my choices? I could either stand my ground and leave Gabriel here, refusing to ever come back, or I could forgive and forget. Could I forget? Was I even capable of forgiving? I didn't think I'd ever really forgiven anyone in my life.

I paused . . . that was *awful*. I was the person who couldn't forgive? That was me?

I looked up at Sam, seeing the melting, anxious expression on his face. He didn't know what to do, and from a little foray into his mind I knew that like me, he didn't know what to think either. Staring into his brown eyes, I mentally pictured each person in my 'family' both present and past. Gabriel was included.

I could do this. I wasn't going to be a horrible person. I needed to sort myself out and move on, concentrating on something else much more important—my own plans for revenge. I couldn't help the slight smile that tugged at the corners of my mouth. *Mnemosyne, the last three Horsemen, Asmodeus.*

I forced my shoulders to relax. "I missed you too." I quirked my lip, and grinned as I realized I wasn't just saying it for effect. "I might not have remembered that I missed you, but I'm sure I did."

Gabriel tensed for a split second before relief spread across her face and she sighed, smiling. She reached through the bars and grabbed hold of my arms that I'd folded across my chest. "I know what you're here for and I'm behind you; just tell me what you want me to do."

"What I'm here to do?" I echoed.

She laughed. "Yes—the reason you're actually here in the Heavens. We might approach things differently but we still have the same goals in mind; we're sisters, not strangers."

"What goals?" I narrowed my eyes.

Her eyes hardened, and she stared at me intently. "Revenge."

That piqued my interest. My sister was a hardened revenge addict too? Who did she have to pay back? I mentally checked myself; duh, she had been locked in a cage for twenty-seven years—that would probably make you feel a little vengeful.

"Who?" I queried.

She turned away and paced the cage, stiffening when she reached the far end, hidden by the shadow. She sniffed. "Let's focus on killing everyone who ever hurt my sister first . . . then we'll get to the revenge that I want."

I narrowed my eyes, trying to see her in the darkness. Was she going to make Raphael pay for having her locked away? Was she going to take down the thrones, who had clearly left her here without judgment? If I were in her place, that was exactly what I would do.

I snorted with laughter and nodded. “Deal.”

The material of her dress rustled as she moved closer to me again. “So, who have you followed here?”

I hesitated, considering not telling her before realizing that if there were anyone I could trust absolutely, it would be Gabriel. Out of everyone here, she was the only one who I knew one hundred percent was herself, not Mnemosyne.

“You trust me to do things my way?” I asked, still thinking. After all, despite being an archangel, she followed the rules of the principality class—what if she tried to take over, convincing me to follow her own plans?

She eyed me thoughtfully. “Fine, let me hear your plans.”

I grimaced. “I don’t really have any *plans* as such . . . but we’re pretty sure Mnemosyne is here.”

Her jaw dropped. Yes, she knew of Mnemosyne. “What are you going to do?” she asked cautiously.

“Kill her,” I said simply.

She shrugged. “How? She’s different to any other foe you will have faced.” She leaned forward, gripping the bars tightly. “I would ask you to reconsider; she’s not someone to be trifled with.”

I nodded. “I know, but the problem is that she’s here for Sam.” I jerked my head towards him. “He’s the Dagger of Lex, and she—”

“Wants to use him to open the gates to Hell.” She looked horrified, gazing up at Sam in something akin to terror. “We have to hide him!”

“That’s why he’s here, only our enemies have also found the Falchion of Tabbris, so—”

“The gates to Heaven are open,” she finished.

If I had thought she looked horrified before, she looked as though she was going to faint dead away now. Guilt and anger roamed free, pouring through my veins like lava.

They had locked my sister away, provided no protection for her, and not told her that anyone could wander into the Heavens whenever they wanted. She was one of their own; how could they do that? What was Raphael thinking? Everything he was doing, everything I remembered him doing screamed to me that there was something wrong with him. Had he fallen, and no one had realized?

I glared at the cage, gripping the bar tightly as thoughts flew through my mind. Images of Drew and Zach flashed through like an electronic photo book; picture after picture. They were gone, dead, and it appeared that Raphael wanted Gabe to join them. So much loss and hurt, so much despair and anger; I felt like I would explode into a million little fragments, never to become whole again. The ground tilted and spun, flashes of gold and black blinding me. I lifted my hands to my eyes, pressing on them hard, trying to ground myself.

Stop! A low voice commanded. Black eyes set in a beautifully masculine face appeared, disappearing as soon as I opened my eyes.

Sam had hold of my left arm while Gabriel had my right. I swallowed deeply, pushing my magic down where it belonged inside. Those eyes. Those eyes were so beautiful, and so lonely. God, I missed him so much.

"Are you okay?"

"What's happening?"

I shook my head free from the dizziness. "I'm fine. Just give me a moment."

I could feel the worry emanating from Gabriel, and I could hear Sam trying to explain my abilities . . . with difficulty.

"She can open portals, yet she's also telepathic?"

I stepped away from them, and jumped up and down on the spot. I turned back and attempted to smile, like I hadn't almost just sucked them into another dimension.

"I was reincarnated as a hybrid," I explained. "Half valkyrie - half fallen angel."

Gabriel's eyes boggled. "Seriously? That's amazing!"

Sam and I looked at each other before turning back to her. "Really?"

"Yes, there's no better combination. With valkyrie abilities you can develop more, making you stronger and faster in a thousand different ways. Combining that with a fallen angel and you appeal to both sides, meaning you can attract allies from both sides of the divide," she gushed.

"Yeah, and I get the additional benefits of rage, hate, and a thirst for revenge, just to mix it up a little." I smirked, pointedly.

She winced. "Okay, so there are a few drawbacks. So, what abilities have you harvested? I've always been so intrigued by the valkyrie; they're so secretive."

"Well, I can open portals—obviously not well—and I'm faster and stronger than other nephilim, I have healing abilities, telepathy . . ."

Gabriel jumped up and down excitedly, clutching at the bars. "Telepathy? How does it work?"

I smiled, unable to be unaffected by her excited energy. "I can hear thoughts if they're projected loud enough, but not the way Sam can. He can literally feel their thoughts, right?" I looked to him for clarification.

He grinned. "Pretty much; I'm not sure how it works exactly, but I can feel the soul inside the body. I knew Mnemosyne was pretending to be Haamiah when she'd kidnapped him."

She scowled. "Wait, what?"

An hour later, Gabriel had been filled in with our tales of love, betrayal and friendship, and I had discovered that not one single angel had bothered to update her on the full situation. During the relaying of our adventures, it crossed my mind that she was probably judging us. After all, as she had pointed out, she had wanted to do this herself. Was she pondering over our escape from Castle Dantanian, and wishing she had been there to do it differently? Did she think she could have killed the zombies single-handedly, and without any casualties?

I sat on the ground at the edge of her cage, looking at the expressions on her face, trying to decipher them. She wasn't projecting any thoughts to me, but I was sure I saw signs of regret, guilt, and maybe even anger.

When Sam finished explaining the argument in the Library of Choices, leading to us coming here to find her, we sat in silence.

Gabriel sat with her legs folded beneath her, eyes open wide with shock, her lips pressed together in a grim line. "I can't believe that happened."

I agreed wholeheartedly. Sometimes I thought I must be dreaming it all, although being trapped in a nightmare would seem more accurate. Or, maybe I was insane and locked in an asylum—a potentially preferable alternative to this.

Gabriel shook her head in wonder. "All of these years I've bemoaned the fate that led me to be locked up here for so long, while I had no idea what was happening to you out there, or if you even remembered us and your life here. I think God made it this way on purpose. They say that God has a plan for everyone, and everything happens for a reason, and it's true; with what you have faced, you have gained more than I ever would have. Despite being in that scary place all alone and without someone to guide you, you have succeeded beyond my expectations."

I felt flattered, but she was painting me in a wrong light for sure. "I haven't," I denied. "I didn't take on your role in the hope of uniting allies; the only reason I went was to save Zach. I was being selfish."

She shuffled on her bottom and stretched her legs out in front of her, turning to sit side on to the bars. “I know you believe that, but following your heart and soul is never wrong, and it is proven by looking at where you are now, and what you have achieved. Follow your heart and you will follow the path to your destiny.”

I groaned. “I don’t mean to feel sorry for myself. I know what I did wrong, and I’ve replayed it a thousand times in my mind. I don’t want sympathy or reassurance, I just want my revenge.”

“Which brings us back to Mnemosyne,” Gabriel said.

I nodded. “I don’t actually have a plan. I was hoping you would have an idea of how to catch her. We’re sure she’s here, probably pretending to be someone else, we just don’t know who.”

“Can Sam listen out and hear her?”

He shrugged. “Probably. I’ve not heard her yet though; everyone seems to be themselves.”

“Who?”

“Well, I haven’t really been with that many people other than the nephilim, but they seem pretty safe, as do Haamiah, Maion, and Zanaria. Oh, and that Bëyander; no weird evil Goddess vibes there either.”

“Which leaves like a thousand other people she could be,” I said.

“She’ll pick someone with access to Sam, and who won’t raise suspicion being in the thick of things.”

We sat in silence for a moment, thinking of who she could be. I knew I was onto something; I had a niggling feeling at the back of my mind. I knew this, something weird had happened—why couldn't I remember what? Who was acting suspiciously?

Raphael.

36

'Sometimes the most productive thing you can do is rest and let your angels wrap you in their loving wings. They've got you covered.'

Anna Taylor.

I sat up straight, my heart pounding. Raphael had acted so strangely when Machidiel and I first arrived. He had been angry, and distant, and kind of intimidating; I couldn't remember him ever being like that. He had always been kind and generous, even if he was set in his ways. When he had visited me in my dreams after the zombie attack he had been gentle. That wasn't the angel I'd seen in the Heavenly reception hall. It was him.

"It's Raphael," I hissed, when I could speak.

Sam and Gabriel stared in confusion.

"What's Raphael?" Sam asked, stretching his arms out in front of him.

Gabriel shook her head. "No, it can't be."

"He was acting so strangely when got here. He was just *different*. I think she's pretending to be him; he has all of the right attributes that she would be looking for. He has the authority to be everywhere and anywhere, nowhere is out of bounds for him, and no one would dare confront him about anything. Why wouldn't she pick him? There's no one else in a better position."

Gabriel sighed. "I agree he would be an excellent candidate, but she would need to make sure he was out of the way—people would notice if there were two Raphaels running around."

That was a good point.

"Maybe he's already out of the way," Sam suggested. "Maybe he's on a job somewhere. It isn't a far stretch of the imagination; you angels are always on some kind of mission."

I tilted my head. "That could be true."

"Of course it could be true," Sam said with a grin.

I bit my lip. "So, we need to confirm it."

"Easy," Sam declared. "Get me near him and I'll read his mind . . . or *her* mind."

"How are you going to get near him?"

I grimaced and exhaled slowly. "I'm not sure. If he's really Mnemosyne I don't want to tip him off."

"What about starting at the beginning, then?" she asked.

I tilted my head, exchanging a smile with Sam. "That would be great, if we knew where the beginning was."

She chuckled. "Find out if Raphael's away or if he's here."

"Ohh." I raised my eyebrows in thought. "Okay, how do we do that?"

Gabriel scooted closer to the bars. "Well, if it's a fight or a war that he's been called away on, talking to Commander Avrail will be your best option. If he's planning strategy or tactics, then Bëyander might know where he is."

"Ugh, I hate her," I grumbled .

Gabriel looked at me in surprise. "Bëyander? Really?"

"I only saw her for a minute, but she really grated on me."

I raised my eyebrows as Gabriel snorted, leaning on the bars as her shoulders shook.

"What?"

She turned her face, and laughed out loud. "She has that effect on people. She's a principality, through and through."

"She's irritating!"

"She was pretty pompous," Sam agreed, grinning as Gabriel laughed harder.

"She's methodic, scheming, always calculating pros and cons—"

"Yeah, that came through pretty well."

Gabriel smiled gently. "She's everything you look for in a great principality. She helped concoct *this* plot, didn't she?"

I grimaced. "I still don't like her."

"You never did."

"I didn't?"

She shook her head. "No. I don't know why, but you never liked her."

Figures.

"Okay, if I have to speak to her then I will, but I prefer the Commander Avrail option," I said. "What are my other choices?"

"We get summons all of the time," Gabriel said. She shrugged. "At least, I *used* to. You could probably look in his rooms and you'd find a stack of papers on his desk. You might be able to find out if he's been called away."

I liked that idea. Not involving interrogating anyone, this would simply be snooping and potentially stealing . . . *that*, I was good at.

"Okay, we'll sneak into his rooms, search through his paperwork, and if we don't find anything, we'll look for the Commander." At Gabriel's look, I continued with a groan. "If I *have* to, I'll speak to Bëyander . . . but that will be my last option."

"You know where his rooms are?" she asked.

I sighed and glanced away. "They're next to mine."

We fell silent. Sam's quiet was probably due to feeling awkward, while Gabriel and I were reflecting on our past, and what could have been our present if things had gone differently.

Shaking myself out of near depression, I took a deep breath and scrambled up to my feet. "Okay, let's do it. How do I break you out?"

Gabriel frowned. "What?"

I pulled on the bars, testing their strength. “How do these come apart? Or, an easier option; where’s the key?”

Gabriel held onto the bars as she stood, staring between them sadly. “They’re unbreakable, and the thrones have the key.”

“They can’t be unbreakable. They must have a weakness.” I clenched my fists around them, and sent warmth through my fingers. Fiery power sizzled into them, heating them up so that they quickly began to glow red.

Gabriel jumped back and bit her lip, watching me.

Sweat beaded on my forehead and I gritted my teeth, sending more churning power through my fingertips. “Why isn’t it melting?”

“Because we’re in the Heavens,” Gabriel answered quietly. “Things are different here. The strengths and weaknesses you have in the human realm will have different values up here.”

I gave one more burst of energy, then let Sam pull me away from the bars, my palms stinging.

I heard the heavy tapping of footsteps; someone descending the stairs into the dungeon. I tensed and frantically turned back to Gabe.

“I’m not leaving you here.”

“You need to go.” She reached through the bars and pulled me closer, kissing my cheek.

I grabbed hold of her hands, refusing to let go. “I’m not leaving you here. There has to be another way out.”

She shook her head. "There isn't. Go, do what you came to do, and go back to the human realm to finish your mission."

"My mission?" I echoed. I angrily rubbed at a tear that tracked down my face. "*You* are part of my mission."

"You want revenge on me?" she asked hesitantly.

I shook my head earnestly, my hair flying around my face. "No. I need to get you out of here, and you can join me. This was your mission, not mine. You need to come back with me, and we can finish it together."

Her face was a mixture of regret and happiness. I didn't need to read her mind to know that she hadn't expected me to want her to be with me. Even as an archangel I hadn't been the most approachable, always hiding my feelings. I had never really been the sister Gabriel had deserved. Well, that would change now. I would get her out of here, and I would make up for all of the years we had lost being close.

The footsteps got louder, seeming to come towards us.

"Go!" she hissed. "Go around behind the cages, and track back up to the stairs. You can come back for me later."

I paused, anxiously looking to Sam for help.

"If you wait too long, you'll get caught, and then we'll both be stuck in here!"

She was right. I let go of her hands and backed away from the cage, letting Sam pull me into the shadows. I desperately wanted to see who was prowling between the cages, but Sam dragged me into the darkness where a path cut between empty prisons until we passed back into the dim light back behind the stairwell. With a final glance towards the path leading to Gabriel's cell, we ran up the steps, treading as lightly as possible.

Out of breath at the top, we slipped around the corner and into the light, taking on a more sedate pace as we left the building, my heart and memories still behind with Gabriel.

We plastered on smiles and forced ourselves to walk silently across the grass, heading back to the building housing the Library of Choices. We could follow the corridor much further through, and there I would find the archangels' bedrooms. With every pulse taunting me, whispering to run as fast as I could towards the far off building with four golden spires rising up through the cloud, I counted my steps. Calm and slow, we neared the building.

"Are you okay?" Sam asked.

"No," I replied. "I'm torn between sprinting back to Gabriel and burning down the dungeon until I can free her, and hunting down Mnemosyne to slice her throat."

He grinned. "I'm glad that Haamiah normally makes the plans; you do realize that if you burn down the dungeon you'll kill her."

I shrugged, and shook my head. "I know. I just can't stand her being stuck in there, completely helpless."

"She's not exactly helpless; she's an archangel, she's got powers of her own."

I groaned low in my throat. "I know. I just have so much energy right now, I want to rip Mnemosyne apart with my bare hands, free Gabriel, and head back to the human realm already."

Sam glanced at me wryly. “Are you that desperate to leave?”

There was a weird tone in his voice. I winced. “Sorry. I know you’re stuck here for now, but it won’t be for long. The sooner I get back there, the sooner I can get rid of the Horsemen, and somehow close the gap in Hell’s gates, then it’ll be safe for you to come back down.”

He linked his fingers with mine, squeezing tightly. “I swear you’re the only person who can get away with making me feel like a little kid needing to be looked after.”

I grimaced. “Sorry. You know I don’t mean it like that.”

He laughed. “I know; I’m playing with you. I love you. You’re the most messed-up bad ass ever, and I wouldn’t have you any other way.”

I rolled my eyes. “I don’t know whether to be flattered or insulted.”

“Ha ha! I mean it; when I tell you I love you, I’m not just saying it. You’re the best thing that ever happened to me.”

I squeezed his fingers tightly, sucking in a deep breath. “I feel the same. It’s okay; we’ll get back home. Me, you and Trev will be together as a family again.”

“And Gwen?”

I tilted my head to look at him. “She left us, remember?”

“I know, but I miss her too. She’s family.”

I smiled sadly. “I know. Like a weird, spoiled cousin, right?”

He laughed. “Yeah, well, you’re the pyromaniac sister who’s just gotten out of juvi.”

I grinned. "Yeah, that's me. Who are you, though?"

He shrugged. "The older, handsome college brother?"

"Pfft! More like the dorky kid brother."

He grunted, smiling, and we fell silent as we passed a group of angels sitting on the grass, singing. They looked up as we passed, reaching out to us, and gesturing for us to join them. We politely shook our heads and hurried on past.

Finally, we retraced our steps, heading up into the building housing my old chambers. We walked down the wide hallway, avoiding the gazes of those who had seen my abrupt exit earlier. At the very end of the hallway, when it forked, we turned right and began to jog up the empty corridor. As we passed closed doors, I felt wave after wave of emotion pour through me as I thought of who could be there, friends and family I hadn't seen in years. I wondered if they would even see through my new appearance and know who I was.

With Sam at my back, I slid to a stop outside one of the doors. Like the others, it was wooden, tall, and had iron trimmings around the edge and slats across the middle.

I turned to Sam. "Is there anyone in there?"

He concentrated for a moment before shaking his head. "No, no thoughts in there. We're good to go." He glanced behind him down the corridor.

I nodded and gripped the thick, round iron knob, twisting it around. I flinched as it squeaked, and quickly pushed at the door. We slid in the gap and shut the door behind us, leaning against it side by side.

I stared into the room, memories washing over me. It was larger than mine had been, probably larger than Gabriel's too. It was shaped in a huge rectangle, the longest wall all glass and beyond it, no sight of anything other than white cloud. In the middle of the room, there was a huge round table with bright multi-colored stools all around it. The floor was covered in numerous deep red rugs. It was sparse, yet beautiful.

While I remained stuck in place against the door, Sam stepped over to the table and pushed aside a small pile of books.

"There's no letters here," he said glumly.

"No?" I joined him and stared down at the table. "What's this?"

A huge map was spread out across the table . . . a map of the human realm, and the books sitting on top were history books detailing human wars. Why would Raphael be interested in those? Yes, the angels had guardianship over humans, but they would never allow them to fight against anything other than other humans and in that instance, they weren't allowed to intervene. It was weird, but not really a link to Mnemosyne; why would she be interested in that either?

"There's nothing here. Nothing relevant," I amended.

I turned away from the table, and stepped towards the glass. I placed my palms against it, feeling the cold.

"It's so beautiful."

"It is," Sam said, joining me.

Together, we turned to face the door in horror as the squeaky handle alerted us we were about to be found.

37

'When life gets harder you must have just leveled up.'

Unknown.

We bolted into the nearest room, closing the door lightly. Spinning in a circle, I searched for somewhere to hide.

"We're in his bedroom!" Sam mouthed.

He looked completely freaked out, and I couldn't blame him. I was pretty panicked myself. Either way, this was going to go down badly. If he was Mnemosyne, we had trapped ourselves in here with no back-up, and no one else knew we were here. If he was Raphael, there was no way to explain ourselves without getting in serious trouble.

Where could we hide? There was a wardrobe consisting of some very thin red material and a pole, a pile of cushions on the floor, an open fireplace, oh, and the bed.

Sam and I looked at each other in panic, and scampered for the bed, rolling under just as the door opened. With my chin on the floor, I could see Raphael's boots as he stomped in. My heart was in my mouth, my whole body throbbing with apprehension. He was going to be furious!

I pressed my lips together tightly and held my breath. Sam shot a fear-filled look at me, and closed his eyes.

Like that would help!

I stared through the hanging sheets, my heart stopping as another pair of feet came into view; dainty feet, in black strappy heels.

As a sultry voice reached my ears, I stifled as gasp. I didn't need to nudge Sam—his eyes were wide open with shock. Bëyander was here.

Fuck! We're screwed! I said telepathically.

Sam's response was an incredibly helpful, *Oh my God.*

How are we going to get out of here?

I don't think that's the issue. I can hear Mnemosyne, he said.

Fuck!

That the Goddess of Memory had fooled Bëyander was shocking in itself, let alone that judging by the noises she was making, she was about to engage in what could only be described as a grotesque, psychologically traumatizing threesome between herself, Bëyander and Raphael's image above us on the bed.

Had Raphael and Bëyander become close while I'd been in the human realm? I couldn't ever remember him showing interest in another female; as a rule, he'd stayed clear of anyone other than his sisters. God, if it was Mnemosyne posing as Raphael all this time, where was Raph? What had she done to him?

I mentally shook myself. No, Raphael had probably been drawn away on a mission of some kind, and Mnemosyne had seen an opportunity and taken it. This didn't have to mean that Raphael was in trouble, or hurt in anyway. He was probably fine.

That's great, Jas, but what about us?

I grimaced. *We just have to wait it out. They'll leave soon.*

"Your nipples are so hard and ready for me." Raphael moaned.

I squished my eyes shut, trying to block his voice out. *Her voice*, I reminded myself. That was definitely not Raphael; he would never say something like that. I flinched when Sam put his hand on my shoulder. If I had to hear my nemesis having sex with someone while I hid under the bed beneath them, I didn't want anyone touching me.

Portal? Sam suggested.

No, it'll alert her that we're here.

So, what's the plan? Isn't now a good chance to catch her off-guard?

I jumped, my eyes so wide they stung, my mouth fixed in a grimace as Raphael's naked body came into view. He laid on his back on the floor, just a matter of feet away from us. His whole body was on display, muscles upon muscles, no blemish, scar or tattoo in sight. His knob stood erect from thick blond hair, waiting. Before my very eyes, Bëyander dropped above him, her knees on either side of his hips, sinking onto his erection until her ass was firmly nestled on top of his groin.

Oh my God. Oh my God. Oh my God.

I covered my mouth with my hand, unable to tear my eyes away. All Mnemosyne had to do was turn her head to the side and she would see us. I was so terrified. I wasn't ready for this at all. Mnemosyne was strong, and almost impossible to beat in a straightforward fight. I had no planning, no back up, and no way out. What the fuck was I going to do? If she saw us and attacked, I had no hope of defending Sam.

Aside from waiting to have my throat slit, I was also beyond disgusted at seeing my brother's body, naked in front of me, being ridden by someone who was supposed to be my ally, but what was I supposed to do? What *could* I do?

I felt Sam stir in my mind. *Nothing; we stay still and quiet, and when they leave we go and find Haamiah.*

Or Machidiel, I felt obliged to say. Haamiah wasn't the only one good at strategizing, and spending so much time with Machidiel had put me firmly on his side. As much as I hadn't liked him—okay, as much as I had hated him at first—he was actually a cool guy, you know, for someone who was, like, a thousand years old.

Haamiah is a principality though; it's his job to find us a way out of this mess. He'll be able to come up with the best solution to bring Mnemosyne down.

I grimaced at the moans coming from a few feet away, and tried to drown them out with my thoughts. *Bëyander is also a principality; should we let her tell us what to do?*

No, but we should probably warn her away from Raphael, seeing as it's not him and she's currently working him like—

Shh! I don't want to hear it—that's my brother! Or at least, it's his image. God, how does that even work?

You mean—

Not what they're doing, gutter-brain; the image thing. I thought she was warping our memories when she was pretending to be Haamiah. I thought she was erasing our memories each millisecond so we would think it was him. How is this working? She doesn't know we're here.

He twisted his face. *I don't know; maybe she's got some kind of magical field around her that affects everyone within a certain distance, or just everyone who can see her. See? Haamiah will have the answer to this.*

Fine, if we get out of this alive we'll go and find Haamiah first. I'm not sure about telling Bëyander though. If she doesn't believe us, she'll go and tell him/her, and then we'll have lost our advantage.

I can't really see that we have any advantage right now. Except, you know, free porn.

Ugh! You're so gross! How are you not even bothered that the evil goddess who wants to drag you down into Hell to let demons and vampires and Hell-spawn loose, is right in front of you, and could see you at any moment?

When there was no reply, I turned my head slightly. My heart dropped when I saw his expression.

Shit, I'm sorry. We do have an advantage, Sam. She doesn't know that we know who she is. When we get out of here we're going to find Haamiah and come up with a plan; something more specific than me ripping her throat open with my hands.

He nodded stiffly. I slowly reached out and pressed my palm onto his hand. *We'll be fine. Like you said, we just need to sit tight and wait it out.*

Raphael flipped Bëyander onto her back and began thrusting hard, eliciting screams of pleasure from her. My stomach twisted and coiled, both disgusted and terrified at the same time. Watching Raphael slam home over and over as Bëyander wrapped her thighs around his waist made me want to vomit. It also made me horny, which was super awkward, as I was lying right next to Sam, who was probably thinking the exact same thing.

Pretty much.

I rolled my eyes, and tried to stifle the blush of embarrassment. We just needed to get over the next few minutes and we'd be fine. After all, how long could a female goddess have sex with a female angel for, while keeping up a mirage?

38

'Wake up every morning and tell yourself you're a bad-ass bitch from hell and that no one can fuck with you, and then don't let anybody fuck with you.'

Unknown.

The answer to my question was three hours and twenty-six minutes. After wearing out the floor just a few feet away from us, Mnemosyne and Bëyander had made excellent use of the bed, groaning and shrieking above us as the mattress bounced within inches of our heads. They then proceeded to use and destroy almost every surface in Raphael's chambers; the dressing table now had cracks across the mirror, the wardrobe lay on a tilt against the wall after the hammering it had received, and even the stools were strewn about the floor.

The two lovers had spanked, whipped, tied each other up, had sex kinkier than I could have ever imagined and then finally, to my uttermost relief they left.

Sam and I remained where we were, somewhat traumatized, but also very aware that either one of them could come back at any moment and catch us creeping out.

After more than half an hour of holding our breath, Sam began to crawl forward, forcing me to slide out from under the bed beside him. He gasped at the mess in the room—it looked worse now that we could see the full extent of the damage. The walls had been ripped, grooves slicing through the material, the door to the bedroom was hanging off the hinges, and there were shards of glass all across the floor.

I briefly heard wonder and excitement in Sam's head, so I switched off and began to make my way silently through the glass, approaching the entrance to the main chamber. We had been such morons to come here without telling anyone; what if Mnemosyne was sitting at the table pouring over the map? What if we had thought we had heard two people leaving, but it had actually only been Bëyander?

I crouched by the wall and slid my shoulder around the edge, peering around the corner. My heart was thumping so loudly that it was all I could hear. No rustle of paper, no clinking of broken glass, and thankfully, no Mnemosyne awaited us.

We stepped carefully into the room and edged towards the door, skirting the mess. After Sam gave me the go-ahead, I gripped the iron ring on the door and yanked it open, darting out. I shut it quickly, and we bolted down the corridor back towards the entrance to the building. We skidded into each other as we rounded the corner. Angels were pouring out of the entrance to the Library of Choices, and also from the corridor opposite the one leading to the chambers, panic on their faces, pushing and shoving past each other in a desperate crush of bodies.

"What's going on?" I called to Sam.

Sam wrapped his arm around my waist and dragged me to the side, out of the flow of fleeing angels.

"They're running!"

"It has to be Mnemosyne!" I hissed. "She has to have done something."

He scowled as he was slammed into the wall. I winced as he stepped on my foot.

"That's a pretty safe bet," he shouted.

We were knocked and dragged along towards the entrance, and had to fight our way back through them towards the doorway to the library, which surely had to be empty by now. I elbowed an angel, earning a glower, and I shoved through, pulling Sam along behind me.

I was right; the library was almost deserted, but fate was smiling down on us and Haamiah remained behind, gesturing wildly with his hands, his voice raised in anger as he confronted another angel, one I didn't recognize.

I didn't wait to find out what they were yelling about; I just barged over and gripped Haamiah by the shoulder, spinning him around to face me.

"I need to talk to you."

"Not now, I'm too busy," he muttered, trying to turn back.

I dug my fingers in, and swung him around again. "No, you're not, fill me in—what the hell is going on out there?"

"I'm going!" Haamiah's companion said with exasperation. He pointed his finger at Haamiah. "There are other much more important things to take care of. Forget the prisoner, and concentrate! We need your head in the game."

The angel glared at me and stomped past, slamming the door closed as he left, leaving us alone.

“What prisoner?” I demanded.

Haamiah looked at me, fully noticing me for the first time. “Forget about it; there are more important things to worry about now.”

Sam put his arm around my shoulder. “Like?”

“Like the fact that a number of fallen angels have been spotted.”

“Here?” I shouted.

He nodded. “Here.”

“It’s what we’ve been expecting,” Sam said, squeezing my shoulder in an attempt to reassure me. “The gate are wide open; we knew this was going to happen.”

I dropped my face into my hands and groaned. “This is all we need! Haamiah I need to tell you-”

“There’s no time! We have to go,” Haamiah said, steering us towards the doorway. “A meeting’s been called, and we need to be there now.”

“A meeting?” Sam echoed.

Pushed out into the corridor, we followed the back of the crowd as they ran down the stairs towards the grassy area in between the buildings. Haamiah drifted in front, and I grabbed hold of his arm to keep us together. We ran down the stone steps and rushed forward onto the grass, following the masses of angels pouring out of every building to converge there.

Angry voices grew louder and louder until I could barely hear my own thoughts. When we finally came to a standstill, unable to be shoved in any other direction, I covered my ears with my hands, grimacing. Sam stood behind me and cupped his own hands over mine, making me smile.

In the distance, figures ascended stairs onto a platform.

I scowled at the first voice I heard—Raphael's.

"Our gates have been breached! The fallen have crept among us like thieves in the night, and are here with us now. We face serious choices; choices we didn't expect to have to discuss yet."

The crowd had fallen silent, each angel staring up at Raphael's tall, intimidating figure in rapture. No one else knew that he wasn't our archangel but was actually Mnemosyne. Anything she was going to say now couldn't be good.

"We need to make a choice; do we close the gates for good, and block out all of the evil creatures descending upon us, keeping our families and friends safe and rejecting the sinful? Or do we allow them to continue creeping in, and hope we can catch them before they kill too many of us?"

Commander Avrail stepped forward. "We seal the gates shut today, and pray for those lost to us on the other side."

To my horror, angels began to shout their approval for closing the gates. Roars of support rang out loudly and angrily. Hands falling away, Sam and I looked at each other in shock, echoing each other's thoughts. They couldn't do that! They couldn't shut the gates permanently—what would happen to all of the human souls? Would they wonder the universe without peace for all eternity? Or, without an alternative, would they be sucked down into Hell?

At least I would be able to get in and out, as I could open a portal, but what about everyone else?

I nudged Haamiah to get his attention. "We need to slip away somewhere private so that I can open a portal. We'll gather everyone who wants to go back to the human plane, and get out of here."

When he frowned down at me, my stomach twisted. Ugh, was he going to give me a lecture now about staying in the Heavens? If it came to it then I would go on my own, but I definitely needed Machidiel to come with me, and if the fallen were already here, surely Sam would be just as safe in the human realm?

"You can't open a portal here," he said gruffly.

I scowled. "Seriously? You're giving me a lecture on rules? I think I can break this one in order to finish killing off evil people."

He leaned closer. "You can't open portals in the Heavenly realm. It's impossible. Lilith and Lamia were the only angels in existence who could summon a portal—when they both fell, the magic surrounding the Heavens was adjusted so that no portal could be opened from or to it."

I glared at him. "You didn't think to mention this before now? How the Hell do I get out?"

He pursed his lips in annoyance. "The only way in or out for anyone or anything is through the gates in the Heavenly reception hall."

"But they're closing them!" I turned away to stare up at the arguing angels upon the platform.

If the gates were closed and there literally was no way out, they were condemning the grigori and the angels still on the human plane to remain there for all eternity. I couldn't quite register that. How could they do it?

On a more selfish note, what would happen to *us*? If they closed the gates with us on this side, we would never be able to get out. Yes, there could be worse things than being locked in Heaven, but what about our mission? What about Trev, my dad, Gwen, and everyone else? I pressed my palm to my forehead in distress. I had allies relying on me; I couldn't be trapped here forever.

"We can't be stuck here!" I hissed at Haamiah.

He turned to me, and winced. "It might be the best option."

I grabbed hold of his arm and tugged until he had to lean towards me. "Mnemosyne is here!" I shouted in his ear over the noise of the crowd.

He turned to me in shock. "What?"

"She's Raphael! She's pretending to be him! Shutting the gates has to be some kind of plan of hers; it's what she wants. We can't let it happen."

I watched as Maion jumped up onto the stage. This wouldn't be good.

He quickly silenced the crowd. "Enough! What of our families still on the human plane? Are we just going to abandon them? And what of our charges—the humans? We were tasked with their care; we have a duty to protect them, yet we're going to leave them to the merciless nature of the evil Hell is currently spewing out?"

I turned my eyes up to Sam in astonishment. As if Maion, of all people, was fighting to save humans! This was unreal. What was happening to everyone?

Sam seemed to be on the same wavelength as me. *I can't believe he just said that. Maybe I was wrong, and Mnemosyne is pretending to be him.*

I tensed. What if he was right? What if she wanted the gates to remain open so she could get Sam out? That would make so much more sense! Why would she want the gates closed if she would then be trapped here with us?

I was joking. I heard Mnemosyne in the bedroom, remember? She's standing up there right now, demanding the gates to be closed.

But it doesn't make sense, I argued.

There must be another way out. That's all it can be.

Maion had been roaring something at the crowd, and the crowd roared back at him. As I hadn't been listening, I had no idea if this was a good thing or not. For some reason, hands began to grab at Haamiah. He deflected them quickly, and turned to me with steel in his eyes.

Another call went out for him to approach the platform, and yet more hands began to tug at him.

I shrieked and grabbed hold of him, digging my nails into his arms as I forced him to remain facing me. I knew my eyes showed my desperation as I saw flashes of panic reflected in his own.

"What should we do? We can't be stuck in here! I need to get out," I hissed.

He bit his lip. I had never seen him look so stuck for words. He knocked another angel away from him. “Okay, we need a plan,” he said.

Duh. We’re running out of time! Sam shouted in my head.

Haamiah quickly turned to Sam. “Find Zanaria, and tell her what’s happening. She’ll be in Jasmine’s chamber; she didn’t want to come here.”

“I don’t have a chamber, but why is *she* in it?” I spat. As I spoke, I realized yes, I did have a chamber, or at least Jophiel had one. Although, apparently not anymore.

Haamiah was oblivious to my sidetracking thoughts. “Jasmine, go to the library. Bëyander is there; she’ll help you find a way out. If Avrail hadn’t been up there on the platform I would have told you to go to him, but Bëyander will have to do. Maybe she can find a short cut to the reception hall, and help you to get out that way.”

“What about you?” Sam cried, shoving past me to hang on to his arm as he was jerked backwards.

He shook his head. “I think it’s too late for me,” Haamiah whispered sadly, emotion flaring across his face.

Sam’s fear was so loud it seemed to reverberate through me. He was devastated and beyond scared, not for himself, but for Haamiah. I bit my lip deeply, fighting back against the pushing and shoving. Haamiah was the only family Sam had ever known . . . and he was losing him.

I joined Sam, and held on tightly to Haamiah’s shirt. “What about Machidiel? I need him to help me finish this mission!” I gasped through tears.

Haamiah breathed heavily, shrugging off the hands grabbing at him. “It’s too late. He’s gone.”

“What are you talking about?” I asked incredulously, my eyes shooting daggers.

“He’s missing. His blood and his dagger were found in the dungeons. There was so much blood, he has to be dead. I’m sorry.”

With a rip, his shirt was torn out of my hands. I stood, gasping for breath, unable to do or say anything as the crowd sucked him away from us, propelling him forward towards the platform where Mnemosyne awaited him.

Sam was in frozen on the spot beside me. I knew I needed to do something; he was right, we were running out of time. I pushed him backwards, forcing him through the crowd of angry angels until we were free and sprinting for the building we had just exited. Sam fought me, trying to turn back.

“Stop fighting me!” I screamed.

“We can’t just leave him here? You’ve never liked him, but he’s family!” he bellowed back.

I punched him in the face, knocking him to the side. “I’m sorry. I know you’re close to him, but we’re running out of time. You’re not the only person who’s going to lose someone. We have friends and family on both sides of that gate, and either way, whether we get through or whether we’re stuck inside, we’re both going to lose people.” I cupped his face in my hands and gazed up into his eyes, tears pouring from them. “What matters here is the mission.”

“*Your* mission,” he spat.

“No,” I denied. “You think I want to chase after psychotic killers?”

“Yes, I do!”

I shook my head and stepped back. “This isn’t just about revenge for Zach anymore. Hell is going to open one way or another. If they can’t get their hands on you, they’ll try something else. Everyone we love on both sides is going to die if we don’t take out the Horsemen, Mnemosyne, Asmodeus, and Lucifer. If we can kill them, then no one else is going to try to open the gate, at least not for another thousand years. They might not know it, but everyone we love is relying on us. If you want to stay here with Haamiah then that’s fine, but I’m getting out of here. Yes, Mnemosyne is on this side, but Haamiah knows who she’s pretending to be now, and he can take care of her. The rest of them are out there with no one to chase them down, so that’s where I’m going to go.”

I took a few steps back, watching as Sams eyes opened wide and wild in distress. He worried at his lip and he stared at me, thought creasing his forehead. His face hardened, and he turned back to the crowd, watching as Haamiah was pulled up onto the platform. My heart sank, my face crumbling as tears freed themselves from my eyes and ran down my cheeks. I was going to lose him for good. Sam, my best friend . . . I would never see him again.

39

'I think hell is something you carry around with you. Not somewhere you go.'

Neil Gaiman.

Staring at the back of his head, I forced myself to turn away. I lifted my eyes and focused them on the steps in the distance. I needed to concentrate. I would find Bëyander, find a way out, and then have a meltdown once I was on the other side of the gate.

I strode forward purposefully, keeping my chin up, even though I wanted to run screaming back to Sam and demand that he come with me. It was his choice to make; everyone should have a choice.

A hand gripped mine. I spun around, my fist clenched.

It was Sam. His face was red and blotchy, and he was blubbering like a baby. He sucked in his bottom lip then said the four most wonderful words I'd ever heard.

"I'm coming with you."

I threw my arms around him, squeezing him so tightly he probably couldn't breathe. I buried my face into his shoulder in the crook of his neck and breathed him in. I pulled away after a few seconds; we had an important mission, and we couldn't waste time. I linked fingers with him and pulled him along with me, thanking my lucky stars my best friend was by my side. I wouldn't let anything happen to him. I would keep him safe, if it was the last thing I did.

Together, we sprinted, quickly closing the distance between the crowd and the library, panting as we ran up the steps and into the corridor. I shouted for Sam to knock on the door five rooms past Raphael's—there he would find Zanaria. I skidded to a stop by the door to the library and threw it open, letting it land heavily against the wall as it swung wide.

Breathing deeply, I scanned the room. It was cavernous; Bëyander could be anywhere. Dozens of pools of various shapes and sizes beckoned, glittering water rippling across their surfaces, and books were scattered about everywhere, chairs were turned over, there were cushions on the floor . . . it was as though a stampede had come through. I ran to the bookcases, running up and down the aisles, shouting for the angel I could only pray knew of a way out without alerting the warriors.

"I'm here," she said in her low, sultry voice.

I spun around as she emerged from behind a bookcase, sauntering towards me. She sailed past, making me turn with her, and I watched as she sat down in a green armchair, opening a book and placing it on her lap. She arranged her dress to cover her legs, tucking her ankles under the seat.

"Well?" She shook her hair loose around her shoulders.

I wrinkled my nose. I honestly didn't want her help . . . but I needed it.

Don't be selfish; she can get us out, and then we can go and protect Trev, and Aidan, and all of the others down there, I chided myself, stiffening in my resolve. Just because I didn't like someone didn't mean I couldn't accept his or her help when I needed it. I could work alongside someone and be civil; yes, I could.

I focused my eyes, and tried to smile. "There's a meeting outside, and they've decided to close the gates."

Bëyander smirked, a comfortable expression on her face which summed up her entire personality. "Are they really?"

I swallowed hard, and nodded. "Yeah, and I need a way out back to the human realm."

She narrowed her eyes. "They've worked out how to close the gates then?"

I shrugged. "I'm not sure, but I imagine they have a whole heap of warriors stationed in the reception hall to stop anyone from coming in or going out. Haamiah said you might know a secret way to leave?"

A muscle in her jaw ticked, sending nerves down my spine. Was she going to refuse to help me? It could just be the bitch in me, but I wouldn't put it past her to refuse to help me out of spite, though I wasn't sure what I'd ever done to her. If she wouldn't help me, whom would I turn to? Gabriel? I couldn't get her out of the cage, but she might be able to give me directions to a hidden passageway.

I paused, waiting for her answer. "Why weren't you in the meeting?"

She smiled, not her usual confident smirk, but a fake cover. Chills raced up my spine and I funneled my power towards her, trying to *hear* her. "I've been busy. I knew someone would tell me what was going on."

"Busy doing what?" I persisted. I glanced over my shoulder towards the bookcases. What had she been doing back there? Was she really my ally? Why had Haamiah sent me here? Were they working on something together—maybe a plot to overthrow Raphael, or another scheme to gain us more allies?

Something was going on, and I didn't like being kept in the dark.

"Bëyander, we're on the same side here. What aren't you telling me?"

She sniffed, turning her face away to look at the door once, then pursed her lips in boredom. "I don't know what you're talking about, and if Haamiah was expecting me to know a secret way out of here then he's wrong. If they close the gates we're all stuck. Of course, as you can open portals you could just magic yourself out . . . You're really not as bright as I thought you were if you haven't thought of that already."

Her words sailed into me and exploded like a bomb. She didn't know that I couldn't open portals from within the Heavens? The part of me that still prayed that God was going to appear and fix everything for us clung onto the hope that she had just forgotten. Perhaps it was pessimism or maybe realism, but the rest of me knew something was very, very bad right now.

I kept my face straight and stepped away from her casually, backing up towards the bookcase she had appeared from. She tensed, and leaned forward in her seat once I had increased the distance enough to notice.

"Where are you going?" she asked in a low, slithering voice.

I flashed her a smile. "Nowhere. I just remembered a book that I needed to have a look at. It might help me with the portals."

I turned side on and slid away, increasing my speed as I caught her movement from the corner of my eye. She slowly placed her palms on the arms of the chair and rose, beginning to walk towards me with stalking, halting movements.

I edged around a corner and pushed off the wall, leaping meters forward to dodge behind another tall bookcase. I almost fell across a rug that had been left half rolled up on the floor. I briefly thought of the rest of the library being left in disarray; that's what happens when hundreds of angels fled a room to attend a meeting dooming humankind . . . mess of every kind.

Recovering, I stepped across it, catching the edge on my shoe. I stumbled and turned back as the edge straightened out, one limp, pale hand falling out.

I hissed in my breath and knelt, flipping the rug over to expose the body hidden within its folds.

She had to have been dead for days and dragged here. Brown hair, matted with blood, was tangled around her face—a face with dark eyes staring up, wide and open, and a mouth stiff in grimace. Her throat had been slit so her head sat at a peculiar angle, though it still remained attached. The rest of her body was stretched out still partially covered with the brown, stained rug. The mole on her lip was all I could see.

I didn't know how long I had been kneeling beside her, or how long it took me to piece it all together, but when I looked up, a mirror image of the angel stood with one arm braced against a shelf, her legs crossed at the ankle, and a wry expression on her face as she ran her free hand through her hair.

Mnemosyne. It hadn't been Raph, she'd been pretending to be—it was Bëyander. Judging by Bëyander's pale, lightly greying skin, she'd killed her days ago, before I'd even gotten here.

The air in front of me shimmered and Bëyander's beautiful, slender body disappeared, leaving a tall woman in tight fitting black trousers and a black crop top with black gloves reaching past her elbows, standing there with a mocking grin. She moved an inch, ropes of muscles rippling across her abdomen. The hand which had been trailing through long brown hair now touched a thick iron band that wrapped around her forehead, keeping her short, black hair off of her face.

I wanted to ask why? I wanted to berate her for sneaking around, and I also wanted to know how she'd managed to hide from everyone so easily. I wanted to know why she'd chosen Bëyander as her guise, and if Machidiel had found out, and that's why she had killed him. I wanted to know if she was the prisoner Haamiah had said had escaped.

But what was the point? She was an evil bitch whore, and I was going to rip out her eyes and shove them so far down her intestines she'd be shitting them as I slit her throat just like she'd done to Bëyander. The angel might not have been a friend, but she had been my ally, and I would avenge her.

The air around me shimmered, rolls of power rippling in waves ahead of me. Sparks exploded I shrieked my valkyrie war cry. Fire shot out in all directions, books bursting into flames, and heat spread outward from me like I was an exploding sun. I elevated, running up the side of a bookcase as Mnemosyne did the exact same to the opposite stack. We reached each other in the air, both going for the throat.

Her fingers dug in, her nails cutting deep as she blocked the air from reaching my lungs. I scrunched up my nose and clenched my hands tightly, trying to grip her neck tighter. We fell to the floor, my hip stinging as I landed heavily on my left side. I scrambled forward and smacked her head down onto the tiled floors. I could feel her struggling beneath me, but was unprepared when she bent her legs underneath my body and straightened, launching me up through the air. I hit the bookcase, knocking it over backwards, and landed in the flames. It took precious seconds to chill the flames.

Mnemosyne took advantage, gripping my hair and dragging me backwards across the floor, throwing me at another bookcase and giggling when I knocked it over, again landing on top of it. I rolled over and jumped away from the books, lifting my fists. I felt a shimmer of power—a warning sign she was going to try to use her magic on me. I resisted, bringing up my own power so that it seethed through my veins, protecting me. I hadn't been expecting it to work, but it did, repelling the magic fireball she shot at me, though tiring my own out rapidly.

She giggled again as she zoned in. I ducked and punched straight forward, catching her in the throat. She coughed and scowled, jumping to the side. She wasn't quick enough as I followed, succeeding in scoring hit after hit to her face. She bent over, gasping and I used her trick—grabbing her hair to launch her over my shoulder to the floor. I kicked her in the stomach, each blow sending thrills of pleasure through me.

"Jasmine!" a voice bellowed. "It's not Raphael!"

I looked up, losing my concentration. A blow to my back sent me sprawling onto the floor. I rolled over and flipped up to my feet, crouching, ready and facing across the room, able to see Sam and

Zanaria rushing towards me. To my relief, when they realized what was happening, Zanaria pushed Sam behind her, her guardian mode kicking in.

"I'm in the middle of something here!" I shouted. "Were you going to tell me that Mnemosyne was pretending to be Bëyander? Because you're a bit late with that!"

Mnemosyne laughed. "So smug, yet you weren't the first one to work it out."

I tilted my head. "I wasn't?"

"Zanaria caught me red-handed." She gave a mock sigh. "I knew I should have ripped her throat out instead of just knocking her out. Looks like the Dagger found her."

I nodded, unable to help the glee that shot through me at the thought of how furious Maion was going to be. If she killed me, which let's face it, was a significant possibility, Maion would hunt her down and destroy her.

Catching Mnemosyne off-guard, I spun, kicking out with my right leg, and booting her in the face. She flew to the ground, narrowly missing falling into a pool. She scowled, and jumped up to her feet, picking up a chair as she did, which she then threw it at me. The heavy weight knocked me over backwards. My head smacked against the floor, and I groaned as the room span above me. My control slipped, gravity moving, angry I couldn't open a portal fully. Flames spread through my skin, boiling and melting, while deep-seated fury rippled through my eyes, releasing mist all around me so that I could barely see.

I reached for the last vestige of control, the only thing holding back the fallen angel inside of me and let it loose, violence spreading through me with intensity. I leaped forward quicker than I had ever moved before and sunk my teeth into her throat, feeling blood gush down my chest. It was the most bizarre feeling, the feeling of someone else taking over my body, the feeling of soft flesh giving way, chewy veins and arteries being crushed beneath my teeth, spurting fluid into the back of my throat.

I clamped down with my molars, fitting a huge portion of her flesh in my mouth, my soul focused on causing as much pain as possible and damaging her in an irreparable way, just as my heart had been damaged. As a side note, hopefully draining her blood would weaken her and give me an advantage, but my main game plan had narrowed to *destroying her.*

Mnemosyne screamed and flailed beneath me. I could hear a shocked gasp from Sam, and I heard the slam of a door as someone—probably Zanaria—fled.

I jerked back, pain shooting though my back. I reached behind me, pulling a sharp, thin blade from where Mnemosyne had embedded it high in my left shoulder. I glared at her, fisting the blade as she staggered away. She looked pale, the blood loss evident. I lifted my palm as if to blow her a kiss and smirked, blowing flames into her face.

Screaming, she threw her body at mine unexpectedly, knocking me backwards into a pool of lukewarm water. Instinctively I spread my arms out from my body and sank under the water as the goddess landed on top of me, pushing me to the bottom.

She held me there, struggling to keep her weight on top of my body. It took a long moment before I realized she was trying to drown me. Panic set in and I tried to roll, attempting to slide from under her. I pressed my lips together, refusing to take in any water.

Shadows poured through the water, a dirty red color obscuring my vision as she kept me held on the bottom of the pool.

I continued to pull against her, twisting and winding, the pressure in my lungs building. Haze pricked at my mind, painful and sharp, as my body began to scream for air. I couldn't shake her. She was too strong, too tough. How had I ever thought that I could defeat her? She was a goddess—I was insane to even think I was as strong as her. I'd said all along that I would need help; why hadn't I run when I'd worked out whom she was? Why did I confront her like an idiot?

Oh my God, I couldn't breathe, and I couldn't escape! I flung my body to the side, ending up in a worse position, facedown at the bottom of the pool, my cheek pressed against the tiles as Mnemosyne forced her body on top of mine, giving me no quarter.

At last my mouth opened and thick, heavy water poured in, filling my body up with lead. As panic left me, regret and sadness took over, and my last thought was a grim awareness that Maion would be the one to get our revenge. He would avenge Zach, Machidiel, and myself, and make her pay . . . and that was something I could accept.

40

'She's mad but she's magic. There's no lie in her fire.'

Charles Bukowski.

I felt my eyes roll, felt my lungs forget their struggle, and my brain and heart accepted that they needed to give up. Numbness crept through me and without any real thought, I lay my forehead on the tiles, my eyelids shutting. My heart slowed, one beat, then pause, then another, sluggish and irregular. Finally, no more came. My blood stopped pumping, my magic began to recede, cooling in my body, retracting into my abdomen.

I was still aware of Mnemosyne, and I knew the moment she stood up, jumping out of the pool, leaving me at the bottom.

I let my mind wander, thinking of my dad, and how lucky I'd been to meet him. I felt a wave of sorrow that I would never know who my biological mother was. All thoughts of revenge had left me. Yes, there were still three Horsemen out there and Mnemosyne, but I had achieved such a lot. I had come from nothing and experienced adventure and excitement, earning friends and finding true love. After all, what was life, if not one long journey filled with a thousand emotions and lives? I had no regrets; it was true that they said that it's better to regret something you had done rather than something you hadn't, but still, I wouldn't change a thing.

At the start of this journey I had been a complete and utter psycho, laughably naïve, and full of self-importance, risking everything for nothing, and now I had risked everything a thousand times over . . . for *everything*. And I wouldn't change it for one more moment.

41

'I don't care what you think of me. Unless you think I'm awesome, then carry on.'

Unknown.

Black eyes flashed at me, angry and insistent. Fury roiled through me.

Boom!

One heartbeat pounded through my chest like a bomb going off. In response, a tsunami of blood flooded through my body, adrenaline electrocuting every fiber.

My eyes shot open and I surged from the water, leaping out of the pool, landing beside Mnemosyne in a wave of energy and vitality. Staring at her frozen expression, I stepped forward and slid the blade I had dropped at the bottom of the pool, prior to my momentary drowning, diagonally up through her chest. I pulled back, keeping the blade in my hand.

She clutched her chest, gasping, and backed away from me with a horrified look. She was frowning as though she couldn't believe what had just happened. She had thought I was dead. I *had* been, and now she would be too.

She coughed blood into her hand, staring at me in panic as I approached her, the blade held up, ready.

"You can't kill me," she said hoarsely. "You haven't finished your revenge. The four Horsemen killed your lover, and you need me alive if you're going to find them. I know you want to make them pay, and I'm the only one who can help you."

Humor tugged at my lips. "There are so many things wrong with what you've just said." My voice was cracked and gruff. "Firstly, there's only three left."

Her face dropped open, alarm evident. She paled, then spat, "You'll never get near the remaining three if you kill me. You'll never get your precious revenge."

"I'll never get my revenge? I've already got it; hearing you beg for your life is as sweet as it gets," I said. I shook my head. "But that's not what I'm looking for anymore. I don't want revenge."

Mnemosyne closed her mouth with a snap, still eyeing me with suspicion, but with more than a hint of relief. "What do you want?" She coughed.

I edged closer. "I don't want revenge for something that I can never change; I want to protect my family and my friends from any harm that might come to them in the future. Right now, you're the biggest threat to them."

With a movement she never saw coming, I brought up the blade I had been heating up in my palm, so it was now glowing red, and slid it through her throat. I dropped it to the floor and gripped her shoulder with my left hand and her neck with my right, pulling her head free of her body. I let go of her head, numbly watching as it rolled into the nearest pool, blood seeping through the water.

"Oh my God," Sam said.

I looked up from the head to my best friend. His arms were hanging loosely by his sides, his mouth open in shock. In fact, he looked as shocked as I felt. Was I dead? Did I die for a moment there? Did I actually just kill Mnemosyne?

I felt the presence of someone reaching my side and instinctively turned, ready to defend myself. I gazed up dazedly as Maion gripped my upper arm, and began to haul me through the library, bellowing at Sam to follow us. He entered the stacks, weaving in and out of the shelves until we were almost at the very back.

"Where are we going?" I asked.

"You need to go," he replied.

"That didn't answer her question." Sam roughly pulled me away from him.

"Stop pulling me! I can walk perfectly well on my own," I complained, glaring at the two of them.

Sam let go instantly, while Maion glowered and gripped my arm tight enough to leave bruises. "You just died."

I shrugged. "So? I'm not dead now." My heart thudded painfully as my eyes widened. "Am I dead?"

He ignored me, instead grumbling to himself, "How the Hell did I get saddled with this?"

Just as I was about to do some grumbling of my own, he silenced me with a finger and pushed me behind a bookcase. He placed his hand in between the books on a high shelf and pushed. A thin door opened in the wall next to us. He slipped in, beckoning for us to follow.

“Wait here,” he ordered. He left us there and disappeared out into the library again, returning a few minutes later, panting lightly. He pulled the doorway closed behind him, and shoved in front of us.

We were in an incredibly thin, dimly lit passageway, a *secret* passageway, evidently. Maion walked in front of me, his shoulders scraping the walls on either side.

“Where are you taking us?” I demanded again.

“I’m trying to get you out of here before they figure out a way to close the gates.”

I rolled my eyes. “Because I don’t belong here?”

Maion spun around, and narrowed his eyes on me. “You *don’t* belong here.” When I glared at him, he continued, “But that’s not the reason I’m *helping* you to get out.”

“Then what *is* the reason?” Sam asked.

“I made a promise to help you out whenever I could,” Maion said to me.

I shook my head. “You didn’t promise me anything.”

“Not you.”

My heart contracted painfully. *Zach*. He was always looking out for me, even when he wasn’t here. I nodded to Maion, and kept my mouth shut. I didn’t want to hear any more. If Maion felt indebted to Zach and it would result in getting out of here, then that was fine by me.

Maion opened his mouth about to say something but at the last minute he changed his mind and turned back, marching off. Sam and I followed closely, so close that we bumped into him when he finally stopped. He crouched on the floor and lifted up a metal grate, exposing a square hole. He pointed down to it.

I peered over his shoulder. “I can’t even see the bottom, and you want me to jump down there?”

“Do you trust me or not?” he asked angrily, his eyes flashing with exasperation.

“Not,” I replied. Still, I stepped around him and sat on the edge, lowering my legs into the hole. With one last look at Sam, I dropped through, pulling my arms in tight against my body.

I landed in a crouch at the bottom. Maion had been right—it wasn’t a long drop, only a couple of meters. I stood up and gasped. I was standing in a huge tunnel, perhaps four meters wide by three tall, and the tunnel went on in both directions as far as I could see, no obvious exits or entries. Was this an escape tunnel?

I shouted up to Sam that I was okay and he soon landed next to me, quickly followed by Maion. Without thinking to explain himself further, Maion turned to the left and began to jog down the tunnel. Sam and I exchanged a groan, and ran to catch up to him.

“You know, I was dead a minute a go. You could at least go a little slower,” I called out, flashing a grin at Sam.

Sam gave me a worried look.

What’s wrong? I mean, besides everything.

You were dead.

I wasn’t dead *dead, otherwise I’d still be dead, if you get me.*

I'm being serious. I reached out to you with my mind, and you were gone.

That chilled me to my bone. *Then how am I still alive?*

I don't know. Maybe an ability?

You think I can't die? That would have to be the best ability I could possibly get, although I think I'd know if I'd been hanging around with someone invincible. Unfortunately, most of the people I've encountered lately I've either killed intentionally, or they've been killed fighting beside me.

There was a slight pause before Sam sent his thoughts to me. *What about Trev?*

Okay, change of subject . . . what about him?

He can't be killed by drowning.

Now *I* paused. He was right. Being a vampire, Trev could be killed with fire or beheading, but he couldn't drown. It wasn't exactly an ability, though; could I really have 'harvested' that?

Jas, that has to be it. There's no other possible explanation. Mnemosyne drowned you and you were dead, then you came back to life.

I sunk my teeth into my bottom lip. *Then I guess I owe Trev a lifetime of blood snacks in thanks, though if he gives me fangs I'll kill him.*

Our thoughts faded away, and we pushed on after Maion. After one or two kilometers we finally stopped running. I leaned against a wall, trying my best not to look exhausted, not wanting to appear weak in front of this arrogant asshole, while Sam leaned over, bracing his hands on his knees, breathing deeply and noisily.

Maion leaped to the ceiling, making me push off the wall and stare up in astonishment. I tutted at myself for being surprised; we had come down through a hole, so why wouldn't we be going back up the same way?

Maion jumped back down, and nodded to me. I grimaced and looked up, stepping closer to him without actually touching him; I wouldn't want his rudeness to rub off on me, or anything.

Sam snorted.

I took a couple of steps back and took a run up before bouncing up to the ceiling, clenching on to the lip of the hole. I lifted my feet up to brace against the side and pushed, scrambling over the edge into a dark, tight, circular space. Sam jumped up, followed by Maion, and Maion replaced the covering on the hole quietly, turning to peer through a crack in our new surroundings.

I was desperate to ask where we were going or where we were now, but refused to be shot down again so I held my tongue, waiting for Maion to produce a way out. As if he could hear my thoughts, he pushed open a part of the wall, letting a small sliver of light pass through. He exited, Sam and I slipping out behind him.

We were in the Heavenly Reception Hall. I was right—that *had* been a secret escape tunnel. It probably ran the whole length of the Heavens, allowing certain angels to slip in and out of anywhere unseen. The space we had exited the tunnel had actually been the inside of one of the glorious pillars that ran up to the roof, branching into the ceiling in a hundred golden strokes.

Maion was already walking away, heading to the gates, which currently stood unguarded.

"Wait, why isn't anyone here?" I demanded. "You were just having a meeting about closing the gates because it was so dangerous here, so where are the warriors?"

Maion continued to walk, unperturbed by my concern. "They are currently all investigating the murder of the Goddess of Memory in the library."

"That's where you went when you shut us in the passageway; to tell them?" I guessed.

He nodded.

"You'd still think they'd leave someone here to protect the gates. That's pretty shoddy," Sam said.

Maion rolled his eyes. "Of course they left someone here. Fortunately for us, my soul mate is an excellent actress, and inspires trust and protection from almost everyone around her." He glimpsed at me.

"So she came here and said she needed help, and they rushed off to save her?" I presumed.

"Do you need me to explain everything for you?"

Ugh, he irritated me so much!

At least he's on our side, Sam laughed in my mind.

We stopped beside the gate and Maion pulled one door open, staring at me expectantly.

"You realize I can't fly, right?" I raised my eyebrows, looking at him pointedly.

"You can open a portal . . . unless that is another talent widely exaggerated," he replied.

I glowered. "You know I can open a portal, just not inside here."

"Then go, jump and open your portal. This is the only chance you'll get."

"You're not coming?"

A smirk played over his lips. "Definitely not."

I shrugged. "Fine, but how's Sam going to get down?"

He scowled. "He's not going. He belongs here."

"The Hell I do!" Sam retorted furiously. "I'm going with Jasmine."

Maion stepped forward, threateningly. "The Dagger of Lex is a weapon to be used against the angels. Regardless of what mission or adventure you think you're going to go on, you remain in the Heavens."

I stepped in front of him protectively. "If he doesn't want to stay then he doesn't have to." I felt Sam wrap his arms around my stomach, and lifted my chin to glare at Maion.

I opened my mouth to say something scathing, but who knew what because it came out a screech as Sam pulled me backwards into him, the two of us falling through white clouds together.

My stomach rolled, vomit crawling up my throat and back down. I clenched hold of Sam, wrapping my legs around his, and holding onto his arms the best I could as we tossed and twisted, falling through the sky. I focused and reached down, managing to draw up my magic. I expelled my mist and pushed us through a portal, praying for home where I could be reunited with Trev, and protected by Caleb.

42

'It's better to cross the line and suffer the consequences than to just stare at that line for the rest of your life.'

Unknown.

As expected, our landing was far from graceful. We landed in a heap of legs and arms on the ground, groaning at the hard impact. I rolled over and looked at the sky; blue with one or two clouds approaching in the distance. I turned my head to look at Sam, grinning as he winced and sat up beside me.

"Um . . . Jas?"

I groaned. What trouble were we in now? I sat up and looked around, closing my eyes to take a deep breath, when I realized where we were. I had been thinking of home, meaning the valkyrie house—only I had taken us to the nephilim safe house.

Hearing voices, I jumped up to my feet, grimacing when my bones protested at the quick movement. I held out my hand and pulled Sam up beside me.

Standing where we were, in the middle of the garden on the grass, we had a clear view up to the back of the house, and could see the two very familiar figures stop on the porch in shock, running towards us when they recognized who we were.

"Jophie!" Gabriel cried, running into my arms.

I braced myself for the onslaught and wrapped my arms around her. I purposefully ignored being called 'Jophie'. Machidiel grinned and shoved his hands deep into his jeans pockets.

I finally extracted myself from her and shook my head. "So you're the escaped prisoner?"

She smiled. "That's me."

I looked up at Machidiel, and raised an eyebrow. "And you're clearly not dead."

He frowned. "Was I supposed to be?"

I shrugged. "That's what they're saying. Your blood was found in the dungeons, and there was an escaped prisoner. Haamiah thinks you're dead."

He pursed his lips. "I will rectify that when I next see him."

When he paused, not offering any further information, I rolled my eyes. "So you broke her out?"

He nodded. "I had help."

"From who? How did you get out of the Heavens while the warriors were at the door, and why was your blood on the floor?"

He laughed. "Any more questions?"

"I'm being serious; I want to know! Maion took us through an escape tunnel while Zanaria planned a diversion, so I'd love to know how you two got out."

"Why did you need to go through the escape tunnel?" Gabriel asked.

"Fallen angels were spotted in the Heavens, so they were guarding the gates. They wouldn't have let us anywhere near them."

Gabriel and Machidiel exchanged a knowing glance.

"What?" I demanded.

Gabriel took hold of my hand and tugged. "Come on, we have something to show you."

I glanced at Sam and let Gabriel pull me up the steps onto the porch. I did a double take as I pushed open the glass door into the kitchen, Gabriel close behind.

"What the . . .?" I gasped.

The house was in the process of being rebuilt. The windows in the kitchen had been replaced, with old worn-out furniture replacing the burned sofa, and table and chairs we had left behind. There was a new stove—nothing near as fancy as the extravagant one the angels had provided, but there was one there, nonetheless.

"Did you do this?" Sam asked, rushing into the room and turning in a circle, delighted.

Machidiel shook his head. "No."

"Then who?"

My jaw dropped as Nikita sauntered into the kitchen, leaning against the counter, making a show of folding her arms across her chest and crossing one ankle over the other.

"Still unable to take a shower?" she mocked.

I glanced down at my torn clothes. Yeah, unfortunately amongst all the fighting and drowning, I hadn't had time to change my clothes.

I crooked an eyebrow. "Still channeling Lara Croft?"

She glowered at me. *Score one for Jasmine.*

Now I had managed to ridicule her, I could admit to myself that she looked good. I could see what Aidan saw in her. Still wearing skin-tight black clothing, her long dark hair was pulled into a plait down her back. Her lightly tanned skin and focused stare honestly did make her look like a ninja. All she needed was a mask and a blade, and undoubtedly she had those hidden in a secret pocket.

Someone else entered the room, capturing my attention. Tall, with ice-blond hair and piercing blue eyes, the newcomer was another person I knew. What *was* this—*This Is Your Life*?

"Blue?" I shook my head and glared at Nikita. "What the Hell are you doing here?"

His eyes twinkled at me. "Joining the party."

I looked at Nikita. "'The party'? As in, the human resistance—*let's go kill everyone who isn't human* party?"

She smirked. "What can I say? We're progressive."

"Some of us are planning on remaining on this plane. The human resistance is an alliance of sorts," Blue Eyes said. "Deshek's here too."

Maybe my death had caused permanent brain damage. Why would demons join with the human resistance, who were intending on wiping out demon-kind?

"And Aidan?" I wondered out loud.

Blue Eyes nodded. "He's fixing the staircase."

Silently I stalked from the room, unsure whether to be pleased that I had tentatively allied myself with the human resistance before I had headed off on a zombie hunt, or whether to be miffed that Nikita seemed to be their leader, usurping my place among both demons and humans. I left the kitchen and headed down the corridor, noting the freshly painted walls and new floorboards. Stopping in the foyer, I looked up to where Aidan was perched, hammering in wooden boards to form the staircase we had crashed through just a few months ago.

"So, you finally decided to fix that?" I called out.

Aidan spun around and grinned, surprise evident in his wide eyes. His jeans and T-shirt were stained with paint splatters, and I could even see paint at the ends of his blond, shoulder-length hair. *From rolling in the paint with Nikita?*

He leaped down the stairs and lifted me up into his arms, squeezing me tightly.

"I'm sorry," he whispered in my ear.

"For the stairs? That's really okay. Besides, it's not as if I live here anymore. Seems like it's the new human resistance's fortress."

"For Zach."

Pain slithered through my chest and I pulled away, refusing to seek solace in another man's arms. I'd bear the pain and the loss forever, and use it to fuel a lifetime filled with destroying evil—not for revenge, but to keep those I loved safe.

I forced a smile on my face, and nodded. "You look well."

He bit his lip, concern etched on his face. "You don't look so good."

I shrugged. "Well a few hours ago I drowned . . . I can't always look my best."

"You drowned?" A female voice came from behind.

I spun around, assessing the newcomer for threat. She was short, probably a few inches smaller than I was, with brown hair wrapped into a bun on top of her head. She looked young—her skin was unblemished and unwrinkled, yet she had an air of mystery and wisdom to her. My mind whispered to me that she was something *other*—she wasn't human.

"Yet you're still alive?" she continued when I didn't answer.

I nodded. "Looks like."

"Magic?" she guessed.

"Perhaps."

"Who are you?"

"Ah, sorry," Aidan said. "Jasmine this is Lana, she's with the human resistance. Lana . . . Jasmine."

Lana held out her hand, and I begrudgingly gave her my own. This was a very human gesture; if she wasn't human, was she a witch? She mentioned magic as though she believed it existed, when most humans wouldn't.

"Witch?" I asked.

She laughed. “Something like that. Come with me, and we can talk more.”

I rolled my eyes. “Aidan, I’ll see you later.”

He hesitated, looking from me to Lana. “Are you sure?”

I nodded and stepped around Lana, heading through the front doors. I looked back to Lana, raising my eyebrows as she stared at me. She soon followed and we stepped out through the newly fixed front door together, pulling it closed behind us.

“What did you want to talk about?” I asked.

She narrowed her eyes on me. “How did you survive a drowning?”

I wasn’t sure if I should confess, thinking to hide my abilities from her for some reason. I snorted. That was ridiculous; Nikita knew what I was, and she certainly wouldn’t be keeping it a secret from anyone.

“I’m a valkyrie, —well, half of one, and I take on other people’s talents.” I shrugged. “Somehow, drowning doesn’t affect me as much as you would have thought. Not entirely sure who I got that from.”

“You’ve suffered a great loss,” she said.

I pursed my lips. “Hasn’t everyone these days?” When she glared at me, I relented. “I lost my soul mate.”

“He was killed?” I nodded. “Then why don’t you bring him back?”

I turned away from her, staring out over the front garden. I leaned against the small wall that ran around the porch. “I can’t. He’s gone.”

I felt Lana step closer to me, saw her hands rest beside mine on the wall. I lifted my head to look at her, frowning when I saw the smirk on her lips.

"Not necessarily," she whispered.

A streak of fear and apprehension ran through me. What was it? What was she thinking? Excruciating hope sprung to life in my body. I pressed a hand to my chest, feeling my heart pounding erratically. No, this couldn't be happening; I had accepted it, and begun to move on.

Her smirk grew wider, her teeth flashing dangerously. "Tell me, have you considered time travel?"

To be continued . . .

Laura Prior

Laura Prior

ABOUT THE AUTHOR

Laura Prior grew up in the northeast of England, and has travelled the world while working as a nurse. She is currently living and working in Melbourne, Australia, with her partner. She enjoys snowboarding, long walks, shoe shopping, and cocktails. She loves reading passionate novels with strong female characters.

Find me:

www.facebook.com/fallingforanangel

Twitter @Falling4anangel

www.laurapriorbooks.com

Made in the USA
Charleston, SC
25 October 2014